DODGE AND BURN

DODGE AND BURN

Ellen Crosby

To Ellen —
with best wishes!
Ellen Crosby

SEVERN
HOUSE

First world edition published in Great Britain and the USA in 2024
by Severn House, an imprint of Canongate Books Ltd,
14 High Street, Edinburgh EH1 1TE.

severnhouse.com

British Library Cataloguing-in-Publication Data
A CIP catalogue record for this title is available from the British Library.

ISBN-13: 978-1-4483-1159-0 (cased)
ISBN-13: 978-1-4483-1160-6 (e-book)

All Severn House titles are printed on acid-free paper.

MIX
Paper from
responsible sources
FSC® C013056

Typeset by Palimpsest Book Production Ltd,
Falkirk, Stirlingshire, Scotland.
Printed and bound in Great Britain by
TJ Books Padstow, Cornwall.

Praise for Ellen Crosby

"Sophie is a principled, smart, well-drawn character in a fast-paced story"
Booklist on *Blow Up*

"Exciting . . . Recommended for fans of Crosby and of novelists who specialize in intricate plots and amateur detectives"
Library Journal on *Blow Up*

"Boldly drawn characters shoulder mysteries set among elite Washington power brokers"
Kirkus Reviews on *Blow Up*

"Sophie is a tough, relatable heroine . . . Just the right amount of thrills"
Library Journal on *Ghost Image*

"Intriguing . . . Compelling"
Publishers Weekly on *Ghost Image*

"A quick-moving mystery with a wealth of fascinating material"
Kirkus Reviews on *Ghost Image*

"Character-driven . . . A good mystery"
Kirkus Reviews on *Bitter Roots*

"A treat"
Booklist on *Bitter Roots*

About the author

Ellen Crosby is the author of the Wine Country mysteries, the Sophie Medina mysteries, and Moscow Nights, a standalone. Previously she was a freelance feature writer for *The Washington Post*, Moscow correspondent for ABC News Radio, and an economist at the US Senate. She lives in Virginia with her husband.

www.ellencrosby.com

For the Rector Lane Irregulars, with much love

Donna Andrews, Carla Coupe, Laura Durham, Val Patterson, and
Sandi Wilson
and *in memoriam* Peggy Hanson and Noreen Wald Smith

'When I have a camera in my hand, I know no fear.'
—Alfred Eisenstaedt, photographer.

Dodging and burning are two of the oldest photo editing techniques and refer to the ability to manipulate exposure by making parts of a photo lighter (dodge) or darker (burn). The terms go back to the era of darkroom film editing when a photographer went through a time-consuming process of manually brightening or darkening segments of a photographic print to get the desired amount of contrast. Some modern digital image editing programs also have dodge and burn tools.

ONE

When Monica Yablonski asked me if I'd drive out to Dulles Airport on what we both knew might be a wild goose chase, I said I'd go because she didn't ask me that often these days, and when she did, it was because she knew the story would be right up my alley: edgy, a bit risky, a challenge. She also asked because she wanted someone who would deliver, and she knew I was that person. 'Just be your sweet, charming self and see what you can get, Medina,' was actually how she put it.

Monica is probably the only person on the planet who can get away with that kind of sexist talk and not get a smart-ass answer in return. It also meant my odds of getting anyone to talk to me, never mind letting me take any photographs, were probably slim and none.

'Who is the newsroom sending?' I asked.

'Kirby. He's a pit bull. New. You haven't met him but he's good.'

I used to work as a photographer for International Press Service, a worldwide news agency that has its headquarters in New York City. IPS produces news reports that are distributed to the newspapers and broadcasters that are their clients, so the journalists and photographers they employ work their tails off to break the story before anyone else has it – including the other news organizations that are their competition. Every so often, Monica, who is the Director of Photography, calls or texts me and tries to pull me back into the fold. But after twelve years of having a packed go-bag at the foot of my bed for those middle-of-the-night summonses to get on a flight to who-knew-where and enough frequent flier miles for a trip to the moon – make that a *round trip* to the moon – I quit my job in the London bureau and moved home to Washington, DC. Part of the reason was burnout, but most of it was to be near my family after my husband, a CIA operative, went missing and was presumed kidnapped – which turned out to be an elaborate ruse. Then, two years ago, he was killed after being outed on a covert assignment he agreed to do as a favor to his old bosses, and that's when I decided I was done with journalism for good.

Monica thought otherwise about me leaving the business and made no bones that she wanted me back at IPS. Perry DiNardo, my former boss in London, did as well. Every so often something would come along that they knew would prick old memories, kick in the adrenalin rush of what it was like to be *first*, to discover something no one else knew about yet that would make news headlines – that shiver-down-the-spine thrill. So one of them would ask me if I'd take on just this one assignment, just this one time. And, of course, I'd say yes.

'OK, fill me in,' I said.

'We got a tip from someone who works at Dulles,' she said. 'Apparently, a couple of baggage handlers lost their cookies on Friday night when they opened the curtain of a luggage trolley – those carts they drive out to the plane with your suitcase on it – and found a guy stuffed inside. Shot dead at point-blank range.'

I'd been sent to war zones when I was with IPS, so I'd seen enough dead bodies and blood-soaked scenes to last the rest of my life. I could get along just fine without doing it again.

'Don't tell me you want me to try to get a photo of that bag carrier?' I said. Because that didn't sound right. IPS wasn't into exploitative journalism. They left that stuff for the tabloids.

'No. Good God, *no*.' Monica is an old-school journalist, also a pack-a-day smoker for years. Now she was down to two cigs a day. The smokes had seeped into her voice, which had roughened and turned gravelly. If she coughed or laughed, she started to wheeze.

'Then why do you want me to go out there?'

'To see if you can get any photos of what he was trying to smuggle in,' she said. 'Our source says a guy who was handling unclaimed luggage from a United flight found two suitcases filled with rings, necklaces, coins, goblets – seriously old stuff. Antiquities. He said everything looked like it was solid gold. The dead guy was a Brit who came in on the same flight. Since it's Monday, by now the Dulles PD probably knows if those suitcases belonged to him. Some of the items had tags on them. He says they were written in Cyrillic. Or at least he thinks it's Cyrillic.'

'So the stuff's Russian?' I said. 'Or maybe – these days – it's Ukrainian.'

'My money's on it being Ukrainian,' Monica said. 'With the Russians stealing everything that isn't nailed down in that country and selling it on the black market to buy more weapons, the odds are probably pretty good. Makes me sick what they're doing, trying to eviscerate that country's culture and its history.'

'Why would someone kill the courier – if that's who he was – and leave the suitcases? People walk off with suitcases that don't belong to them all the time. No one stops you. No one would have said boo.'

'Beats me. Look, bring me a couple of shots of what was in them, OK? You remember the photos you took for a piece back in 2016 on the ancient burial ground a couple of archeologists found in the Caucasus?'

Monica has a photographic memory. Pun intended. She probably didn't even have to look up the date of that story. The Caucasus Mountains run along an isthmus separating the Black Sea and the Caspian Sea, a place where Europe and Asia converge. The burial ground, which had been located on a farmer's field at the base of the mountains in southern Russia, had belonged to the Scythians, a nomadic tribe that founded a rich, powerful empire lasting from the eighth century BC to the second century AD. Because they didn't have a written language, almost nothing had been known about them before this discovery. What little information there was had come from the Greeks, who didn't like the Scythians much, calling them 'mare milkers' and drunks. The cache of items found in the burial ground told a different story.

'Sure, I remember taking those photos. I nearly got pneumonia tramping around that field for a few very cold days,' I said. 'Why?'

'Because what our guy described to me sounds not only like what they found at that burial site but also the things you photographed later at the museum in Melitopol,' Monica said. 'So I figured you'd be the perfect person to send for this one.'

If Monica ever went on *Jeopardy*, she'd ace every geography question hands down. Melitopol was a city in southern Ukraine with a museum that possessed a collection of exquisitely worked necklaces, rings, arm bands, goblets, hair combs, shields, and other items that had been made from gold by the Scythians. The Ukrainians claimed the Russians had staged a bizarre heist – a man in a white lab coat had shown up accompanied by Russian soldiers at the home of a museum caretaker who was forced at gunpoint to accompany him to the Melitopol Museum of Local History. The white-coated thief then cherry-picked nearly two hundred priceless items belonging to the Scythians and disappeared. The items he'd taken had vanished and no one knew where they'd gone.

'Monica. A guy was murdered. The suitcases are evidence. Do you think anyone from Dulles PD is going to let me take pictures of what are probably stolen goods? That person would have their head handed to them by whoever is in charge of the investigation. *After* they got canned for stupidity.'

'I have faith in you, Medina,' she said. 'You can be very persuasive when you want to be.'

She disconnected and I stared at my phone. Like I said, this was probably going to be a wild goose chase.

I went anyway, my journalistic curiosity getting the better of me.

The graceful curl of the gull-wing main terminal at Dulles Airport came into view as I rounded a corner on the access road an hour later. Vince Kirby, who looked like he'd graduated from J-school all of about ten minutes ago, met me on the lower level by the baggage-claim area near a door that led to the airport manager's office, a conference room, and a small warren of offices – cubicles, really – that were used by the Metropolitan Washington Airports Authority and the Dulles division of the MWAA police department.

Dulles is vast, sprawling over 12,000 acres of land in northern Virginia. Most of its facilities are invisible to the millions and millions of passengers who fly in and out of that airport each year. Hidden in a remote field with a view of the low-slung Blue Ridge Mountains in the background is an airplane fuselage and a truncated control tower with the capacity to set fire to the plane as if someone is turning on a gas grill for a barbecue. It is where firefighters, airport staff, airline crews, and law enforcement authorities regularly run drills and practice the what-if scenarios of everyone's nightmares. I photographed one of the triennial emergency drills every airport in the country must run for an IPS story years ago. As the professionals practice these drills in eerie silence, passengers at the main terminal are sublimely oblivious to the hellish scene happening a few miles away because all lights, sirens, and emergency horns are turned off for just that reason. But, let me tell you, an airplane with a fire raging through the cabin, shooting flames out the windows and the cockpit – even if you *know* it's a simulation – is something you don't forget.

Ever.

Kirby had already done his homework before I got to the airport.

'There's going to be a presser late this afternoon, maybe tomorrow morning,' he said. 'A cattle call where they'll share what they know about the dead guy and what was in the two suitcases that belonged to him.'

'Asking for the public's help?' I asked.

'Yep. I nudged a bit, asked if we could get an early peek at the contents of the suitcases.'

'Who'd you talk to?'

'A lowly secretary who couldn't – and wouldn't – promise diddly. We have to plead our case to whoever talks to us from Public Affairs. At least she didn't tell me to go pound sand.' He sounded hopeful.

I indicated the door to the offices. 'Well, then, shall we?'

Kirby opened the door and held it for me. 'Why not?'

The secretary Kirby had talked to led us down the hall to a small windowless conference room, told us that Rex Morgenthau from Public Affairs would be in momentarily, and shut the door on her way out. Kirby and I found two seats around the conference table and sat down, checking out our surroundings. The only decoration in the plain vanilla room was a series of model airplanes parked on a shelf that ran along one wall. Each plane had the logo of an airline that flew out of Dulles.

Kirby got up and picked up a plane with an Emirates logo. 'Wow, do you know what this is?'

'An airplane,' I said. 'A big airplane.'

He gave me the *Thanks-wise-guy* look. 'It's an Airbus A380-800, the largest airplane in the world. If it's configured as a double-decker, it can hold more than five hundred passengers. Eight hundred and fifty if it's a single level. It can fly eight thousand nautical miles at a max speed of six-hundred and seventy-five miles an hour. Price tag nearly half a billion dollars. Built in France.'

He went down the line, picking up each plane and examining it, geeking out telling me the model number and explaining its history, how big it was, and how fast it could fly. Something in the way he held each plane told me this was more than a childhood hobby, that he'd done more than build model airplanes as a kid.

'How do you know all this stuff?' I asked.

'My father was a Navy pilot. Based on the *USS Independence* in the Mediterranean, flew all over the Middle East. My grandfather flew missions in Vietnam.' He shrugged. 'Unfortunately, I've got anomalous trichromacy so no pilot school for me.' He saw my puzzled expression. 'Color blindness inherited from my mother's family. In my case, protanopia. I can't see the color red.'

I could tell he'd rehearsed that speech dozens of times to cover up how much not following his father's and grandfather's footsteps had hurt.

'So, journalism instead?' I said, and my heart tugged for him. 'It must have been a tough second choice.'

He shrugged again, still stoic. 'It wasn't a choice, and at least I'm lucky I don't see only in black-and-white, but yes, journalism instead. I figured I'd still get to see the world. Just not from the cockpit of a plane.'

The door opened and Rex Morgenthau walked in as Kirby set a Singapore Airlines Boeing 747 back on the shelf. Morgenthau was tall and broad-shouldered, and looked as if he could have moon-lighted as a linebacker for the Washington Commanders.

He introduced himself and said, 'What can I do for you folks?'

Kirby was the journo. He did the talking, explaining about the tip we'd gotten and asking if we could get a preview look at the contents of the suitcases as well as any additional information Morgenthau could share with us in advance of the press conference.

Morgenthau pulled out a chair at the head of the conference table, sat down and leaned back. 'Where'd you get the tip?'

Kirby shook his head. 'Sorry. We promised our source anonymity.'

Morgenthau looked annoyed but he said, 'So it was a person and not something on social media?'

'It was a person.'

'What did this person tell you?'

Kirby recited what we knew.

'Can you confirm if it's correct?' I asked.

Morgenthau nodded. 'It is.'

'Anything else you can tell us?' Kirby said. 'By now, maybe the next-of-kin have been notified so you have a name?'

'The victim's next-of-kin haven't been located yet so we're not giving out a name,' he said. 'We contacted State once we saw the passport showing the victim was a resident of the United Kingdom. The British Embassy confirmed it. That's all I can say.'

'We heard a couple of suitcases containing what might have been really old artifacts – antiquities – maybe all solid gold were found by someone at United. They were from the same flight that guy was on. Were they his?' Kirby asked.

Morgenthau arched a surprised eyebrow that made me wonder if he was going to make it a personal mission to find out who our source was, who had blabbed so much to the press.

'They were.'

'Do you have any information on who killed him?'

This time he shook his head. 'We do not. The Dulles PD is checking security cameras, who badged in for work Friday night, the usual stuff. As for why the suitcases were left at the airport, we figure the luggage handlers who found the guy did so right after he was shot, based on what the ME told us about the probable time of death. It's possible the killer might have needed to get away quickly and didn't have a chance to collect the suitcases, which is why we think it's one person who acted alone, no partner to get the luggage. He or she might have hoped to come back and retrieve the bags later. The victim had already cleared customs in New York, so there wasn't that hurdle to go through in DC. We were lucky someone from United happened to open one of the suitcases and saw what was inside, realizing it was valuable. Otherwise, there's a good chance the bags would have gone to Lost and Found before the police got to them. And maybe been picked up by the killer.'

'Have *you* seen what was inside them?' I asked.

'I have.'

'Our source told us some of the artifacts had tags written in Cyrillic,' I said. 'Meaning they might be Russian. Or Ukrainian.'

'I'm afraid I don't read Cyrillic – if that's what it is – so I can't help you there.'

'My husband's grandmother was Russian,' I said. 'Nick spoke Russian and taught me to read Cyrillic. I'm not fluent but I know a little. If we could see those items, I might be able to read the tags.'

He started to give me the *nice try* look, but then his expression changed, and I'd clearly piqued his interest. Now he looked as if he were wrestling with the show-them/don't-show-them voices in his head.

'We're going to release a couple of pictures of items that were in the suitcases at the presser. Ask for the public's help, see if anyone knows anything or can identify any of the items,' he said. 'I suppose I could let you see the photos a bit early.'

He pulled out his phone, clicked it on and started thumbing. OK, photos. Damn. But, better than nothing. When Morgenthau found what he was looking for, he held out the phone to me.

'You can take a look at these,' he said. 'We unwrapped a couple of things because we had no idea what we were dealing with. When we realized it was jewelry and antiquities and how old this stuff might be, we decided we'd better get an expert out here, someone from the Smithsonian, to take a look at it. We're waiting for that person to come by. Given the physical weight of what we found, it's possible those items were solid gold.'

Which is what our airport source had said.

'At least the guys who stole this stuff were careful, unlike the morons who hacked that Iranian relief carving out of a damn cliff with a pickaxe and thought they could waltz it through airport security at Stansted,' Morgenthau added.

I'd read about that incident. The British security officers caught the shipment because it was so poorly packed – a flimsy wooden crate held together by a couple of nails. The ancient stone had broken into two pieces during transit, but fortunately conservators at the British Museum were able to put it back together. By way of thanks, the Iranian government had given permission for the carving to be exhibited for three months at the British Museum before they sent it to the National Museum of Tehran.

I scrolled through Morgenthau's photos. A pair of rings, a woman's hair comb decorated with a filigreed carving of a warrior on a rampant horse surrounded by two men carrying shields, and an elaborate many-tiered necklace that looked like a collar. I went back to the first photo, zoomed in so I could read the tag on the necklace and smiled.

Numbers and dates. The first thing Nick had taught me because it was so useful. And the handwriting was clear and precise.

'It's Cyrillic. This necklace dates from the fourth century. The fourth century BC.'

Kirby said *holy crap* under his breath and even Morgenthau's eyes widened. I scrolled to the next photo. 'The rings are from the first century AD. And the hair comb is from the late fifth to early fourth century. Also BC.'

I looked up at Morgenthau, who reached his hand out for his phone. I gave it back to him.

'Thanks for the information,' he said. 'So the stuff *is* really old.'

'You're welcome,' I said. 'One more thing, though.'

'What's that?'

'Those items look a lot like jewelry I photographed years ago at a museum in Ukraine. Since then, the Ukrainians have said the Russians raided that museum and no one knows what happened to what they took. I'm no expert, so it's very possible I'm wrong about what you've got here. I'm sure your Smithsonian expert will know for sure.'

'Thanks. I'll mention it. And now if you give me your emails, I'll send you both the photos.'

We did and a moment later the quiet whoosh of emails landing in our inboxes sounded. I checked mine.

'Got them. Thanks.'

'Me, too,' Kirby said.

We were done. Kirby and I stood up and thanked Rex Morgenthau for his time.

As we started to leave, he said, 'Before you go. Do either of you realize how much stuff comes into this country illegally *every day*?'

I said, 'Not specifically.'

Kirby said, 'A lot.'

'I'll tell you how much.' Morgenthau started ticking items off on his fingers. 'In just one day, the guys from Customs and Border Protection seize almost three thousand pounds of drugs, more than two hundred thousand dollars of illicit currency and eight million dollars of products with Intellectual Property Rights violations – your fake Rolexes and knock-off Hermès bags, among other things. They arrest at least forty people and that's not counting those who are inadmissible or have already been expelled and are trying to get back in.

'They process nearly nine hundred thousand passengers and pedestrians who come in over borders, on ships, trains and planes. Then there's private vehicles, trucks, boats and all the products and merchandise that come in as well. That's just one day and it's also *every day*. Then you get this guy who shows up and probably would have waltzed in with who knows how many thousands or maybe millions of dollars of priceless stuff if somebody hadn't decided to kill him and shove him in one of the cans – *and* we found the luggage before the killer picked it up.'

Kirby said, 'I'm sorry,' as if he were talking to a bereaved relative at a funeral.

'At least this one's a win,' I said. 'Isn't it?'

'A dead guy and suitcases full of gold trinkets older than Jesus Christ?' Morgenthau smiled the ghost of a smile. 'Yeah, chock one up for our side. This one's a win.'

TWO

Kirby and I parted company in the parking lot. I knew he'd file his story as soon as he got in his car. Updates to follow. I'd come up empty-handed, but Kirby had the photos of the items Morgenthau had emailed us, so I called Monica and gave her the news that, as predicted, Rex Morgenthau had said *no dice* to taking actual photos.

My phone rang as I was crossing the Teddy Roosevelt Bridge, leaving Virginia and entering DC. Today, on a blustery mid-March afternoon, the Potomac River was the color of tarnished pewter, gleaming dull and sullen. The boxy white Kennedy Center was immediately to my left; further up the river, the spires of Healy Hall, the Neo-Romanesque and Victorian Gothic centerpiece of Georgetown University, stood out on the skyline like a fortress on a hill. The Washington Monument was ahead of me, a bit off to the right.

The display on the screen in my car read *Max*.

Maximillian Katzer lived in the basement and first floor of the four-story Victorian gingerbread we rented from India Ferrer, a sweet, eccentric woman of an uncertain age, who lived a couple of doors down from us. Max got the back deck, which was off the first-floor dining room, and the walkout patio; we both got to use the small fenced-in backyard. His duplex had the original carved woodwork from the 1890s and stained-glass surrounds in his front windows. I got the second and third floors, which included a witch's hat tower room that I'd turned into my bedroom and a beautiful floor-to-ceiling bay window in my living room that overlooked the 1800 block of S Street, Northwest, the street we lived on. When I moved in, Max had been renting the carriage house across the alley as a place to store furniture and items that either needed minor repair work or he didn't yet have room for in the antique gallery he owned in Georgetown. After he moved to a bigger location and didn't need the storage space anymore, India rented it to me, and I'd turned it into my photography studio.

'Sophie, darling.' Max's voice was as fine and smooth as

hundred-year-old Macallan Scotch, with a hint of refined Charleston, South Carolina drawl. 'Are you out somewhere? It sounds as if I caught you while you're driving.'

'You did,' I said. 'I'm on my way home from Dulles. IPS sent me out there for a story.'

'Do you have to work?'

'The reporter does. We got a story, but I wasn't allowed to take photos.'

'What a pity. Where are you?'

'By the State Department. I'll be home in fifteen minutes, depending on the traffic. Why?'

'There's somebody I'd like you to meet. He's coming by tonight, and I wondered if you could join us for dinner. It's nothing fancy – I'm ordering takeout from the Bombay Club. I know it's last minute, but I really want you to come – actually, I *need* you to come.'

It had been nearly two years since Nicholas Canning, my husband of fifteen years, had been killed while he was on a business trip to Vienna, Austria. As far as my family, my friends and most of the world knew, Nick was hit by a car as he was leaving a bar late at night and died instantly. What really happened was that he was assassinated by a Russian agent in one of the city's many under-ground tunnels because he was there as a covert operative on an assignment for the CIA.

Covert is covert. The CIA would never admit what happened – *could* never admit it – so everyone I knew believed the invented story about the hit-and-run. Max hadn't exactly been trying to set me up with someone since Nick died, but recently he'd been drop-ping a few 'you need to get out there again' hints. Not with him, mind you – Max was like a favorite older uncle and treated me like a beloved niece even though he wasn't married and had no kids of his own.

So now I asked in a wary voice, 'Who is *he*? And why do you need me to come to dinner?'

'*He* is Robson Blake,' he said. 'And he wants to hire you.'

I was still looking at the Kennedy Center. Robson Blake was one of its biggest benefactors. He also gave a lot of money to Georgetown University, which was still visible on the skyline. He had paid for part of the repair work and the cleaning of the Washington Monument after the 2011 earthquake. If I continued driving up Constitution

Avenue once I crossed the bridge, I'd be driving along the National Mall and its iconic museums. Robson Blake had probably contributed money to most of them – or else he'd contributed to their collections. Also to the National Gallery of Art. The Library of Congress. Cleaning and repair work of the Jefferson Memorial across the Tidal Basin. The same for the Lincoln Memorial. The 2016 restoration project to re-seed and renovate the grass on the Mall itself.

'Why does Robson Blake want to hire me?' I asked.

'I'll let him tell you,' Max said. 'But I will say that it's a photo shoot, and he needs someone who can be discreet. So I immediately thought of you.'

I probably shouldn't have been surprised that Max knew Robson Blake well enough to have him over for Indian take-out. In the circles he moved in, he knew a lot of politicians, diplomats, cabinet secretaries and Washington's elite and powerful. The White House, under a previous administration, had been a client when the First Lady hired him to decorate the family quarters. After her husband left office, Max had furnished and decorated their homes in New York City, DC and Martha's Vineyard.

So now I said, 'What time is this dinner?'

'Seven,' he said. 'Ish.'

'Can I bring something? Wine? My portfolio?'

'Nothing, just yourself. Anyway, Robson's already looked you up, done his homework on you. You don't need to bring a thing.'

I made hay of my closet trying to figure out what to wear to meet one of Washington, DC's wealthiest and most generous philanthropists who wanted to hire me for a discreet assignment. It wasn't like he was going to interview me – or was he? Maybe he wanted to check me out in person. But it was *definitely* not a date. So I discarded an LBD and a fire-engine red sleeveless sheath that fit me like a glove. Also the black trouser suit I often wore for high-end photo shoots. Eventually, I settled on a pair of fitted camel suede trousers, an ivory silk blouse and a pair of caramel slingbacks. Brushed my hair so it fell loose around my shoulders, put on some blush, eyeliner, mascara and tinted lip-gloss. Looked in the full-length mirror.

Decided I'd do.

Which seemed to be what Robson Blake was thinking when I

followed Max into his masculine antique-filled living room where a fire crackled in the fireplace and Blake's dark-blue eyes lit up when he saw me. He crossed the room, extended his hand and said, 'Sophie. Robson Blake. My friends call me Robbie. It's nice to meet you, especially after everything Max has told me about you.'

I cast a sideways *What-did-you-tell-him?* glance at Max, who returned it with a benign smile, and put my hand out to shake Robbie Blake's. He held on to it a little longer than he needed to, and I started to wonder if maybe this was a date after all, and I'd been set up.

'It's nice to meet you, too,' I said. 'I've read about you in the news, of course, but all Max told me about this evening was that you're interested in hiring me to take some photos.'

'Let's have drinks first, shall we, and then Robbie can fill you in?' Max steered me toward the sofa. 'Have a seat, darling. And what can I get you?'

I sat. 'A glass of white wine, please.'

'Pinot Grigio or Sauvignon Blanc?'

'Pinot.'

'Robbie, I assume you want your usual?'

'Please.'

Robbie had a usual and Max knew what it was. They seemed quite comfortable around each other. Chummy, good friends. I had no idea Max knew Robson Blake so well.

He sat down next to me as Max left the room to get our drinks. Yep, this was feeling more and more like a set-up. The only one who hadn't been in on the plan was me.

'How do you and Max know each other?' I asked before Robbie could take over the direction of the conversation. Nice. Safe. Easy.

'Through Gil. He introduced us a few years ago,' he said.

Gil Tessier was Max's business partner, handling the antique gallery's finances and its media and advertising. He also took care of the logistics of getting furniture and antiques they'd purchased delivered to the gallery, filling out customs forms and making arrangements for items they bought abroad. He and Max were opposites in almost every way, but they were a good team. Gil liked being behind the scenes; Max thrived as the gallery's public face and its celebrity interior designer. Gil performed the unseen wizardry that kept the business humming, giving Max and the gallery its aura of privileged exclusivity. In a city like Washington where money, power and connections were the holy trinity that people worshipped, that kind of cachet was a big deal.

'How do you know Gil?' I asked.

'We met in London at an antiquities auction.'

Robson Blake seemed to be studying me with acute interest as if I were some rare item he might be interested in acquiring.

I shifted in my seat and put a bit more distance between us. 'My husband and I lived in London for twelve years,' I said. 'I love that city. It was home. We were really happy there.'

Robbie's eyes flickered and I knew he'd correctly read the subtext in what I'd just said. *I was married. Now I'm a widow. I'm still a bit fragile.*

He said in a kind voice, 'Max told me about your husband. I'm sorry for your loss, Sophie. I understand he was killed in an automobile accident two years ago. That must have been rough.'

I still couldn't talk about Nick without my voice wavering, but this time I'd been the one who'd brought him up, wearing my marriage like a suit of armor.

'It was,' I said. 'It is.'

'I'm sorry,' he said again.

Max returned with our drinks, catching my eye and then Robbie's, instantly aware that something had happened, and we hadn't gotten off to a great start. He handed me my wine glass. 'Pinot for you, my love. Robbie, a dirty Martini for you. Vodka, not gin. Two olives.'

He took the club chair across from us and set down his own drink on a side table. His usual was a Scotch on the rocks. I was the lightweight with the glass of white wine.

He crossed one leg over the other. 'Before you got here, Sophie, Robbie was telling me about his latest acquisition, a previously undiscovered painting by Jean-Michel Basquiat that seems to have been part of his 'Skull' series.'

I'd read about Robson Blake's wide-ranging eclectic art collection: it was worth north of a billion dollars. Then there was the art and antiquities he'd given away, donated to museums and galleries. His wealth came from his businesses; he had started out with a small import-export company and built it into a juggernaut, turning it into one of the biggest in the world, buying a cargo shipping business, railroad cars, a fleet of airplanes, a trucking business. And, of course, containers.

'I read that you have a talent for finding paintings or works of art that were previously unknown or undiscovered,' I said. 'How do you do that? How do you get so lucky so often?'

He smiled as if he were going to let me in on a tantalizing secret, though I had the fleeting feeling my remark about his uncanny, repeated good luck had annoyed him. 'I am endlessly curious, and I travel extensively. I'm always on the prowl for something new, looking in places that don't seem obvious to others. As a result, I often find unexpected things. It's more about dogged searching than luck.'

The tiniest wrist slap for my impertinence. 'Is that how you began collecting art?' I asked.

'It is. The first piece of art I bought was in a shop on a dusty street in Marseilles, a series of rough sketches on two pieces of paper. It was years ago, so I paid for them in French francs, the equivalent of about thirty dollars. They turned out to be by Eugène Delacroix, part of the series of sketches he did during the time he spent in Morocco. I sold those drawings later for nearly forty thousand dollars.' He shrugged and smiled. 'After that, I was hooked.'

'So is it about the art or about the discovery?' I asked.

He gave me a sharp-eyed look. 'That's a very astute question.'

'Which you just very neatly sidestepped.'

He laughed. 'I did, didn't I? Honestly, it's mostly the latter. I love the thrill of the hunt. It's addictive, like a drug. To possess something no one else in the world owns – an object of incredible beauty that doesn't demand anything from you. Only that you enjoy it, treasure it.'

'Which has something to do with the reason Robbie would like to hire you, Sophie,' Max said, giving Robbie a look as if I'd passed a test. 'But before we discuss that, our dinner is waiting in the dining room, and I don't want it to get cold. So why don't we talk about everything while we eat?'

The mahogany sideboard was filled with platters and covered dishes sitting on a couple of hot plates, food Max had ordered from the Michelin-starred Bombay Club near the White House. Tandoori salmon, chicken tikka and lamb vindaloo. The vegetables were mushroom matar, saag and an eggplant dish called *bharli vangi*. There was also vegetable biryani, lemon-cashew rice and basmati rice. Finally, there was an assortment of homemade chutneys.

'Who else were you expecting for dinner?' I asked. 'You ordered enough to feed a small army.'

Max grinned. 'I love leftovers.'

We sat down and Max poured the wine, a chilled bottle of pale gold Kabinett Riesling that he said was perfect with Indian food. He sat at the head of the table; Robbie and I sat across from each other.

Robson Blake was not at all what I expected. He seemed restless, as though he were here with us but felt he should be somewhere else and at the first available moment was going to bolt. His edges were rougher than I imagined they would be for someone who was such a generous patron of the arts. Somehow, I thought he'd be more urbane, a bit cultured: instead, I found out he was a bit of a hustler. He bought art for the adrenaline thrill of owning something he alone possessed, which was different from buying it because a painting or a sculpture or an antiquity was something you loved, something that spoke to you. There also seemed to be a ruthlessness about him, not that he had shown it tonight, but it was something I sensed.

We made small talk about the food, which was delicious, and told stories about places each of us had visited in India. I wondered when we were going to get around to the real reason I was here.

Finally, Max set down his fork and said, 'Go ahead, Robbie. Why don't you tell her?'

'Tell me what?' I said. 'It's about time, I think.'

'I'd like you to photograph a recent acquisition I've made,' he said. 'In the strictest confidentiality.'

'I never violate my clients' confidentiality,' I said. 'I wouldn't be in business long if I did.'

'I understand, but I would have to have all your pictures. *All* of them. Don't worry, you'll be well compensated for your work. But you would need to delete everything of mine from your computer. You would have no record of any photographs you took for this project.'

No record of my photographs. Delete everything.

What was he talking about? Pornography? Something he'd stolen? Now it was my turn to glance at Max, except he was telegraphing me a look that said *don't worry, it's all copacetic.*

'I see,' I said. 'In that case, you're going to have to give me more information before I say yes. I need to know what it is you want me to photograph.'

Max stood up and got the bottle of Riesling from a silver wine cooler on the sideboard. 'More wine?' he asked me.

Was I going to need it for what came next? Because he was clearly totally clued in.

'Yes, please,' I said.

He filled my glass, then his and Robbie's. After he sat down, Robbie said to me, 'Have you ever heard of the X Patents?'

'I don't think so. What are they?'

'The very first patents filed with the US Patent Office in the early days of the United States,' he said. 'Before the government started numbering them.'

'You're talking about the 1700s?'

'The *late* 1700s. The first patent was issued in 1790. The first *numbered* patent was issued in July 1836. A few months after that happened, in December 1836, a fire burned the wooden hotel where the patent office was located – not far from the White House – to the ground destroying every patent the US had ever issued,' he said.

That blazing fire, the entire US Patent Office in a hotel in the days when DC was still a rough-and-tumble city going up in smoke. *That* story I'd heard.

'Since the X Patents weren't numbered, does that mean nobody knew how many patents had been destroyed?' I asked.

'They had an idea. The best guess is that there were around ten thousand of them – nine thousand nine hundred and fifty-seven to be precise,' he said. 'Ever since that fire, the Patent Office has been trying to recover what was lost, asking people to look for something – anything – that might be a drawing or the description of an invention that was patented. Sometimes it's something hanging on a wall in someone's office and the owner has no idea of its importance except it's the design for something Great-Great-Great-Uncle Horace invented and then he filed a patent for it. All the Patent Office is looking for is a copy – a scanned document, a photocopy, whatever. They're not asking for the original. They just want to rebuild their archives.'

'So I take it you've found an X Patent?' I asked.

A flicker of annoyance crossed his face as if I were rushing him to the conclusion and he wanted to tell the story his way and in his time.

'Oh, come on, Robbie, don't leave her hanging,' Max said. 'Tell her.'

'It's not that simple,' he said. 'First, she needs to know some history.'

'She's listening,' I said.

'All right,' he said. 'A few months ago, I was in Paris for a friend's birthday party. Every time I visit that city, I haunt the stalls of the *bouquinistes* – I take it you know who they are?'

I nodded. The used and antiquarian booksellers with their green wooden stalls along the banks of the Seine were so famous they had been classified as a UNESCO World Heritage Site.

'You can probably guess where this is going,' he said. 'In one of the stalls, I came across a complete set of *The Four Books on Architecture* by Andrea Palladio. Not in very good condition, unfortunately, but published in the early 1800s. Are you familiar with Palladio?'

'He was an Italian architect who lived in the fifteen hundreds,' I said. 'I photographed an Italian shelter magazine's story on Palladio's influence on American architecture – specifically the classically designed buildings in Washington, like the White House and the Capitol. Also, Monticello and the University of Virginia. Thomas Jefferson was a huge Palladio fan.'

Robbie looked pleased. 'Correct. In fact, Jefferson owned five separate editions of Palladio's books on architecture.'

'You bought the books from the *bouquiniste*?'

'I tried to haggle because they weren't in very good condition, but I did buy them. When I got back to my hotel, however, I discovered the back flap of one of the books looked padded, as if something had been inserted between the cover and the marbled paper. So I got a knife and pried it open. What I found were two pages of drawings of what looked like a design for a clock. A tall case clock with weights, a pendulum and a minute and hour hand. What caught my attention was that some of the writing on one of the pages was backwards, a mirrored handwriting that Leonardo da Vinci was famous for. There was also a third page, a letter to a Countess de Tessé asking for the return of the drawings. It was signed by Thomas Jefferson.'

'What—?'

He held out his hands, palms out. *Wait.* 'I'm getting there. To cut to the chase, I had the documents vetted. One of the drawings was, in fact, Leonardo's, so I was right. The other – which looked as if it had taken Leonardo's design and made some changes, a few

improvements, belonged to Thomas Jefferson. Madame de Tessé
was a good friend of Jefferson's; they wrote hundreds of letters to
each other over decades. I read later that she had a huge influence
on his love of and knowledge of architecture – especially Palladio.
Jefferson was also an admirer of Leonardo da Vinci, who spent his
final years in France living in a villa not far from Paris where he
was the architect and artist for the king of France. And Jefferson,
as you might remember, was our ambassador to France in the years
leading up to the French Revolution.'

'Do you think Jefferson might have found the da Vinci drawing
the way you did, in a bouquiniste's stall, when he was living in
Paris?' I asked.

He smiled. 'He could have done. The *bouquinistes* have been
around since the sixteenth century. Anyway, after Jefferson returned
to America, George Washington asked him to be his Secretary of
State. One of his responsibilities, believe it or not, was to vet or
examine requests for patents in the days before we had an official
patent office. Jefferson's letter to Madame de Tessé asked for the
two drawings to be returned to him because he was considering
filing a patent for the clock. Although, if you ask me, improving
on an invention by Leonardo da Vinci is like telling God you'd like
to take a stab at improving what He'd done after He created heaven
and earth.'

Max caught my eye and winked. As in *I told you so*.

'Why do you think she didn't return the drawings?' I asked.

'I don't know. The best I can figure is that they fell out of contact
for a few years while he was president, as well as the years she and
her husband lived in Switzerland during the French Revolution.
Maybe she forgot about them when they finally got back in touch.
And so did he.'

'Those drawings must be worth a lot of money,' I said.

'I imagine they are. When I had them vetted, no one I consulted
– a friend at Sotheby's who looked at the da Vinci drawing and
someone I know at Monticello who looked at the Jefferson drawing
– was aware that the other drawing existed. So except for Max, Gil
and me, you are now the only other person who knows the whole
story. And I suspect you understand now why I don't want you to
say anything about this to anyone.'

'Of course. Though there's one thing I'm curious about.'

'And what would that be?'

'I'm no expert on Jefferson, but I've been to Monticello several times, including that photo shoot on Palladio. Thomas Jefferson was adamant that his inventions were for the public to enjoy – just like Benjamin Franklin. Neither of them wanted to keep their ideas to themselves or make money from them. Thomas Jefferson and Benjamin Franklin didn't file *any* patents.'

'You're right,' he said with just enough irritation in his voice to let me know he wasn't used to being challenged. Or contradicted. The ruthless streak I'd imagined earlier on restrained display. 'The only US president who ever filed a patent was Abraham Lincoln. It was for a device to lift boats over shoals, but like so many patents, it was for an invention that was never manufactured.'

'So how do you explain the X Patent? Or Jefferson's intention to file what would be an X Patent?' Because so far, he hadn't.

'Obviously, he was prepared to make an exception no one knew about,' he said as if he couldn't believe I hadn't drawn the same conclusion. 'First of all, the clock wasn't an original invention – it wasn't *his* invention. Instead, he was expanding on a design that belonged to Leonardo da Vinci, a polymath – a genius – a man Jefferson admired immensely. My guess is that Jefferson planned to file a patent as a matter of integrity, even though the clock was never built and nothing ever came of it. Later, of course, he designed his own clock – the Great Clock, which is at Monticello and works to this day. You've seen it if you've been there to take photographs.'

'Anyone who visits Monticello sees that clock. It's amazing. The cannonball weights are so large they had to cut holes in the floor so the weights could descend into the basement. A Chinese gong chimes the hour.'

'That's correct.' Then he added with a tiny bit of sarcasm, 'Now, have I explained things to your satisfaction?'

'I'd like to be clear,' I said. 'You want me to take photos of these drawings and the letter and that's it?'

I expected him to say now I was the one sidestepping the question, but he nodded. 'And turn everything over to me. *Everything.*'

'Not to talk myself out of a job, but you've got a cellphone. You can do this without me.'

Max got up. 'I'm getting another bottle of wine.'

When he was gone, Robbie said, 'I want professional photos. I've donated art, sculpture, antiquities to many museums and cultural institutions over the years, but I've also loaned works of art from my personal collection. When something is on loan, I have a framed photograph of it on the wall or wherever it would be as if I still had it. It's an eccentricity, I know. Especially when I have a man who keeps track of all this for me. But it's an indulgence I figure I'm allowed to have.'

Max came back with an open bottle of Sauvignon Blanc. 'Sophie? Another glass? I've switched wines.'

I'd already drunk more than I usually did, but this evening seemed to need alcohol to lubricate it. 'Yes, please.'

He poured wine for the three of us and sat down. 'Have you two worked this out?'

'Almost,' Robbie said. 'There is one more thing. Olivia has asked me for a new author photo – make that *demanded* a new author photo. She told me it needs to look like I do *now*, not the one I've been using from twenty years ago. To quote her, "when you had less weight and more hair."'

Max and I laughed, and I said, 'You want me to take a portrait you can use for a book jacket?'

'Yes. And I'll pay whatever your fee is to own all the rights.'

'Alright, but in that case, I'll need two sessions with you. One for the documents and one for the portrait.'

'Fine,' he said. 'No problem.'

'I didn't know you and Livvie were working on another book,' Max said. 'What's this one about?'

'It's called *Gilded Splendor: The Influence of Byzantine Art in the Modern Age*,' he said.

'You're an author as well?' I asked.

'A co-collaborator, not an author. You've heard of Olivia Sage? Doctor Olivia Sage? She's the author.'

'Her name sounds familiar.'

'She's probably the world expert on Byzantine art,' he said. 'Livvie has been extremely helpful in verifying the provenance of many of the items I acquired that date from the period of the Byzantine Empire – which, strictly speaking, began during the Middle Ages and ended with the fall of Constantinople in 1453. As far as art goes, though, many countries preserved Byzantine influences in their art and architecture for centuries afterwards. I own a number of items from the actual Byzantine era, but I also own a significant amount from the later years. It's a period of history I find fascinating, much of it thanks to Olivia.'

'Olivia teaches at Georgetown,' Max said to me. 'She has her own chair. Jack O'Hara probably knows her.'

I nodded. 'That's right. That's how I know her.' To Robbie, I added, 'Jack is a Jesuit and an old friend who teaches ethics at the law school. A few years ago, he inherited an icon from a woman he counseled as her spiritual advisor. It was beautiful but it was also damaged, so Jack took it to Olivia Sage. She told him it was quite valuable and that it had probably come from an Orthodox church or a monastery in Eastern Europe. She put him in touch with someone at the National Gallery of Art who specialized in restoring icons. Now it's in his suite at the Jesuit house of studies in Stanton Park. It's stunning.'

'I'm not surprised. Olivia is incredibly well connected,' he said. 'She's also a brilliant scholar.'

'Two years ago, she and Jerome hired me to decorate an addition to their house in Georgetown,' Max said. 'A sunroom and a library. They were wonderful to work with – especially Olivia – and their place is beautiful, filled with art and a fabulous collection of icons.'

'Do you mean Jerome Sage the Broadway producer?' I asked.

Max stood up and nodded as he began collecting our dinner plates. 'They have an apartment overlooking Central Park along with the house in Georgetown. They go back and forth between DC and New York City, especially if Jerome has a show on. They've also got a summer place in the Hamptons.'

I started to get up. 'Let me help you with the dishes.'

'Sit. You, too, Robbie. I'm bringing dessert.'

Dessert was *gulab jamun*, an Indian dish of fried khoya dipped in saffron-infused sugar syrup and coffee. We made small talk and Robbie – apparently not one to let grass grow under his feet – asked me if I could come by his house tomorrow morning at eleven to take photos of the X Patents. I said I could.

Inevitably, we left Max's apartment together and I knew Robbie wanted to walk me home, even though it was only up a flight of stairs. A black Lincoln Town Car sat idling in front of the house. Robbie hadn't called anyone or even texted anyone that I was aware of, so I wondered how long the driver had been waiting there at his beck and call.

'He'll wait,' Robbie said, indicating the car. 'I want to make sure you get safely inside.'

Nothing was going to happen on my front steps. And this evening *had not been a date*. It had been a *business* meeting. So Robbie shouldn't expect a goodnight kiss or anything beyond a handshake and a simple 'goodnight,' even though his body language said the former was exactly what he *did* expect. I unlocked the outside front door, and he followed me into the small vestibule with its black-and-white harlequin-tiled marble floor. It was just big enough for two people. I turned around before I put the key in the lock to the interior door that led to a staircase up to my apartment and held out my hand.

'Goodnight,' I said. 'It was nice meeting you, Robbie. I'll see you tomorrow.'

He took my hand and brought it to his lips. 'Goodnight, Sophie. It was nice meeting you, too. I'll see you tomorrow at eleven.'

'I should go.' I extracted my hand. 'I still have some work to do tonight, so I'm going to be up for a while. Thank you for walking me to my front door.'

He accepted the brush-off with grace, smiled and said he hoped I wouldn't be up too late. After I opened the interior door, I closed and locked it behind me. Then I leaned against it, shut my eyes and wondered what the hell had just happened.

THREE

I have never been able to say no to Finn Hathaway. He asks, I say yes.

Although I wasn't going to say yes this time, not after what he just asked me to do.

He figured it out lightning quick, reading the expression on my face and saying as if he couldn't believe it, 'Wait a minute – you're not going to turn me down, are you, Sophie? I could get somebody else for this – it would be a piece of cake – but I want *you*. You're great with kids. You speak Spanish. But mostly you're the best damn photographer I know.' He smiled, a slow, teasing smile. 'Come on, it's going to be fun.'

Fun.

It wasn't going to be fun. It was going to be more like picking at a scab that had never really healed, but Finn didn't know that.

Finn was tall, lanky, easygoing, engaging. Kind eyes, brown hair lightly sprinkled with gray, usually wearing nicely pressed jeans and a dress shirt, sometimes a vest, unless he had a meeting with someone in which case he dressed more formally: he tucked in the shirt. He was really good with people – actually, he was great – possessing an almost preternatural ability to understand what made someone tick as if he could see right through your skull into your brain. Which, in turn, made it easy for him to get people to do what he wanted. He could also make you believe it's what you wanted, too.

So he didn't understand why I might say, *No, thanks.*

'I don't do sports photography,' I said. 'You know that.'

Finn brushed me off. 'This isn't really sports. It's an afternoon soccer camp for homeless kids. And it's going to take place on the Mall, thanks to the Vice-President getting involved. Usually, it requires an Act of God for the National Park Service to agree to let their grass be trodden on by a lot of people. Especially if they're wearing cleats.'

'The Vice-President of the United States is interested in this?'

'He is.'

The bells of the Church of the Epiphany began tolling as they'd done for nearly two centuries. They had also tolled for the inauguration of every incoming president since Calvin Coolidge. Abraham Lincoln once attended a funeral here. Senator Jefferson Davis was a parishioner before he moved to Richmond to become the president of the Confederacy. Later, the church became a Civil War hospital. So these bells had weight and they had history.

Finn and I stopped talking to listen. I had met him in the little park that was adjacent to the church, a tranquil place of dappled sunshine and greenery dwarfed by the high-rises of downtown Washington, DC that loomed over us like bullies on a playground.

In the mid-1800s, the church established a home to help the poor and the sick, and ever since then that had been its mission: helping the indigent, the neglected, the homeless. So it was appropriate that the offices at the back of the little Gothic church with its bright-red arched doors were where Streetwise was located, a resource and cultural center for DC's homeless population. It was also the office of the weekly street newspaper for and *by* the homeless, and Finn was its Editor-in-Chief.

Weekly, that is, until last week. Now it would be bi-weekly, a matter of fewer donations and no way to make the math work. The homeless who sold the papers – some made as much as six hundred dollars a week selling papers on the street – would now have their meager incomes cut in half. When Finn told me – before the news was officially announced and made the front page of both *The Washington Post* and *The Washington Tribune* – it was one of the rare times I'd seen him despondent. Taking the decision personally, as if he could have done something to make it turn out differently. Like winning the Mega Millions jackpot or finding a pot of gold at the end of a rainbow.

So he had thrown himself into this new project as a way of raising visibility – and hopefully bringing in donations – for Streetwise: organizing a soccer camp for homeless kids who were going to have the opportunity of a lifetime to run drills and pass balls for a few hours with some of the best soccer players in the world.

The bells finished tolling and Finn said, 'Don't tell me this is the first you've heard of it – Real Madrid coming here for a friendly with DC United?'

'I don't really follow soccer.' *A lie.*

'You don't need to follow soccer. You don't even need to know what "offside" means or what the advantage rule is. The US, Canada and Mexico are hosting the next World Cup in a few years, and FIFA and the US Soccer Federation are trying to gin up interest. Americans don't get that an entire ninety-minute game of a sport with so much running around can be played and the final score is one-nil. This is the first international friendly the Soccer Federation is sponsoring, but it won't be the last.'

I knew what offside meant and I knew what the advantage rule was.

'What's up, Sophie?' Finn asked. 'You're not telling me something. What's the real reason?'

He wasn't going to let me off the hook. I picked at an imaginary piece of dirt under a fingernail. Then I looked him in the eye.

'My father played soccer for Real Madrid,' I said. 'My biological father. Antonio Medina.'

Finn's eyes were saucers. '*You're* Antonio Medina's daughter? Are you serious? Jesus, he's soccer royalty. *Was* soccer royalty. I had no idea . . . I'm . . . jeez . . . I'm sorry for your loss.'

My loss. He didn't know the half of it.

'Thanks, but I'm sure I found out he died the same way you did.' I shot him a sideways glance. 'In the news.'

A motorcycle crash in the Sierra Guadarrama Mountains outside Madrid when I was fourteen. Blood alcohol as high as an IQ score. One of Spain's top fashion models was with him. Their bodies were found tangled together at the bottom of a very deep ravine. The country had held a national day of mourning.

'I'm sorry,' he said again. 'I had no idea.'

'My mother moved us back to the States when I was two. She got a divorce – *and* an annulment. So it's not like I knew him. Or even remember him.'

Though I hadn't stopped thinking about him. *For years.* Wondered if someday he'd come for me, rescue me and take me back to Spain after my mother – who had always seen me as a *mistake* – remarried. Within a couple of years, my blond, blue-eyed, all-American half-brother and half-sister were born.

I look like the Spanish maid's kid or else like I've been adopted. *I look like Antonio Medina.* Dark hair, skin the color of a caramel latte, dark-brown eyes flecked with gold. My mother and I had never discussed my father – a regrettable episode of her young life as a college student studying abroad who got knocked up and then married the father when she discovered she was pregnant because that's what you did in those days, especially if you were living in a severely Catholic country.

After we left, I never saw my father again, and my mother and my grandparents raised me. Until Harry Wyatt, my stepfather, entered my life. I adore Harry. And I know he adores me, too, loves me as fiercely as he loves Tommy and Lexie. Maybe even spoiled me a little more than the two of them as if he were trying to make up for Antonio not being there. For forgetting all about me.

Harry saved me.

'It's OK,' I said to Finn. 'How would you know?'

'So that's the reason you don't want to take photos at the soccer camp? Because of your father?'

'I don't want anybody connecting the two of us. Nobody knows about me – nobody knows that Antonio had a daughter – at least, I *think* no one knows. Or remembers. I'd like to keep it that way.'

'Nobody has to know who you are.'

I gave him a skeptical look, but he wasn't giving up.

'I really need you for this.' His tone was light, cajoling. 'Please? I *promise* no one is gonna know who you are if that's how you want it. You've got nothing to worry about.'

I sighed and said, with some reluctance, 'All right, if you can keep it that way, I'll do it.'

'Thank you. I knew you wouldn't let me down.'

I didn't tell him that it was really the *kids* I didn't want to let down. Hardly any of them had fathers that were involved in their lives or even fathers that were still around – and if they were in the picture, well . . . they were *homeless*.

So these kids and I had something in common.

I'd traveled to Spain on business with IPS; Nick and I had been there twice on vacation, to Nerja on the Costa del Sol and Andalusia during Semana Santa – Holy Week – to watch the processions of religious fraternities in colorful hooded robes wind through the streets carrying crosses and candles as they marched alongside floats depicting Mary the Mother of God or the Passion of Jesus Christ.

But I'd never gone to a Real Madrid football match, not once.

Now I'd finally meet some of the players on the team where my father had been a superstar, an idol. No one who played for them now had been there when Antonio was on the team – it had been too long, too many years, nearly twenty-five since he died.

'Don't worry,' Finn said again as if he were reading my mind. 'I promise no one will know you're Antonio Medina's daughter.'

Although it was against my better judgment, I believed him.

'All right. And now I'd better go,' I said. 'I've got an appointment across town at eleven to take photographs at a client's house.'

'I think I'll stick around here for a while and make a few phone calls,' he said. 'Reach out to some people who've been generous donors in the past and see if they might be able to help us out.'

If he didn't want to make the calls in his office where someone might overhear him asking for money, the situation was probably more dire than I realized.

'Is it that bad?'

He tilted his head as if considering his answer. 'We'll get through this.'

Which sounded like it *was* that bad. 'Let me know what I can do to help.'

'You're already working for us pro bono, so you couldn't possibly do any more, Sophie. The rest of us are taking pay cuts, cutting expenses where we can.'

'*Finn.*' He and the rest of the staff didn't make much money to begin with.

'It's OK,' he said, pulling his phone out of his pocket. 'It's just temporary. We'll be fine.'

'Call me if you get together to practice with the kids who will be at the soccer camp before the real thing, OK? I'd like to spend some time getting to know them and for them to get to know me before I show up on the day with a camera.'

'A practice beforehand is probably a good idea,' he said. 'I'll let you know.' Then he turned to his phone and started punching numbers.

I said goodbye. He didn't hear me.

I left the park and headed for my car which, by a stroke of luck, was at a meter on the street near the church rather than in the garage where I usually had to park and fork over a usurious fee to the robber barons who owned it. A couple of tents and a shopping cart filled with someone's life possessions were clustered together on the sidewalk across from the entrance to the park. Even though the DC Department of Human Services had recently tried to clear out the little encampment claiming the sidewalk needed to be cleaned, and passersby needed better access, the residents had returned the next day to set up their tents near the curb edge of the sidewalk where they weren't bothering anyone who wanted to walk by. During months of working with Streetwise and taking photos, I learned that the homeless, or *unhoused* as Finn referred to them, sought to stay in places where they felt safe and protected. Next to a church was such a place. Near the Streetwise offices was even better; the staff looked out for them. On the day when the DHS officials had tried to move the little tent village, Finn told me one of his editors had stood *right there*, stone-faced with arms folded across her chest, watching the officials do what they came to do but making them clarify that this was just a street *cleaning*; once it was finished, no one was going to have to leave permanently as long as they allowed others plenty of access to the sidewalk.

This morning, most of the tents appeared to be unoccupied – homeless individuals might not have a proper home, but many had jobs – except for a bright-green tent that had the flap open. Its owner, an elderly man wearing a red-and-white knitted cap, a red Nationals tee-shirt and black nylon track pants sat in a camping chair in front of the tent. I knew almost all the regulars who lived there; he was new. A black Labrador Retriever that reminded me of my parents' dog Ella lay next to him. Another man who had his back to me was bent over the dog. I slowed down to get a glimpse of the Lab and say hello to his owner, which turned out to be a mistake because the dog caught my eye and instantly leaped up, barking and lunging at me to protect his master.

The owner jerked the dog's leash and shouted for him to sit as the younger man swiftly stood up and stepped back as if he were ready to turn around and see what had upset the dog. I was dressed for my appointment with Robbie – black trousers, white short-sleeved silk blouse, two-inch stiletto heels. One of my heels caught in a crack in the pavement as I tried to sidestep the Lab. At the same time, the man who had been caring for the dog and its owner swung around and bumped me, sending me flying. I hit the ground hard and slid like a baseball player trying to get to base before being tagged. I landed on my right side and my arm took the brunt of the fall.

It took me a stunned moment to catch my breath and not yelp with pain because my arm hurt like hell. The man who had decked me was already kneeling at my side, the words of apology tumbling out as he tried to help me stand up. 'Are you OK? I'm so sorry – I didn't see you. I was afraid Bruiser was going after something and I meant to move whoever or whatever it was out of the way, not knock you over. I'm so sorry,' he repeated.

Bruiser. Good name. 'I'm bleeding,' I said in a faint voice and lifted my arm. A bloody abrasion along my forearm looked like raw meat that had been through a grinder.

'That wound needs to be cleaned so it doesn't get infected,' he said. 'Let's sit you down somewhere so I can take care of it.'

I shook my head. 'Thanks, but I've got an appointment across town and I'm going to be late if I don't leave right now. I've got tissues in my car and hand sanitizer. It's just a scrape, not a deep cut. It'll stop bleeding eventually.'

I checked my blouse and trousers to make sure I hadn't torn or bled on something and saw the long white scuff mark on my trouser leg. I could probably brush it off and maybe Robbie wouldn't notice. At least my suit jacket was in the car. Once the cut stopped bleeding, I could put on the jacket so he wouldn't see my arm.

'Hand sanitizer is going to sting like hell. I've got something better, and I promise I'll only take a moment. Hang on. Let me get my bag.'

'No, really—'

'*Wait here.*'

I did as I was told while he went back to the camping chair where the owner was sitting with Bruiser who now lay peacefully next to him. 'Thanks, Doc,' the man said. 'See you next week?'

'I'll be by to change that bandage,' he said. 'Try to keep it clean and don't let Bruiser pull it off.'

He came back to where I was still standing. 'Your turn. Come on, that arm is bleeding like crazy and you don't want to get blood all over your nice clothes. We can sit on the bench inside the park.'

He opened the gate and held it for me. 'You're a doctor? I asked. 'And you're awfully bossy.'

'I'm a vet, and you wouldn't be the first person to tell me that.'

'You weren't treating that man?'

'I was treating Bruiser,' he said. We sat down on the bench, and he opened a small medical bag, pulling out a bottle of pale-blue liquid. He set it on the bench and reached back in, removing a packet of gauze squares and peeling off a few pieces. 'This isn't going to hurt but it will clean the wound. And, like I said, it won't sting.'

'What is it?'

'Nolvasan.' He squirted some of the liquid on to the gauze compress and gently cleaned my arm.

'There. All done. Now I'm going to put some sulfadene cream on it. Cover it with gauze and tape till it cauterizes. It'll do for now.' His touch was gentle. I looked down at his hands. There was a pale line on the tanned third finger of his left hand where a wedding ring would have been. Until recently, by the looks of it.

He had curly brown hair and the bluest eyes I'd ever seen. If I had to guess, he was probably a few years older than I was. Maybe early forties.

'Is that cream for dogs?'

'And cats. It's all I've got and it's fine for humans in a pinch. Once that cut stops bleeding, the best thing to do is let it heal naturally. You can also put cocoa cream with shea butter on it. You'll want a piece of chocolate every time you get a whiff, but you won't have a scar.'

'Sophie? Landon? What's going on?' Finn had crossed the park from the bench where he and I had been sitting in a few quick steps.

'Nothing. Everything's fine,' I said. 'I had a near run-in with Bruiser over there and I tripped and fell. This, um, gentleman was just treating a little scrape I got. Do you two know each other?'

The vet – Landon – looked from me to Finn. 'Do *you two* know each other?'

'Sophie, meet Doctor Landon Reed, a veterinarian who moved here from San Diego a few months ago,' Finn said. 'He just opened a clinic in Adams Morgan, but he's also spending time on the streets with our people looking after their pets. And Landon, this is Sophie Medina. She's an international photojournalist who has been kind enough to help us, doing pro bono work. You've probably seen some of her photographs in the newspaper. We got lucky. We've got an award-winning ringer on our staff.'

'Nice to meet you, Doctor Reed.' I held up my bandaged arm. 'Thanks for the first aid. I'm sorry to run but I'm going to be really late for my meeting. Finn, call me and let me know when the kids are going to get together for a practice scrimmage, OK?'

Finn nodded and Landon Reed said, 'Hey, wait. It's Landon. Doctor Reed was my dad. Nice to meet you, too, though I'm sorry about the circumstances. Would you like an escort to walk past Bruiser?'

I gave him an *Are-you-kidding?* look. 'I've been sent to war zones in a previous job. I think I can handle walking to my car.'

'Oh.' He reddened. 'Sorry.'

Still, I slowed my pace when I passed the green tent so I wouldn't startle Bruiser again. This time, the dog just sat there next to his owner, placidly watching me.

'You OK?' the man said to me. 'Bruiser don't mean nothing. His bark is worse than his bite.'

'I'm fine,' I said. 'He's a good watchdog.'

'That he is. Doc took care of you, too, huh? He's a good man. Heart of gold. Won't take no money, either.'

'Yes,' I said, 'he does seem to be a good man.'

I looked back over my shoulder.

Landon Reed was still watching me, a thoughtful look on his face that for some reason made me vaguely uneasy.

FOUR

Robson Blake lived in Kalorama, a neighborhood of beautiful old homes and one of Washington's wealthiest and most exclusive. Although it wasn't far from the commercial bustle of Connecticut Avenue, it was a world unto itself of graceful stone and brick houses built in the late nineteenth and early twentieth centuries. Kalorama was on the list of National Historic Places, a neighborhood of presidents. The Obamas owned a home here. Woodrow Wilson, William Howard Taft, Franklin D. Roosevelt, Warren Harding and Herbert Hoover all lived here at some time before or after their presidencies. The embassies of twenty-eight countries and a few ambassadors' residences were located here; the largest and most elegant was the residence of the French ambassador, a palatial nineteen-bedroom Tudor Revival mansion that overlooked Rock Creek.

Robbie's house, a redbrick Georgian that was lush with ivy growing halfway up the façade, was down the street from the French ambassador's residence on Kalorama Road. An enormous saucer magnolia, its branches heavy with pink flowers the size of large teacups, graced the side yard along with drifts of yellow daffodils. An espaliered rose bush grew on a trellis in the front garden. It was only mid-March but already a few roses had bloomed. I parked the Mini in the tiny driveway in front of the garage, gathered my equipment and camera bag, and walked up the flagstone path to the front door.

Last night, Robbie had named a sum of money for my fee that was at least five times higher than I would have charged and asked if it was acceptable. I didn't blink. I said yes but asked him to clarify what exactly he wanted me to do so we were on the same page. He repeated that he wanted me to take photos of the Jefferson and da Vinci drawings of the clock and the letter to Madame de Tessé. After that session, once I sent him my photos, I was to delete everything from my computer and my camera. I would return another time to take his author photo. But most importantly, he reminded me, his fee bought my silence: that I wouldn't reveal anything about the X Patent drawings.

After I said I agreed, he told me he'd have a contract drawn up for me to sign, which was odd. Usually, I prepared the contract for my client, not the other way around. I said OK and wondered if I was going to have to sign it in blood.

Robbie's housekeeper, a petite pretty woman with skin the same color as mine, opened the door after I rang the bell. She knew my name. I was expected.

'Follow me, please,' she said with a light Hispanic accent. 'Mr Blake is in his study.'

We left the art-filled foyer with its beautiful spiral staircase that wound dizzily up three floors and a crystal chandelier that sparkled like diamonds from Cartier. I recognized the runner in the hallway from my trips to the Middle East – an Isfahan, very expensive – as we walked by more paintings that I knew were originals: two Monets, a Degas, a Constable, a Picasso and one I didn't recognize. I wanted to linger to take them all in and see if I could read the signature on the unrecognized painting, but the housekeeper was walking briskly ahead of me, her head swiveling to make sure I was following. I hurried to catch up.

A photographer will tell you to take as many pictures as you can the first two days after you arrive someplace you've never been before. The reason is that two days is roughly how long it takes before even the most exotic, breathtaking vista – the snow-covered peaks of the Himalayas, a herd of elephants by a lake at sunrise in Botswana, the iridescent blue, turquoise and purple of the tropical waters of a beach in Turks and Caicos – becomes familiar and less jaw-droppingly special. The newness wears off like new-car scent. You don't see or notice things with the same awestruck wonder you felt when you first got there. I wondered if Robbie's housekeeper had become so inured to the priceless art her boss owned that she no longer stopped to stare and appreciate it.

Halfway down the hall, she knocked on a heavy oak door. I heard Robbie's voice on the other side of it. 'Come.'

He was seated behind a massive desk that reminded me of the Resolute desk in the Oval Office. We were in his study, a room filled with books and more art, the walls painted a rich shade of vermillion. Two windows looked out on the blooming magnolia in the sideyard. Behind Robbie's desk hung a large painting of a Madonna and Child that I guessed probably dated from the Renaissance. The scenery behind the two figures reminded me vaguely of Venice. Whoever had been the dark-haired model for Mary, she couldn't have been older than thirteen, her eyes downcast as if ignoring the artist or maybe keeping a secret she would never reveal. Her chubby-legged, pink-cheeked baby had eyes that already looked world-weary, as if he knew the weight of his destiny and what was to come. The painting was a surprise – somehow I would have expected a Gilbert Stuart portrait of George Washington or a Winslow Homer seascape or a Remington, which would have seemed more in character for Robbie. Still, the painting was breathtaking. Probably worth millions of dollars. Many millions.

He got up as the housekeeper closed the door, leaving us alone. Today, he was dressed more casually in a burgundy cashmere V-neck sweater over a blue dress shirt and jeans. He came around from behind his desk and shook my hand. All business, last night's awkward goodbye apparently swept under the carpet as if it hadn't happened.

'The painting behind your desk is magnificent,' I said.

He turned around and looked at it. 'The del Verrocchio,' he said. 'Thank you, it is one of my favorites. Do you know his work?'

'Not really. Not well.'

'Andrea del Verrocchio was a fifteenth-century painter, sculptor and goldsmith from Florence. Leonardo da Vinci was one of his apprentices. Leonardo may even have done some work on this painting, although it's attributed to del Verrocchio.'

'Can you tell me about the other paintings in here?' I asked.

He nodded, a pleased smile flitting across his face. 'Of course. This is my Renaissance room.'

He gave me a slow tour as if he were a museum guide, telling me about each painting, expounding on its history and provenance. Each one – Ghirlandaio, Perugino, Bellini, Jan van Eyck, Pieter Brueghel the Elder – a masterpiece. He also told me some fascinating, arcane and occasionally scandalous fact about the artist or a previous owner. The last painting hung on the wall next to the door and didn't seem to belong with the others. It wasn't Renaissance. It wasn't even a painting.

'This is an icon,' I said. 'It looks Russian.'

Like the del Verrocchio, it was a Madonna and Child, except only the faces and hands were painted and then heavily varnished in the flat, sad-eyed way of icon-painting. Everything else – the ornate embellished border, the folds of their robes and the two halos, hers like a diadem, his like a crown – was intricately worked in burnished silver and gold.

'This,' Robbie said, 'was one of Olivia's finds.'

'Olivia Sage?'

He nodded. 'It's a very good copy of Our Lady of Kazan, though probably only from the mid-eighteen hundreds. The original – which was brought to Russia from Constantinople in the thirteen hundreds – was stolen from the monastery in Kazan in 1904. To this day no one knows what happened to it.'

'I thought it was presumed destroyed.'

'You know the story?'

'My husband's grandmother was Russian Orthodox. I know a lot of stories.'

He gave me a curious look. 'So you must know that when you are dealing with the Russians, you never know what is true or what is made up. What did Madame de Staël say? "In Russia, everything is a mystery, but nothing is a secret."' He pointed to the icon. 'It's not the first time that icon vanished. The original, I mean. It disappeared for several hundred years and magically reappeared in the fifteen hundreds. It's not impossible that it could turn up again.'

'That story about Our Lady of Kazan being discovered in the fifteen hundreds is a legend. The Virgin supposedly appeared to a little girl and told her where the icon was hidden. Under a house in perfect, pristine condition.'

'Just as someone could come across it now in a grandmother's attic,' he said. 'Where it has been hidden and gathering dust for more than a century.'

'Perhaps,' I said. 'Considering you found two Delacroix sketches in Marseilles and drawings by Thomas Jefferson and Leonardo da Vinci in Tours, I imagine something like that seems quite possible.'

For some reason, the remark seemed to rub him the wrong way and I saw a flash in his eyes that might have been anger. 'The Jefferson and da Vinci drawings are downstairs in the vault,' he said in a curt tone. 'That's where you'll take your photographs. I'll escort you and then Bernard can help you get set up.'

'Wait— I'm going to be inside a vault? And who's Bernard?'

'The vault is not what you're expecting, I assure you. And Bernard is the caretaker of my art collection.'

'Before we go,' I said, 'I'd like to take a couple of pictures of you in this room.'

'Why? I've already hired you to take formal author photos. Not here, not now.'

'Because I believe this room is your sanctuary, where you come when you want to close off the rest of the world. Because you're probably your most authentic self when you're in here.'

He looked startled, but then he gave me a shrewd look and I knew he'd figured out exactly why I wanted to do this. These photos would probably look nothing like the posed photo he wanted for the book jacket.

'You're very perceptive,' he said. 'But I still want proper author photos taken. Formal ones.'

'Of course,' I said. 'I'll take those another time. But you might like the ones I take here as well.'

'We'll see about that,' he said, though he indulged me for about fifteen minutes.

When he seemed to be growing impatient, I said, 'I think I have enough. Why don't you show me where your vault is so I can get started?'

The elevator to the lower level was at the end of the hallway. As he'd done before, he murmured the names of the artists of yet more paintings as we walked by. Frans Hals, Peter Paul Rubens, Caravaggio, Diego Velázquez. I wondered what the rest of the house looked like if this was only the hallway.

He pushed the call button for the elevator, and I heard the hum of a motor as it rose to the main floor. Just before the door opened, his phone rang.

He pulled it out of his pocket and frowned at the display. 'Dammit, I've got to take this. Bernard's downstairs. He should have everything set up for you.' He turned away, an abrupt dismissal, and I heard him say into his phone, 'What the hell happened?'

The elevator door opened. I stepped inside and reached over to push the button for the lower level. There were *two* lower levels. Robbie hadn't mentioned that, nor had he said which floor the vault was located on. I said *eenie-meenie-miney-moe* and pushed the button for the lowest level. Where else would a vault be?

When the door slid open on Level −2, I stepped into a small but very beautiful room decorated much like the upstairs. An Oriental carpet, a love seat, an oval coffee table, two matching upholstered chairs pulled up for an intimate gathering. A few small paintings on the walls and a marble bust on a console table – an eyeless woman with a cap of tightly ringed curls, a robe draped low across her breasts, her sightless face tilted up with an expression as if she were staring at something rapturous and wonderful. I took a guess. Greek. Or maybe Roman.

Across from the elevator, a door was open to a room that was softly lit as if by candlelight. I went over and peeked inside. Icons, dozens of icons, their frames shimmering gold and silver were lit by tiny spotlights that made the flat two-dimensional faces and bodies of saints, of Mary the mother of God, of Jesus as a child, a teacher and crucified on the cross all look otherworldly.

In the center of the room a kiot – a carved wooden shadow box – rested on a stand containing an icon of the Virgin of Vladimir, the most famous, most venerated icon in the Orthodox Church. Like Our Lady of Kazan, it also depicted a Madonna and Child, the painting of the two figures cracked and crazed with varnish, a dark yellowish black as if they'd been preserved in amber. It wasn't hard to guess why this icon was the star of the show: the exquisite intricately-worked gold and silver frame was also encrusted with rubies, sapphires and emeralds that sparkled where the light caught them. It had to be worth a fortune, and I wondered where Robbie had acquired it.

I started to pull out my phone and then shoved it back into my pocket. Bernard was nowhere to be seen, so I was definitely on the wrong floor. Although it had been an honest mistake, I wasn't supposed to be here, and I had no right to take a picture – even a personal candid – of something Robbie kept hidden in a vault that would give Fort Knox a run for its money.

The door to the elevator had closed but it was still on the second lower level. I went back and pushed the button. The next time the door opened, a tall, stern-faced man with snow-white hair was waiting for me on Level –1. I stepped into another anteroom that was almost a duplicate of the room on the floor below.

'Ms Medina.' It sounded like a reproach.

So this was Bernard. He knew I'd been on the lower level.

'Yes.'

'Where's Mr Blake?'

'Taking a phone call. He said you'd show me where I can set up my equipment.'

He picked up my lighting kit and one of my tripods: a gentleman.

'Follow me.'

The conference room could have been in any office – a law firm, a consulting firm, a hotshot DC lobbyist. It was plain and sterile, set up for meetings, video conferences, a place to do business. No art on the walls, no awards, no photographs, no books on book-shelves. No *nothing*. No hint that this room was where Robson Blake conducted business, did deals, bought art.

'In here,' Bernard said. He set down my equipment. 'Before you arrived, the elevator stopped on the lower level. And stayed there.'

The question was implicit.

'I apologize. I wasn't aware that there were two floors when I got in the elevator, and I assumed a vault would be on the lowest level.'

'You were not supposed to be there.'

'I'm sorry,' I said again.

'If Mr Blake finds out . . .'

'Would that be a problem? His icon room is very beautiful.'

'. . . I could lose my job.'

'Seriously?'

'Very seriously.'

'Why?'

'Because no one is allowed in that room unless Mr Blake is present as well.'

'Look, Bernard, if he asks me, I'm going to tell Mr Blake the truth. I didn't touch anything, I promise. I'll explain and apologize. Like I said, it was an honest mistake. It's not your fault.'

'It is. The door to that room should have been closed.'

'I don't want you to get fired,' I said. 'So let's just not say anything, OK?'

'Did you take any photographs?'

'I did *not*.'

For a moment, I thought he was going to ask to see my camera and my phone, but he gave me a grim nod and said, 'All right. Let's get you set up.'

He helped me with my equipment, but he also stayed to take care of handling the drawings, placing them where I asked him to, surprisingly without wearing white cotton gloves as I'd expected he would.

'Mr Blake doesn't believe in wearing gloves when you handle books or old documents,' he said. 'He says it's easier to damage or tear paper – especially if it's very old and fragile – if you can't feel it. He believes gloves are an impediment, whatever the glove-wearing purists will tell you. Besides, they don't wear gloves to handle Shakespeare's First Folios at the Folger Library across town, so Mr Blake says that if it's good enough for the Bard, it's good enough for him.'

'Either way, I'm glad you're the one taking care of these drawings,' I said. 'They're extremely fragile.'

He left me briefly, and I heard the elevator descending to the lower level, so I figured he was probably closing the door to the icon room and locking it. By the time Robbie showed up, noticeably irritated and distracted after his phone call, I had finished taking all the photos I needed. I showed him a few pictures off the monitor on the back of my camera, but he barely seemed to register seeing them.

'These are fine,' he said. 'Thank you.'

We were done.

'Do you want to set up a time and day for me to come by and take your author photo? Or do you want to contact me, and we'll work something out? And there's a matter of the contract you wanted to draw up for me to sign?'

'Yes, yes, it's done, but we can take care of that next time. And I'll call you. Bernard will see you out. Forgive me, but I need to take care of something down here.'

'Of course. I'll send your photos once I edit them. Give me a day or two.'

'Sure,' he said. 'That'll be fine.'

I finished repacking my camera bag. Bernard collected the rest of my equipment, carrying it into the elevator.

On the ride upstairs to the main level, I said, 'Is he often like this?'

He didn't even bother to ask what I meant by 'like this.'

'He has a lot on his mind lately,' he said. 'At least he won't find out you were downstairs. I erased the video.'

'There's a video?'

'Of course. With the value of everything in this house, there has to be. The insurance company insists.'

He helped me carry my gear to the car and stow everything in the Mini's compact trunk. I thanked him and watched him walk, erect as a soldier, back into the house.

I wondered who had called to set Robbie off and what had transpired during their conversation to make him so upset and irritable. Bernard had tried to brush it off, but if the boss was in a bad mood, some of that anger was going to rain down on him as well. Which would explain the somber, troubled look on his face when he said goodbye to me just now.

Maybe Bernard knew exactly who had called – and why.

Finn Hathaway promised no one would know I was Antonio Medina's daughter when I agreed to take photographs of the soccer camp, but, of course, someone *did* know.

Almost immediately.

I checked my messages after leaving Robbie's home and found one from someone named Enrique Navarro who said he was with *El País*. Spain's top newspaper.

It doesn't take a genius.

I listened to the message, my heart beginning to thud against my ribcage like war drums. Enrique Navarro not only knew *exactly* who I was, he also knew my father. At least that's what he said. I racked my brain, but the name didn't ring a bell.

Then he said, 'I was wondering if you might give me a call because I would like to talk with you about your father, who was a friend of mine.' He paused, and for a second, I thought that was the end of the call. I looked at the text translator on the phone, which showed something garbled. There was more to his message.

'I could also tell you about your brother.'

He said a polite goodbye and disconnected, and I thought, *I have a brother?*

FIVE

I waited until I got back to my studio to return Enrique Navarro's call. It wasn't a conversation I wanted to have in my car while driving. For one thing, I was upset. For another, I hear other people's phone calls projected from their cars all the time, especially at a stoplight or in a parking lot. They're not private. I wanted this call to be private.

I wanted to know how Enrique Navarro found me so fast.

He answered on the second ring.

'Sophie,' he said right away, 'I'm so glad you called back.'

As if we were picking up where we'd left off earlier, instead of total strangers.

'Mr Navarro—'

'Enrique. Please.'

'Enrique. How did you know who I am?' I was surprised at how angry I sounded. My question came out like an accusation.

'Like you, I'm a journalist. I found out the usual way. I looked you up.' He seemed unruffled by the edge in my voice. 'Imagine my surprise when I found out you were Antonio's daughter.'

'Yes, well, imagine *my* surprise when you called me. I had no intention of letting anyone know who my father was.' I was still angry. Combative. It had only been – what? – a few hours since I told Finn I'd take photographs at the soccer camp. 'What made you even *think* I was his daughter? Medina is not an uncommon name.'

'I happened to stop by Streetwise this morning to talk to the director about the soccer camp before the upcoming friendly between Real Madrid and DC United. While I was waiting for him, I saw one of your photographs in the latest edition of the newspaper. I knew Antonio had a daughter who had returned to the United States with her mother years ago. I knew your name and that your grandfather was a famous photographer. I asked the gentleman about you, but he was reluctant to give me any information – which only made me more curious. So I did some checking on my own.'

'I see.' At least Finn hadn't given me away. But if Enrique Navarro had figured it out that fast, who else would do so once Real Madrid and its entourage came to town?

'I can tell you about Antonio,' Navarro said. 'I knew him well.'

He and my father had been *friends*. It hadn't been a professional relationship. I wasn't expecting that.

I snapped back at him, still angry that he seemed to presume so much about me, as if *we* were friends. 'What makes you think I want to know anything? I never saw him or heard from him again after we moved back to the United States.'

'That's not true,' Enrique said. 'He wrote you. He sent letters.'

For a moment, I couldn't breathe. *He couldn't be right.* I never got any letters. *Letters.* More than one.

'What did you say?' I asked.

He repeated himself, and when I was silent, he said, after a poignant pause, 'Ah. You never read them.'

'I never *got* them.'

'I see. I'm so sorry.'

Jesus. I got up from my desk. Started pacing back and forth in my studio. *Sorry.* I felt like he'd just cut me open and yanked out my heart. My mother must have intercepted my father's letters and either kept them or destroyed them. All these years, I thought he didn't want me. Remember me.

But he did.

And my mother didn't want me to know.

I needed to change the subject, derail this conversation. Not talk about my father anymore. Or think about my mother.

'You also said I have a brother. A half-brother.'

'Yes. Danilo. Antonio never remarried after he and your mother divorced, but he had another child with a woman he was living with for a while. She was beautiful like your mother. In fact, she was a double for Caroline, or "Carolina" as Antonio called her – blonde, blue-eyed, gorgeous – Antonio's women were always stunning. Elsa was British. She returned to England before the baby was born, so Danilo grew up there. He goes by Daniel. And he took his mother's surname. Worth.'

'Did Antonio – my father – ever see him?'

'He did,' Enrique said, and that hurt. Danilo knew his father. My father. I did not. Enrique went on. 'His mother wanted her son's father to be part of his life, so occasionally Antonio flew to London or else he arranged for Danilo to spend time with him in Spain.'

'You knew Danilo, too?'

'I met him a couple of times when he was a little boy.'

'Are you still in touch with him?'

'No,' he said, 'but I'd like to be. I wondered if you were, but now that I understand you didn't know about him, you obviously wouldn't have been in contact.'

'If I didn't know my father wrote me letters,' I said, 'I certainly wouldn't have known I had a half-brother.'

'Danilo knew about you. I should say that he *found out* about you.'

'What do you mean?'

'He was going through some of Antonio's papers after he died and came across photos of you and your mother. So he asked Elsa who you were, and she told him.'

'How do you know that?'

'Why, from Elsa, of course.'

Then why didn't he try to contact me, find me? I almost said it, but I didn't want Enrique's pity. Didn't want him to know it hurt to learn my half-brother didn't care enough to seek me out once he found out he had a half-sister. Because if the shoe had been on the other foot, I would have tracked him down. I would have tried to find *him.*

As if he read my mind, Enrique said, 'I'm surprised he didn't get in touch with you. You were both journalists, both living in London, although Danilo didn't spend much time there. He's a foreign correspondent for *The Guardian* – mostly traveling to war zones, so he's rarely there. I should say he *was* a foreign correspondent for *The Guardian.*'

Daniel Worth. I recognized the byline. Surely he would have seen my photos?

'What do you mean? Was he fired? Did he quit?'

'I have no idea,' he said. 'He disappeared a few months ago.'

When I first started working for IPS, my boss, Perry DiNardo, sent me to Scotland for a weeklong course in hostile environment training designed specifically for naive, inexperienced journalists that was taught by British ex-Special Forces operatives. Along with a dozen other reporters, cameramen, producers and translators, I learned the most rudimentary survival skills they could cram into our heads in one week, including basic battlefield triage in case we were caught in a firefight and what to do if we were kidnapped.

Disappeared and *war zone* sounded as if maybe he'd been detained somewhere.

'Disappeared how?'

'I don't know. That's what I'd like to find out. Frankly, I have a suspicion he's been involved in several high-profile international art thefts.'

He dropped that into the conversation as if he were merely filling in a few more timeline details about Danilo's life. I stopped pacing.

'Whoa. Wait a minute. What do you mean *involved*? Do you mean a half-brother I never heard of is a thief? An art thief?'

'It's a long story,' Enrique said. 'Have lunch with me tomorrow. I'll explain everything then. I'll answer all your questions. Do you know Del Mar?'

'The Spanish restaurant on The Wharf? I know it. Look, you can't just drop a bomb like that in the middle of my life and then say, "Wait until tomorrow for the rest of the story."'

'It's complicated.'

'I've got time.'

'Unfortunately, I do not. Look, meet me at Del Mar at noon. I will tell you about your father and what I know about Danilo. But I also have a request.'

'And what would that be?'

'If *you* find him, I'd like you to tell me how I can be in touch with him.'

'What makes you think I'm going to find him? Especially if he has "disappeared" as you said.'

'Because now that you know about him, you *will* try to find him.'

This total stranger – someone I'd never heard of until twenty minutes ago – had pushed himself into my life and just *presumed* he knew me and what made me tick.

I hate being manipulated. I hate being played. Right now, I was almost sputtering with anger. 'How do you know that?'

'Because I believe you are your father's daughter. Antonio never walked away from a challenge. He confronted things, looked for answers. *Got* answers. I've looked at your photos, Sophie. You don't walk away from anything, either. Now that you know about Danilo, I am certain you *will* find him.' Then his voice grew soft. 'And when you do, I am asking this one favor: tell me how I can contact him. *Please*, Sophie.'

Even the *please* didn't change my mind. I would *not* help this man.

'Why would I do that? If Danilo – Daniel – has disappeared, maybe it was his choice, his decision. You call me out of the blue, announce that you knew my father and tell me I have a half-brother who, apparently, is an international art thief and I don't even know what you mean. Besides, I don't know *you*, Enrique.'

'I can help him.'

'Help him with what? How? Who are you *really*, anyway?'

'Look me up. I know you will. And you'll look up Danilo, too. Meet me tomorrow at Del Mar, Sophie, and let's talk. I'll tell you what you want to know.'

After he disconnected, I held the phone in my hand as if I couldn't figure out how it got there. Then I went back to my desk, closed out the computer file I'd been working on of Robbie's photos, locked the door to the carriage house and walked across the alley to my apartment.

I needed to do something – *anything* – to deal with a roiling sea of emotions from anger to regret to just plain heartache. Enrique Navarro – a complete and utter stranger – had insinuated himself into my life like the serpent slinking into the Garden of Eden and he'd blown it up entirely. My father, who I thought had forgotten me entirely, wrote to me. More than once. My mother had kept his letters and let me grow up *not knowing he cared*. I had a half-brother who *did* know about me – we even lived in the same city – but he never tried to find me or look me up. Plus, he was missing, and Enrique told me he might also be an international art thief.

I pulled on my running clothes with sharp, angry tugs, laced up my sneakers and went for a long, punishing run. I live in the Dupont Circle neighborhood of Washington, a mostly residential area of numbered streets and streets with alphabet letters that are just about at the end of the ABCs. I live on S Street and there is no letter street after W, but then the progression continues through two-syllable alphabet names and so on. A few embassies are located here, the small countries that don't have the cash to fork out for a palace on Massachusetts Avenue, which is known as Embassy Row. But residential Dupont Circle is quiet, and the streets are flat, easy for running.

I did my usual neighborhood loop but I wasn't done flushing the anger out of my system. I turned a corner on to 16th Street and ran up the hill to Meridian Hill Park, where I often go. It is a place that is not on any tourist destination map, which I'm glad of, because it's a lovely park known almost exclusively to locals and designed by architects who had in mind the lush stair-stepped gardens of the palace of Victor Emmanuel III, the last king of Italy. Its centerpiece was a spectacular waterfall consisting of thirteen cascading basins that connected the upper and lower parks. By the time I sprinted up one of the symmetrical staircases that ran alongside the waterfall, I had a stitch in my side. I bent over until it subsided and pulled out my phone. Then I sent a text to my mother asking if I could drop by this afternoon.

My mother and Harry live in Middleburg, Virginia, a charming village in the middle of Virginia's horse-and-hunt country, about fifty miles from DC, or a ninety-minute drive. So I didn't usually 'drop by' and she was instantly suspicious.

Is everything OK?

I wrote back. *I haven't been out there for a while.* Dodging the question, but it was true.

Harry's out this afternoon and I know he'll want to see you, so you'll stay for dinner, of course.

Mom rarely asked. She just presumed.

I wrote back and said I would. But I wanted to have our conversation before dinner while Harry was out and not there to act as a buffer between us as he had done so often over the years. What we were going to talk about was just between my mother and me, although when we were done, dinner might be iffy because Mom probably would want a Valium and she'd need to lie down. Harry would take care of her as he always did.

I jogged home, showered and changed into jeans and a sweater. My mother had some of the answers I needed. Maybe even all of them.

Beginning with *why*.

SIX

About twenty miles before I reached Middleburg, Route 50 – the road I'd been on most of the way from DC – stopped being a multi-lane highway of strip malls and turn-offs to newish subdivisions and became a pretty two-lane country road. Fifty, which traverses the United States from Ocean City, Maryland, to Sacramento, California, has been called "the loneliest road in America" when it winds through parts of the Midwest. Here, though, it is lined with Civil War-era stacked stone walls and post-and-board fences that surround fields where cattle and Thoroughbreds graze peacefully. The homes and farmhouses that dot the landscape date back one, maybe two, centuries. It is a lifetime away from the congested streets, wailing police sirens and noise of Washington. I always feel myself grow calmer the further I am from the city, as I get closer to the home where I grew up.

Mayfield is a horse farm that belongs to my stepfather Harrison Wyatt, and it has been in his family for generations. The house, a graceful Georgian mansion made of stone quarried on the property, was built shortly after the Civil War. Much of the two hundred and fifty acres is fields and forests. The aptly named Blue Ridge Mountains frame the western view, and Goose Creek, a meandering creek that flows into the Potomac River, cuts diagonally across a corner of the farm. Harry raises Thoroughbreds so there are stables, living quarters for the stable hands, an indoor training track for the horses, a guest cottage and a couple of barns. Harry renovated one of the barns so Charles Lord, my grandfather, could store his vast collection of photographs, negatives and contact sheets there after he came to live with Mom and Harry a few months before he died.

I turned off Route 50 on to Sam Fred Road and eventually into the long gravel driveway that led to Mayfield. Ella, our sweet black Labrador Retriever, barked a greeting when I opened the front door. I bent and scratched her between her ears. Her tail thumped madly.

'I missed you, girl.' More tail thumping. 'I met a buddy of yours in Washington, but he wasn't as friendly as you are.'

'Sophie?' My mother's high-pitched voice trailed from somewhere outside the house. 'I'm in the garden. Side yard.'

I opened the gate to the side yard with Ella trotting beside me. My mother was on her hands and knees, pulling weeds in a garden where clumps of yellow, white and orange daffodils rioted happily. She sat back on her haunches and brushed a strand of shoulder-length blonde hair off her face with her forearm.

The first thing she said was, 'What happened to your arm?'

'I fell on the sidewalk in front of Streetwise. My heel got caught in a crack, and a vet who happened to be there caring for the dog of a homeless man cleaned the cut. It's healing. I won't even have a scar.'

'I worry about you in Washington,' she said. 'There's so much crime in that city.'

'Mom. I tripped. No crime was committed.'

'People are always being shot there. Daily. It's all you hear on the news. Do you carry mace? You should.'

'No. I do not. I'm fine. I live in a good neighborhood, not Hell's Kitchen.'

She sighed and gave up. We had this discussion all the time. Unfortunately, now she was right. Since the pandemic, the crime rate had skyrocketed, everything from violent crimes to robberies to carjackings to homicides. The resulting front-page headlines and news stories had provoked Congress enough to poke its nose into DC's business, refusing to approve a crime bill drafted by the city council that they said was way too lenient. It also reignited the long-simmering feud that Congress would never cut the cord and allow Washington to become the fifty-first state.

So my mother had a point.

'Could you get my shears, sweetie?' she asked. 'I left them on the patio table.'

I got the shears and watched her cut a handful of daffodils, which she passed to me.

'These will be for the dinner table,' she said. 'Harry loves them.'

She held out her hand and I pulled her up. 'What's going on?' she asked. 'You've hardly said an unnecessary word since you got here. Something's bothering you. I've been wondering ever since you texted me.'

Of course she had. She was my mother.

'Maybe we should go inside,' I said. 'Put these flowers in water.'

She studied my face. 'Should I make us some tea? Or is this going to be a conversation where we need a glass of wine?'

'I'm fine, Mom,' I said. 'I don't need anything.'

We sat in the sunroom, which was warmed by late-afternoon sunlight pouring in through the west windows and lighting the leaves of my mother's ficus, the schefflera, the lemon tree and her peace lily so they turned lovely translucent shades of green. She had recently redecorated the room so everything down to a table lamp that looked like a sinewy green vine and a glass-topped coffee table that sat on a base of crisscrossed pieces of driftwood was meant to make you think you were outdoors. She sat in the chaise where she always worked on her needlepoint; I took the sofa where Harry sat each morning to read his newspapers with a cup of coffee.

My mother folded her hands in her lap. 'So what's going on?'

'Do you know someone named Enrique Navarro?'

She stiffened. 'No. Should I?'

'I don't know. I didn't know him until he contacted me this morning.'

Her voice grew wary. 'About what?'

'He knew my father. He knew Antonio. Real Madrid is coming to Washington for a friendly with DC United in ten days. Finn Hathaway – you've heard me talk about him, he's the editor of the Streetwise newspaper – is organizing a soccer camp for some of the homeless kids to practice with the players. Finn talked me into being their photographer. Enrique Navarro, who is a journalist with *El País,* came by Finn's office to talk to him since Real Madrid was involved. He said he saw my name as a photo credit on one of the pictures in the newspaper, did some research and added two and two. Figured out I was Antonio's daughter.'

She nodded and didn't say anything.

'He wants me to meet him for lunch tomorrow so he can tell me about Antonio.'

She exhaled. 'Are you OK with that?'

'Why wouldn't I be? He's my father, Mom. I don't know anything about him other than what I read in magazines or articles I found on the Internet. Videos of him playing soccer. That's it.'

Her eyes flashed. '*Harry* is really your father, Sophie. Harry loves you with his heart and soul, as if you're his flesh-and-blood daughter, not his stepdaughter. You *know* that. And I know you love him, how close you two are. I always thought that would be enough. That it was enough. Antonio was never part of our lives. You know as well as I do that we got married because I got pregnant.'

'With me.'

'Yes, of course, with you. But there was no chance our marriage was going to last. We were a couple of hormonal teenagers. We had nothing in common from the beginning.'

'I know that. You've always told me that.'

'Then what?'

'He wrote me letters. Enrique told me about them.'

In the haunting silence that followed, I knew our relationship had just tilted on its axis and that it could never go back to what it was before this moment. Already we'd been through rough times when it was complicated, precarious, fraught. And always fragile.

'I can explain.'

Which meant she *couldn't.*

'It's a little late for that, don't you think? I don't know if it's possible, anyway.' There was an edge to my voice, but I couldn't help it.

'Sophie—'

'*Why*, Mom? Why didn't you let me read the letters my father wrote me? Or at least let me know about them? Give me the chance to decide if I wanted to see them or not?'

Her voice was anguished. 'You were just a little girl. I thought it would only confuse you, make your life more difficult and complicated. *I* was the adult. *I* had to make the decision for you. I did what I thought was the right thing.'

'What about when he died? I was old enough then.'

'By then Harry was in our lives. How could I tell you about Antonio when he was *gone*? Especially the way he died – that gruesome accident and so many photographs of him and his girl-friend, of the place where it happened splashed all over the news. And then Spain held a national day of mourning for him.'

'You didn't think I would like to have known that he thought about me? Remembered me? *Cared* about me? It would have mattered. It would have made a difference.' I sounded like a hurt child. 'It still matters.'

She rose from the chaise in one swift, graceful motion and left the room. Which is when I knew. *She still had Antonio's letters. She had kept them all these years.*

When she came back, she was holding a small bundle of

onion-skin airmail envelopes with red-and-yellow borders – the colors of the flag of Spain – tied together with a red grosgrain ribbon. She held them out to me, and I placed them in my lap as tears rolled down my face.

'I'm so sorry, honey,' she said. 'I never meant for you to be hurt.'

'You didn't want him in your life, so you didn't want him in my life, either.' I swiped at my eyes with the palms of my hands.

'That's not true.'

'I have a half-brother. Another brother besides Tommy. Did you know that, too?'

Once again, she didn't say anything, so I already knew her answer. It was *yes*.

'Did you ever meet him? How much do you know about him?' I was pushing, *pushing* for answers, but also hoping hers were *no* and *nothing*. That all she knew was that Antonio had another child, a son. Nothing else. I didn't want to know she kept *that* from me, too.

'Why don't I open a bottle of wine?' she said, so I knew this wasn't going to be an easy conversation. 'Red or white?'

'I have to drive home. Nothing for me, thanks.'

'Well, *I* need a drink,' She got up again. 'Let me get something and then I'll tell you what you want to know.' She got a tissue out of a box on the end table next to the chaise and handed it and the box to me as she left the room.

When she returned, I saw she'd skipped the wine and gone straight for Scotch. After she sat down again, she said, 'I'm so sorry you're learning all this from a stranger, Sophie. I know I should have been the one to tell you.'

'But you didn't.'

'No.'

'Why not?'

She drank some Scotch. 'I don't know . . . though that's not much of an answer. But you love Harry and Tommy and Lexie so much, and they love you. I thought – hoped – it was enough.'

It was an honest answer. Besides, I knew from years of living with her how much she disliked confrontation, conflict, any messiness in her life. My mother liked tidy edges, neat borders and boundaries. She hated spontaneity or being surprised. We were total opposites, and I wondered now if I was more like Antonio than I was like her, especially after what Enrique said to me on the phone earlier today. I also knew I had just dropped a bomb into our lives, as he had done with me. My mother looked as stricken as if it had already exploded.

'So you knew about Danilo,' I said. 'Or Daniel, as he goes by now. What do you know?'

Her eyes skidded away from mine. 'I never met him or his mother if that's what you're asking. But my roommate from the year I studied in Madrid also married a Spaniard – because she fell in love, not because she had to. We're still in touch, and she stayed in contact with Antonio for a while, at least until his career took off and he became famous. She knew he had a son and that he and his mother had moved back to England where Danilo . . . Daniel . . . grew up.'

'Do you know anything else about him?'

She took another long drink of her Scotch and shrugged. 'It was easy enough to find out about him on the Internet. From time to time, I checked up on him.'

'Then you know he was a journalist. A foreign correspondent. That he worked for *The Guardian*.'

'Yes.'

'I didn't even know he existed until Enrique told me about him. He was stunned that I had no clue. Also surprised that you never said a word to me.'

'First of all, this *Enrique* has no right to pass judgment on me and my decisions. He doesn't even know me. And honey, I'm so sorry. I just didn't want you to be hurt.'

'Or maybe you thought I'd never find out.'

'That's unfair.'

'But not untrue.'

When she didn't answer, I said, 'Is there anything else I should know that no one told me? Any more surprises? Who else knew about the letters, Mom? Chappy? Nonna Gina? Harry?'

We had lived with her parents – my grandparents – for a while after she moved us home from Spain before Harry came into our lives.

She looked uncomfortable. 'The letters came to a different address, so your grandparents never saw them. They never knew about them. By the time I met Harry, Antonio had stopped writing, so there was no reason to bring the subject up.'

No reason.

I was the reason.

'Are you going to tell Harry now, Mom? Because if you don't, I will.'

'Tell me what?'

Harry had been so quiet that neither of us heard him until he was standing in the doorway. His eyes went from my mother whose face was filled with remorse and unhappiness to me with my red-rimmed eyes. Then he saw the bundle of envelopes on the coffee table.

'What's going on? What happened?'

When neither of us said anything, he said, 'One of you had better tell me.'

'Mom?' I said.

She shot me an anguished look and shook her glass so the ice cubes tinkled. When she looked up, she said, 'I gave Sophie letters that Antonio wrote her when she was very young. She didn't know about them until just now.'

'Because you didn't tell me about them,' I said, my voice stiff with anger again. 'Because I had to find out from a *stranger.* A journalist with *El País* who knew my biological father. *Not from you.*'

Harry came over to the couch and sat down next to me, throwing his arm around my shoulders.

'Why didn't you tell her, Caro?'

'I made what I thought was the right decision at the time, Harry. *That's* why. I thought the letters would only upset and confuse her.' She sounded defiant, holding her ground that it had been the right decision. A mother protecting her young daughter.

Harry had always been the peacemaker between the two of us.

'Sweetheart,' Harry said to me, 'you know your mother would never do anything to purposely hurt you. These letters were written – what? – more than thirty years ago. Looking back now, it probably was a mistake not to show them to you.' He glanced at my mother. 'Right, Caroline?'

When she spoke, her voice was barely a whisper. 'Yes.'

'But that was then,' he said. 'You were a little girl. She was a single mother. Don't hold it against her, Sophie. Please, honey. She kept the letters all these years. You have them now.'

'*Because I asked her about them.*'

Harry closed his eyes as if he couldn't bear to think about what

I'd just said. I reached for the stack of letters and an envelope slipped out of the bundle and fluttered to the carpet. I bent to pick it up and turned it over. The envelope was unsealed.

I looked up and met my mother's eyes. They were filled with tears.

'*You read my letters.*'

She nodded.

I opened my mouth to say something I knew I'd regret, so I closed it. Harry shot me a grateful look.

'I need to go,' I said.

'Stay for dinner, Sophie,' my mother said. 'Please. We should talk about this some more.'

'I . . . can't.'

As I closed the front door, I heard my mother start to sob. And wondered how we were ever going to fix what had just broken between us today.

SEVEN

The drive from Virginia back to DC was rough. Antonio Medina died twenty-five years ago. I never knew him, and he never knew me, though now I was aware that he had tried, he *wanted* to know me. How I was going to handle the tsunami of regret and sadness that had swept me up, I had no idea.

What I did know was this: *I was going to find Danilo*. He could tell me about our father, what he was like when he was home being a dad and not a world-class soccer star. Was he the kind of father who read bedtime stories, taught you how to ride a bicycle? Did he help with homework? What was his favorite food, color, season, type of music? What made him laugh? Did he ever cry? Did he sing in the shower? All these things I never knew.

Danilo did.

And before I met Enrique tomorrow, I intended to read the letters my father had written me. All of them.

I waited until I was in bed and there was a full glass of Cabernet Sauvignon on the nightstand before I opened them. I untied the red ribbon my mother had bound them with and looked at the postmarks. Of course, they were in chronological order, with the newest one on top. I was ten years old when he wrote the last one. I flipped over the pile so I could start at the beginning. My father wrote me for the first time when I was five. The letter was in the simplest, most basic Spanish, perhaps because he was hoping I could read it for myself. It was short and sweet. He missed me and wondered how my life was going. Did I like school? Did I have a favorite subject? He wrote that he had injured his arm at soccer practice the other day – he called it *fútbol* – and there was a little drawing he'd made of himself with his arm in a sling standing next to a soccer ball. It was very good – not just sticks for arms and legs and circles for the head and body, but a drawing, a likeness of how he really looked in his soccer posters and magazine photos. I read more letters, and in every single one, there was a drawing. Eventually, he switched from pen and ink to watercolor. A little painting of his dog – a sweet-faced German Shepherd – lying on the chair my father liked to read in. The view from his kitchen window – he lived in an older section of Madrid. A *barrio*, he called it where elegant Neoclassical apartment buildings were mixed in alongside neighborhood shops that sold newspapers and tobacco, a bakery, a butcher, a café, a churrería. He'd drawn more scenes of Madrid, chosen especially for a little girl: a flamenco dancer, the giraffes at the Aquarium Zoo, a stall filled with colorful pottery at the Rastro flea market, the façade of the Palacio Real – "the most beautiful royal palace in Europe" – people eating and drinking at an outdoor café in the Plaza Mayor.

There was no drawing in his last letter but there was a photo. My father in jeans and a collared shirt sitting at a table in an outdoor café looking tanned and relaxed and happy and as devastatingly handsome as he was in all his publicity photos. He was smiling directly at the camera, at whoever took the photograph, and I was certain, looking at his smile which also lit up his eyes, that it was a woman. He didn't say it was his last letter, but unlike the others that were signed '*Abrazos y besos, Papa*' – hugs and kisses – this one was signed with his name. *Con cariño, Antonio Medina.* With affection. By now he'd probably decided either I wasn't reading his letters, or I didn't want to answer him, didn't want him in my life.

So he stopped writing.

I leaned my head back against my pillow and *wept*.

I slept poorly, and the next morning, I looked like it. Thank God for makeup, especially concealer. After breakfast, I got out my laptop, poured a third cup of coffee and climbed into my favorite armchair tucked into the bay window in the living room. The trees on S Street were just starting to bud out, the first being the red-tipped maples. In a few weeks when everything turned the soft, promising green that only happened in spring, the branches on either side of the street, which arched toward the light and toward each other, would form a leafy overhead canopy that felt like being inside a cathedral.

I searched first for Daniel Worth, and then, for good measure, I searched for Danilo Medina. There was nothing – absolutely nothing – on Danilo Medina. As if he didn't exist. But Daniel Worth's life was laid out for me in bylines, photos, a paper on the history of the Benin bronzes written when he attended Oxford, an official *Guardian* biography and another small bio when he had a year-long fellowship at the British Museum.

I wondered if he looked like his English mother, because he didn't look very much like Antonio or me, although he did have Antonio's dark eyes and dark hair like I did, except his hair was straight, not wavy like ours. And where Antonio and I were olive-skinned and Mediterranean-looking, he was light-skinned and fair as the English are – the kind of skin that burns easily in the sun, unlike mine which turns a golden bronze. If you stood us next to each other, I doubt anyone would have taken us for siblings – or even half-siblings. There were other photos in places where the background looked as if it had just been bombed or set on fire, probably taken when he was in some war zone or hellhole for *The Guardian* because they clearly weren't vacation photos. Or so I hoped.

I clicked on more links, none of which were in chronological order. In the photograph that went with his *Guardian* bio, he looked like a kid who was still getting carded. At Oxford, he'd read Computer Science and Art History, graduating with honors. During his fellowship with the British Museum, he'd focused on analyzing data on artworks that had been damaged either by human careless-ness, while in transit to or from the museum, or just from simple wear and tear. After that, he'd written a paper recommending ways for museums to better safeguard their masterpieces – especially from the carelessness of patrons who were responsible for more incidents of breakage and damage to priceless items than I'd realized.

I found a lot of stories he'd written for *The Guardian*, the earliest ones with London bylines and a few with bylines of cities in Spain – Madrid, of course, but also smaller towns like Santiago de Compostela, Salamanca and Jerez de la Frontera. His more recent stories had bylines of cities or towns with exotic, nearly unpro-nounceable names in countries that were at war: Iraq, Afghanistan and, more recently, Ukraine. Sometimes he wrote about the troops, a battle or who controlled what territory, but the majority were – not surprisingly, given his background – focused on the devastation the war was causing to the cultural and religious institutions: bombed and looted museums, churches, archeological and historical sites. Things that couldn't be rebuilt or replaced. He wrote heartbreaking accounts about what was being lost because of invaders who were attempting to erase history and art and culture as a form of psycho-logical warfare, destroying everything that gave people their national identity as a country – leaving them with nothing, a huge void.

Enrique Navarro had said it was possible Daniel – by now he had become Daniel to me – was involved in several high-profile international art thefts. What did that mean? The difference between writing about stolen art and stealing art was night and day. You couldn't possibly compare them.

I looked up Enrique next, first a photo. He had a mane of snow-white hair, a goatee that gave him a vaguely devilish look, piercing blue eyes, slim and ascetic-looking. Like Daniel, he had an impressive bio, winning two Ortega y Gasset Awards, the highest prize a Spanish-speaking journalist could win. He'd been with *El País* for nearly forty years, and it appeared he'd done just about everything – editor, beat reporter, foreign correspondent, special assignments reporter. Lately, it seemed he wrote cultural features, along with the occasional sports story.

Was that why he was interested in talking to Daniel? Because both of them wrote for their respective papers about culture – about art – and he was curious about these supposed thefts?

I can help him, he'd said.

With what?

It was time to leave for my lunch with Enrique Navarro. In an hour – maybe less – I'd know.

Or at least I hoped so.

The Wharf is one of DC's newest and most expensive rehabilitation projects, completely transforming a once-rundown, weary part of the city along the Washington Channel into a high-end, upscale residential, business and commercial center. I parked the Mini in an underground garage that wasn't far from the restaurant, climbed a staircase surrounded by a rushing waterfall and reached the upper level where the plaza was located. The Wharf had been designed as a meeting place, a gathering place for people – a *destination*. But because so many tall, mirrored glass-and-stone office buildings loomed overhead, dwarfing the restaurants and shops and casting the cobblestone walkway into shadow, this slick redesign didn't really work for me. I liked the openness and more human scale of Old Town Alexandria, Virginia, or my absolute favorite, The Queen's Walk along the South Bank of the Thames in London. The overall feeling I got each time I came to The Wharf was that it was designed for business and commerce. *For making money*.

Del Mar was on my left across from the Capitol Yacht Club and the Washington Channel. The wind coming off the water gusted sharply, cutting like a knife and scattering dry leaves that still skittered around from last fall. I pulled my blazer tighter and wished I'd thought to bring a jacket or a scarf.

When I walked into the restaurant precisely at noon, I saw Enrique Navarro seated at a table next to a window with a view of several dozen cabin cruisers and large sailboats that bobbed up and down in their slips next to the yacht club. He stood as soon as he saw me, but I would have recognized him anyway – the shock of white hair, the indefinable way he carried himself that marked him as Old World European.

'Sophie.' He took my hand and held it in both of his. 'How nice to finally meet you.'

'Thank you.' A waiter appeared and pulled out my chair. I sat down, glad for the distraction since I wasn't ready to say, 'Nice to meet you, too.'

'You look so much like him.'

If only he hadn't started this meeting by telling me *that*. Talking about Antonio, especially after what I'd just learned about my father, was almost like talking about Nick. *Hard.* Enrique Navarro had pierced my armor with a sure, sharp blade right through to my vulnerable heart in less than a minute.

'I don't remember him at all.'

The waiter who had seated me reappeared with a pitcher of water, introducing himself and asking if we'd like anything else to drink while we studied the menu. I wondered if he sensed how uncomfortable I was and then decided that he did.

I gave him a grateful smile and asked for sparkling water. Enrique ordered a beer.

'Have you eaten here before?' he asked after the waiter left.

'A few times.'

'I come here quite often,' he said. 'It's one of my favorite places.'

'I thought you lived in Madrid.'

'I do,' he said. 'But I also have a small condo on the waterfront in Georgetown. My ex-wife was American and my daughters and their families – my grandchildren – live here. So I'm in DC quite often.'

'I see.'

I lowered my eyes to study my menu since I didn't feel like making small talk or pretending that he was a long-lost family friend. And just now, I wasn't even sure I liked him. Enrique Navarro was the one who had sought me out, baited me, getting me to agree to meet him by promising information about my father and explaining his final disturbing comment about my half-brother. I was here because he wanted something from me.

'The tapas are excellent,' he said.

'Yes. I've had them before.'

The waiter returned with our drinks and took our orders. Pulpo a la plancha: Galician-style octopus, smoked potato and spiced black garlic sauce for him. Andalusian gambas al ajillo – shrimp with garlic and arból chile – for me.

After he left, Enrique said, 'You're not happy about this meeting.'

It wasn't even a question.

I pulled the photo from my father's last letter out of my purse and set it on the table, so it was facing him.

'Where did you get this?' he asked.

'My mother kept all the letters my father wrote me. She gave them to me yesterday afternoon after you told me about them. The photo was in the last one,' I said. 'You track me down out of the blue, announce you and my father were friends and tell me that I have a half-brother. Plus, my mother and I did not have the easiest conversation when I asked her about his letters. Right now, it seems as if everyone knows about my father – and Daniel – except me.'

He held up his hands to stop me from saying anything more. 'Please. It's not like that.'

'Then tell me what it *is* like. You found me because you're looking for Daniel,' I said. 'It has nothing to do with me or you and my father being old pals.'

'That's not true.'

'Why are you trying to find him?'

'You looked him up, I presume?'

'I did. I also looked you up.'

'As a good journalist, I expected you would.'

'You said Daniel might be involved in several high-profile international art thefts. That's a hell of an introduction, the first thing I learn about him. Are you saying he *is* a thief?'

'Not exactly.'

'Could you be a little more specific and stop with the semantics?'

'Have you read any of the stories he wrote when he was still working for *The Guardian*?'

'The ones about stolen and plundered art in countries that are at war, like Afghanistan and Ukraine?'

'Yes,' he said. 'Those stories.'

'I did. What about them?'

We were silent while the waiter returned with our tapas, wished us *buen provecho* and left.

Enrique picked up his fork. 'Please. You must eat.'

'You were saying something about the stories Daniel wrote for *The Guardian* concerning plundered and stolen art.'

He nodded. 'He also wrote a story about six extremely valuable sixteenth-century tapestries that were stolen from a cathedral in the town of Cuenca. It's a provincial capital in the *comunidad-autónoma* of Castilla-La Mancha. The thief – or thieves – apparently walked in, cut the tapestries down and walked out. There was no security, no security camera. It's a *church*. Cuenca is also a UNESCO World Heritage Site, so you might have heard of it.'

'I have.'

'Did you know about the tapestries?'

'No.'

'Well,' he said, 'a few months later, they were mysteriously returned to the church. A priest found them there when he arrived for early-morning Mass. Daniel also wrote that story. In fact, he was the first journalist to write about it. A scoop.'

'And?'

'He wrote several more stories about stolen art – always items taken from a small town, a museum, a church or an archeological site. And then a few months later, as if by magic, the stolen items were returned. He wrote those stories as well.'

'I don't understand.'

'How did he know the items were going to be returned?'

'Maybe he didn't.'

'No.' He shook his head. 'The first time, OK, he got lucky. Twice could be a coincidence. More than that and it's a *pattern*.'

'Are you saying Daniel is involved in some kind of elaborate plan to steal stolen items – re-steal them, actually – and return them to their owners?'

'That's what I want to find out.'

'You don't think that's a little far-fetched?'

'I do not.'

'Even if it were true, whoever is responsible for returning those items is no thief,' I said. 'They're like . . . I don't know. Robin Hood. Sort of.'

He snorted. 'Don't be naïve.'

I sat back and folded my arms across my chest. 'The people who loot and steal those items are criminals. Especially the ones who steal from countries at war – like Ukraine and Afghanistan. They're ruthless thugs. Do you really think Daniel would get on the wrong side of people like that and then live to tell about it if he did? They would hunt him down.'

Just like whoever put a bullet through the head of the courier who showed up at Dulles with two suitcases of stolen fourth- and fifth-century BC gold artifacts.

'Maybe that's why he disappeared.'

I didn't have an answer for that.

'Which is why,' he went on, 'I'd like to talk to him. I know people in the art world. I might be able to help him. And I'm not saying – or even implying – that he's behind the return of these stolen items. But I do have a sense that he plays a role somehow. At a minimum, he knows something.'

'And this is where I come in? You want me to find him and then let you know how to get in touch with him? For what, a story?'

He steepled his fingers. 'Obviously, I would protect him. If you have looked me up, you know I can do it, too. I *am* that good. But it is a fascinating story, and I think Daniel knows something about it. Plus, I have a connection with him as an old friend of his father's. Of your father's.'

'No.'

'No, what?'

The waiter stopped by our table. 'Terminado?' he asked.

Enrique and I nodded. We were finished with our meals. The waiter took our plates and said, 'Algun postre? Dessert?'

'Sophie?' Enrique said. 'Dessert? Coffee?'

'No dessert, thank you. But I would like a coffee.'

I ordered a cortado, an espresso with a splash of milk. Enrique asked for a café solo – strong black espresso. He also ordered flan with Moro blood orange and asked for two spoons.

After the waiter left, he said, 'You said "no." No what?'

'First of all, Daniel disappeared, as you said. So what makes you think I could find him? Second, he'd be nuts to talk to you and discuss anything about a role he may or may not have in re-stealing stolen art and returning it to its owners. Because if you've figured out he's part of this whatever-it-is, the people he's stealing from have as well. *That* would explain why he disappeared.'

'I think you have this wrong. I think you have the wrong idea about me. I want to *help*. And I would never do anything to jeopardize Daniel's safety or betray him in any way. I swear this on your father's life.'

A different waiter set down our coffees; then our waiter returned with Enrique's blood orange flan and the two spoons. He set the flan in the exact middle of the table.

Enrique was a good journalist, a *very* good journalist. You didn't win two Ortega y Gasset prizes if you weren't one of the best. And I got why he was pushing me so hard because he wanted to write this story. When I worked for IPS, I was just as aggressive in getting the shot I needed as he was being with me. But there were boundaries I wouldn't cross – potentially endangering someone's life was one of them – and right now, sitting across the table from him as the boats in the harbor across from us rocked side to side, the lines that anchored them to the dock growing taut in the sharp, cold wind, I didn't have a good feeling about him.

I finished my cortado and set my napkin on the table. I was done.

He looked dismayed. 'Won't you try the flan? It's excellent.'

I shook my head. 'I'm sure it is, but I should go. And I'm sorry, but I don't think I can do what you're asking.'

'This isn't just about the story. Please. If you find him, at least tell him I want to talk to him.'

'You're assuming I'll find him.'

'I *know* you'll find him.'

'*If* I find him,' I said, 'I'll pass on your message. It will be up to him if he wants to be in touch. But I wouldn't count on either of those things happening.'

As soon as I was outside, I turned around and looked through the window. Enrique Navarro was still sitting there, holding his espresso cup in one hand and staring at the boats on the water.

He didn't look happy. In fact, he looked angry because I had just told him I wasn't going to help him find my brother.

It also occurred to me that he hadn't told me a single thing about my father. But maybe that didn't matter. Because, like it or not, I hadn't seen the last of Enrique Navarro.

He would seek me out again. We would have more opportunities to talk.

EIGHT

If Daniel Worth had gone missing after taking an extended leave of absence from *The Guardian*, I had two options if I wanted to try to find him. The first was to go to London to see if I could learn where he'd gone and maybe why he'd gone off the grid. That was also the expensive option, but when it came to a city that had been home for twelve years, I agreed with Samuel Johnson: if you're tired of London, you're tired of life. It wouldn't take much of a nudge for me to pull out my credit card and book a ticket on a flight from Dulles to Heathrow that left tonight, however outrageously expensive it was.

Option two was easier, faster and more practical: I could call Perry DiNardo, my former boss, and ask him what he knew about Daniel. Perry was the unofficial dean of the foreign press corps in London, partly because he'd been there so long and partly because he was a damn good journalist who knew everything about anything that had to do with our colleagues. And if he didn't know, he knew people who did, people who owed him favors.

Last fall, he'd come to DC for a day of meetings, and we'd gone out to dinner. After that, we'd gone to bed – a reckless, somewhat alcohol-fueled impulse that was also driven by the fact that we'd been shot at as we were leaving the restaurant. Having sex with Perry had changed everything between us. He still wanted me to move back to London and work for IPS again, but after that night, he could never be my boss. If I went back to look for Daniel now, Perry would expect me to stay at his place. And I knew what would happen if I did.

We had been in touch a few times since then, but our relationship had never gotten back on keel, never returned to what it used to be. I missed our old friendship, the way we could talk to each other about everything, however raw and unvarnished. We were better as friends than lovers.

When I got home from Del Mar, I called him.

Three p.m. in Washington was eight p.m. in London. Perry could be at work at that hour – he was a workaholic – or he could be home in front of the television eating takeaway fish and chips and drinking a couple of beers. He picked up immediately when I called. I could hear the buzz of the television in the background. His voice sounded tired and a bit blurred. He was home.

'Long time no hear, Medina,' he said. 'I thought you'd forgotten me.'

Rough start.

'I know,' I said. 'I'm sorry.'

'What's going on?'

Getting right down to business, skipping the personal banter and figuring – correctly – that I'd called because I needed something. No awkward questions or comments like 'I miss you' or 'When are we going to see each other again?'

'I'm trying to find out what happened to a journalist who might still work for *The Guardian*,' I said. 'Daniel Worth.'

Silence for a moment as he was probably digesting that this *was* a business call. Or something like it. I was asking for information.

'I know the byline, but I don't know him personally,' he said, and if he was disappointed I hadn't called just because I wanted to hear his voice, he hid it well. 'Why are you looking for him?'

'Why don't you pour yourself a beer?' I said. 'It might take a while to explain.'

I told him everything – I would trust Perry with my life – and when I was done, he said, 'That's a helluva story.'

I'd also heard the click of keys on a keyboard as I talked. He had been checking out what I'd been telling him.

'I just texted the managing editor of *The Guardian*,' he said. 'He said Daniel took a leave of absence. Which you already knew.'

'That was fast. Did he say how long he planned to be away?'

'Yeah. An undisclosed amount of time. Unquote.'

'So he's not going to tell you why, either.'

'Nope.'

'I wonder if he's still in London. I already wrote him using his *Guardian* email address and got an autoresponder that he's out of the office, so that's no help. I can't find a phone number or a personal email address. He could be anywhere.'

'Especially if Navarro is right that he's involved in tracking down stolen art and getting it returned to its rightful owner – which sounds pretty daring and ballsy, if you ask me. If it were me, I wouldn't want anyone to know where I was. The guy probably has a target on his back the size of Liverpool by now.'

I shuddered. He probably did. Besides, if Daniel hadn't reached out to me before this, why would he want to be in touch if he was playing the dangerous game Enrique said he was? Maybe this was a fool's errand.

'You know' – Perry paused and I could hear him take another sip of beer before going on – 'someone with ICIJ might know how to get in touch with him. Now that I think about it, one of the subjects they've taken on is stolen and plundered art.'

'That,' I said, 'is a brilliant idea.'

'I have them sometimes,' he said.

'So modest.'

'That's why you love me.'

Had that just slipped out, something the old Perry would have said as a teasing joke, or was he fishing?

'That's why everybody loves you,' I said, stepping over that landmine. 'Your staff worships you.'

ICIJ was the International Consortium of Investigative Journalists, a group of journalists who worked together to shine a light on the dark corners of the world. According to the vision statement on their website, ICIJ exposed wrongdoing 'so the world can make it right.' They collaborated with more than one hundred newspapers, television and radio stations, and media outlets to write stories about injustice and abuse of power. They had even been nominated for the Nobel Peace Prize in 2021. What made ICIJ unique was its ability to persuade rival news organizations to work together to uncover corruption, abuses of power and grave harm inflicted on the world's most vulnerable people.

And although they had offices all over the world, they were based in Washington, DC. I could walk from my studio to their main office on Rhode Island Avenue in about twenty minutes. And as Perry had said – he wasn't the only one clicking on a keyboard – one of the topics they shone their spotlight on was looted and plundered art. I clicked on their website and went to a page called *Our Staff*.

And got lucky.

'Valerie Zhou is working for them,' I said. 'She used to be with the *International Herald Tribune* in their Paris bureau. I know her. She's working in the DC office.'

'Are you writing her right now?'

'I will be in a minute.'

'Let me know what you find out,' he said. 'In the meantime, I'll poke around and see if Worth confided in someone at *The Guardian* about what he's really up to on that so-called leave of absence.'

'Thank you,' I said. 'I owe you.'

I shouldn't have said that.

'I know you do. And I intend to collect.'

'You always do.' I shouldn't have said that, either.

'He might still be in London, you know. If he is, you ought to come over here and meet him.'

'If he's still in London, maybe I will.'

'You've got a place to stay if you do.'

'Perry—'

'What?'

'Thank you for the offer . . .'

'But . . .?'

'Can we talk about this some other time?' I asked.

'What happened that night was good,' he said. 'You know it was good.'

'It was. But it changed our friendship.'

'Only if you let it. And it doesn't have to be for the worse, you know.'

'I know.'

'Medina,' he said, 'you know how I feel about you. Why don't you give us a chance?'

'I . . . I don't know.'

There was a long silence on his end. Finally, he said, 'Think about it, OK?'

'I will. Goodbye, Perry. And thanks.'

'Sure,' he said. 'Any time.'

He disconnected. I didn't want to hurt him. I didn't want to lose him, either. But if I told him that I didn't see any future for us together – I didn't feel the same way about him that he felt about me – I would definitely hurt him.

And I might lose him forever.

I found Valerie Zhou's email address on the ICIJ website and wrote her, asking if she could meet because I wanted to talk about a subject they had written about extensively: looted and plundered art. I didn't mention Daniel, which I knew was disingenuous on my part, but I was afraid if I did, she'd shut me down completely before she knew the real reason I was trying to find him. *If* she had any idea where he was or how to contact him. I hit send as a text from Finn Hathaway dinged on my phone telling me there would be a scrimmage with the kids from the homeless camps Friday afternoon after school in Meridian Hill Park.

What time? I texted.

Three. You coming?

I wrote that I was, hit *send* and went over to my studio. Two hours later, I finished editing Robbie Blake's photos of the da Vinci and Jefferson drawings. I emailed him a link so he could access them. He called at once, said the photos were great and asked if I was available Friday afternoon to take his author photo.

'I've got another commitment, but I could make it at five if it's not too late for you.'

'Five is fine,' he said and disconnected as my phone dinged again. An email from Valerie Zhou.

She wrote that she was glad to hear from me after so many years and what a surprise that we were both in Washington now . . . blah, blah, blah. ICIJ was an invitation-only organization for investigative journalists, she wrote, and she loved the work they were doing. She'd be happy to talk to me about their project involving looted and plundered art. Would tomorrow at ten a.m. at the Enid Haupt Garden at the Smithsonian Castle work?

I wrote and said ten at the Haupt Garden was fine, realizing she still thought I was working for IPS and maybe this meeting was work-related. Tomorrow, I'd tell her that I'd left a couple of years ago but right now I didn't want to say anything that might give her pause about why I was asking to meet.

She might not know anything about Daniel Worth, but she was my best hope.

In fact, she was my only hope.

NINE

When I saw Valerie Zhou, she was standing next to a bench by the entrance to the Smithsonian Castle, head bent over her phone, speed typing with both thumbs. Still one of the most stunningly beautiful women I'd ever met. She looked up as if she instinctively knew I was watching, and her face broke into a smile.

Val was a knockout in the kind of exotic head-turning way that made people stop and look twice – and maybe one more time. Half-Chinese, half-French, slender and long-legged, flawless skin, almond-shaped dark-brown eyes that she always made up to look cat-like, jet-black hair skimming her shoulders so when she turned her head, it caught the light, flirty and a bit sexy. She knew it, too. Used it. Her clothes – a black shirtwaist dress under a red shawl-collared jacket, black heels – were undeniably Parisian. I could tell by the cut and the way she wore them, with the effortless chic French women seem to be born with. I had on jeans, a white V-neck sweater, and my favorite black leather jacket.

We hugged and did what the French call 'faire la bise' – two quick kisses, one on each cheek. In France, men do it, too. No one thinks it's weird.

'The invitation didn't specify that I needed to dress,' I said, and she laughed. 'You look gorgeous, Val.'

As always.

'Thanks,' she said. 'It's good to see you, too, Sophie. You look great, but you've lost weight. I looked you up after you got in touch yesterday. I didn't know you'd left IPS and I'm so, so sorry about Nick.' She spoke English with a hint of a French accent.

I froze as I always did when someone blindsided me by bringing up Nick and forced a smile. 'Thanks,' I said. 'I'm doing better. I'm OK.'

She reached up and touched my cheek with her hand. '*Ma pauvre.*'

I can just barely handle sympathy, but pity unravels me all the way to my core. I did what I always do: change the subject. 'What are you doing in Washington working for ICIJ? I didn't think any job in the world could make you leave Paris.'

She held up her left hand and flashed the large diamond I hadn't noticed on her ring finger. 'Alexandre was named AFP bureau chief in Washington. I followed him.'

Val had had a string of boyfriends and a few affairs with married men when I knew her in Paris. None of them ever lasted long. As one relationship ended, she sailed effortlessly into the next one. If she had followed Alexandre, who was the bureau chief for Agence France Presse and obviously a damn good journalist to be named to a plum assignment, he must either be quite incredible in bed or else he was a minor god to have captured her heart and kept it. Probably he was both.

'Congratulations,' I said. 'I hadn't heard.'

'You'll have to meet him. Now that I know you're here, we should all have dinner.'

'I'd like that. We should.'

'Come on. It's chilly, so let's walk and you can tell me about your interest in ICIJ – and plundered art.' She arched an eyebrow. 'I'm curious. Is this something new you're working on?'

'In a way,' I said.

Of course she was curious. I knew Val; she was canny, a good journalist. If I wasn't working for IPS, what was I doing seeking her out and, more than likely, planning to pick her brain?

'Tell me.'

The Enid A. Haupt Garden was not crowded this early on a cool spring morning, partly because it is an out-of-the-way place for most tourists, even during cherry blossom season, which was happening right now. The throngs that pour off the tour buses clogging the streets on the Mall side of the Castle mostly keep to the big museums and the art galleries; few venture here. You have to know about it.

The garden is laid out in an elaborate geometric design known as a Parterre, a style dating back to the Victorian era. A fleet of gardeners change its shape and color palette with the seasons. Today two large interlocking diamonds were filled with pink ranunculus planted among dark purple and white pansies. Two smaller gardens, also diamond-shaped, on either side of the main garden were filled with yellow pansies, surrounding low, sculpted boxwood. Across from the garden, Yoshino cherry trees and saucer magnolias, their branches heavy with flowers, curved over the walkway, sheltering visitors from the pale sunshine like a lacy pink curtain.

'I promise I'll tell you,' I said to Valerie, 'but first tell me why we're meeting here, what made you choose this place. I mean, it's lovely, but why?'

'Take a look around.' She pointed to two small pavilions that flanked the garden. The Museum of African Art and the Museum of Asian Art. 'Those museums have had items in their collections that don't belong to them – that's why. Fortunately, they're beginning to make amends, returning what's not theirs to the rightful owners, although it's taken years to get that to happen. People writing about it, speaking out, protesting, clamoring for someone to pay attention. Massive guilt-tripping, I guess you could call it. The Met in New York is the worst offender in the US. By some accounts, they have thousands of items that are rightfully someone else's or the patrimony of another country. And don't get me started on the British Museum and some of the other European museums.'

I'd been inside the Museum of African Art and the Museum of Asian Art, two gems, many times. When they were built as twin buildings in the 1980s, the idea was not to obstruct the view of the Smithsonian's landmark castle or its greenery, so only one floor of each museum would be above ground. The other floors would be subterranean. A tunnel would connect the museums and an information center. Neither museum would be visible from the National Mall, which was the intention, but which also made them less frequently visited. And if you didn't know better as you walked around the Haupt Garden admiring the beautifully manicured flower beds, you probably had no idea that you were also walking on the roofs of both museums.

'I didn't know you were so passionate about art,' I said.

'I studied Art History at the Sorbonne. I always thought I might work in a museum after I graduated, spend my days surrounded by history and beauty. What a life that would be.' She sounded wistful. Then she shrugged. 'But it wasn't to be and the pay – if you can believe it – is even worse than journalism. So since I also loved to write, I went down that road instead and eventually landed a job at the *Trib*. What I'm doing now at ICIJ has given me an opportunity to do both – be a journalist *and* write about art.'

'Do you like it? More than working at the IHT?'

We had reached the end of the garden where enormous cast-iron gates – the Renwick Gates – led outside to Independence Avenue. Cars sped by – Capitol Hill was only a dozen blocks away – on

their way to or from places where decisions were made, deals were
done, and powerful people worked. Here it was a calm, beautiful
oasis. A different world.

Valerie traced a finger along the red sandstone of one of the
pillars that anchored the gates. 'I feel like I'm doing something
good, something worthwhile. But there are days when the destruction – people looting sacred places, eradicating cultures, destroying
history and items as old as time that can *never* be repaired or replaced
– just guts me. It's so senseless, so stupid. So . . . brutal. Art and
antiquities are the fourth most stolen and trafficked items after
money, drugs and arms. Did you know that? The *fourth.*'

The despair in her words reminded me of what Rex Morgenthau
had said at Dulles. *It. Doesn't. Stop.*

'I did not.'

'You're not the only one. A lot of people have no idea. Come
on. Let's walk back and we can sit and talk in the Moongate Garden.
It's quieter there and we might have it to ourselves. Then you can
tell me what's really going on, Soph. Because something *is.*'

She narrowed her eyes, making them look even more mysterious
and cat-like. She *knew.*

'All right,' I said.

The Moongate Garden was next to the Museum of Asian Art
and had been inspired by the gardens and architecture of the
Temple of Heaven in Beijing. I'd been to the one in Beijing; it
had once been a sacred place where emperors went to pray for a
good harvest and had been built by the emperor who also oversaw
the construction of the Forbidden City. Now it was a public park,
open to everyone, just like this garden. Val and I entered through
pink granite gates shaped like two halves of a moon. She was
right; we did have it to ourselves. I followed her over to a bench
in the far corner that overlooked a circular pool of black and pink
granite.

When we were seated, she said, 'Okay, talk to me. You don't
really want to discuss plundered art, do you?'

I smiled half-heartedly. 'I do and I don't.'

'I don't understand.'

'Do you know someone named Daniel Worth? He worked for
The Guardian until a couple of months ago when he took a leave
of absence. No one seems to know for how long or where he went.'

The startled flash of recognition in her eyes before she composed her face into a benign look of mild interest gave her away. 'I know of him. I know his byline.'

'Val, come on. You *do* know him. More than his byline.'

'Why are you asking about him?'

If I wanted – *needed* – her to be honest with me, I was going to have to be honest with her.

'I found out we're related. Like, two days ago.'

'You found out *what*? Are you serious? How?'

'He's my half-brother. His real name is Danilo Medina, but he anglicized his first name because he grew up in Britain and took his mother's maiden name as his last name.'

Her mouth fell open. 'Danny is your half-brother? And you *just* found out?'

Danny. She did know him well.

'It's complicated.'

'It must be.' She leaned back so she could study me. 'You're not kidding.'

'No.'

'I take it he doesn't know about you, either?'

Of course she would zero in on that right away. I looked her in the eye and said, 'I was told that he does know.'

She shook her head. 'No. That can't be right. Danny is a sweetheart, a good person. If he knew he had a half-sister out there somewhere, he'd track you down. I know he would. Besides, how hard would it be? You both lived in London and you're both journalists.'

Right on all counts. Laid out in harsh clarity.

'I know,' I said. 'But he didn't. I don't understand why, either. That's part of the reason I'd like to get in touch with him.'

I watched her do lightning-quick mental math and come up with more correct answers. 'Why did you come to me, Sophie?'

Asking, even though she'd figured out I also had found out about Danny's possible connection to a scheme to return stolen art and antiquities to the rightful owners. First, though, she wanted to know how much, or what, I actually did know. She wanted to test me, friendship or no, before she told me anything.

If she told me anything.

'Because I've been led to believe that he might be involved in several high-profile art thefts,' I said, and her eyes flickered again. Bingo. I went on. 'Not exactly thefts but locating art that had been stolen and returning it to the original owners. I wondered if his leave of absence from *The Guardian* had something to do with that. I also thought you might have some idea how to get in touch with him.'

Valerie looked past me, her eyes skimming the garden as if she were searching for someone specific. I shifted in my seat and followed her gaze. A couple of kids were walking on the granite stones that crisscrossed the pool, clowning around, pretending they might fall in. A woman, presumably their mother, let them be goofy.

'That's a hell of a theory. Or an accusation. How did you hear about this? Who told you?' Her voice rose, and the children's mother briefly cast a worried glance at the two of us, as if she might be wondering if there was reason for alarm.

'The same person who told me Daniel – Danny – was my half-brother. Someone who knew his mother and our father, plus he knew Danny when he was a child. He's looking for Danny himself, so he tracked me down. He figured I'd know where he was. Instead, he found out I had no idea I had a brother.'

'Who is he, Soph? I need a name.'

'I know you do.' And I was going to tell her, too. Otherwise, she didn't owe me anything. 'He's a journalist named Enrique Navarro. Won two Ortega y Gasset awards and he's been with *El País* since Ferdinand and Isabella sent Columbus to look for the Indies.'

She smiled at the little joke before giving me a serious, worried look. 'So he's looking for Danny, and he wants to go through you? He wants *you* to find Danny?'

'He does. But the reason he wants to find him and the reason I want to be in touch with him are entirely different.'

'You told me his. What's yours?'

'Mine has nothing to do with stolen art and everything to do with family,' I said. 'Can you help me, Val? Please?'

'Sophie—'

'Do you know where he is?'

'I can't answer that.'

'Which means yes.'

'Which means I can't answer that. He's moving around. I have no idea where he is now.'

'But you could get in touch with him.' Not a question. She could.

She shook her head, like *Please don't ask me to do this.*

'Val,' I said, 'I just want to talk to him. *Meet* him. Ask him about my father. Our father. I grew up completely estranged from both of them. It's been a hell of a lot to deal with since Navarro told me I have a half-brother.'

She gave me a look like she was going to wait me out until I explained what exactly *a hell of a lot to deal with* meant. We weren't the closest of friends, but over the years we'd had a couple of *nuits blanches* – white nights, all-nighters that lasted until whatever bar we were at closed – talking over drink after drink at some dimly lit place in Paris or London as we slowly lost our inhibitions and bared our souls to each other. Saying things we knew would never leave that bar. That table. So even without the lubrication of a few cocktails, I told her about my father's letters. When I was done, she looked like she might start crying.

'I'm *so* sorry.'

'Now you know why I want to find Danny,' I said. 'He knew our father. I didn't.'

'What about Navarro?' she asked. 'What are you going to tell him?'

'Nothing. *If* I meet Danny, I'll tell him that Navarro wants to talk to him and explain why. Whether Danny wants to get in touch, whether he actually even *knows* him as Navarro claims – it's up to him. He can make his own decision about what he wants to do. It's not my call.'

She nodded, a look of relief crossing her face. But I knew she was still worried. Alarmed. Because what I had told her about Navarro had probably shaken the foundation of what I suspect Danny had believed was an airtight scheme no one had figured out.

'How did Navarro connect Danny with the stolen art that was returned?' she asked.

'Apparently, he began following Danny's stories after he wrote about the theft of the tapestries from a small church in Cuenca – and how they were "mysteriously" returned. Danny wrote a few more stories about plundered art that was also returned to its owners with no explanation. Navarro figured it happened enough times to be a pattern. So he got curious.'

'*Merde.*'

'Meaning he's right?'

She looked up at the sky and blew out a long breath. I waited. Her turn for soul-baring.

'Yes,' she said, 'he is.'

'Tell me,' I said. 'You already know it won't go any farther than me.'

'It's a long story.'

Weren't they all?

'I'm listening,' I said, as an overwhelming feeling of dread started to drip through my veins like a poison. My half-brother *was* an international art thief.

'When Danny was a student at Oxford, he read Art History as well as Computer Science,' she said, her mouth twisting into a knowing smile. 'Yeah, yeah, I can tell by that look that you already knew this, but I need to start at the beginning for you to understand.'

Did she really mean *understand*? Or justify?

'Sorry. Go on.'

'While he was at university – and later while he had a fellowship at the British Museum – he started putting together a database of art that had been stolen and later ended up being found and returned to its owner. He compiled statistics about similarities in thefts, where the art – or antiquity – had been stolen from, where it had traveled and finally ended up before it was recovered. He went back and looked at historical records, found every scrap of information he could get his hands on. I'm talking about a couple of years of him doing this – while he was at uni and later during the year he had the fellowship. He even worked on it when he first started with *The Guardian*.

'He began finding patterns, and the more data he collected, the more patterns he uncovered,' she said. 'Eventually, he was able to build an algorithm *predicting* where a stolen painting or sculpture or antiquity would end up.'

'He *knew* who had stolen something?'

'*No*. Definitely not. But he could predict with a fair amount of accuracy *where* it probably would end up – the route from theft to dealer. Who was interested, what country or countries it would probably transit, who the big dealers were in a particular city. I'm not talking about big thefts – a theft from the Louvre or the Met – but small museums, churches, archeological sites that were poorly guarded or had no security at all.'

'That's an incredibly valuable algorithm.'

'You have no idea.'

'And I imagine if certain people knew it existed, they'd want to get their hands on it.'

'You'd imagine right.'

'So that's why he disappeared?'

'Yup.' She pursed her lips together in a tight thin line and surveyed the park. We were alone again. 'There's something else.'

'What?'

'Danny . . . got hooked up with some people.' She held up her hand. 'Wait – let me finish. It's probably not what you're thinking.'

'OK.'

'Well,' she added, 'it is and it isn't.'

Back to square one. I'd said something like that to her at the beginning of this conversation. She was equivocating, just as I'd been.

'Go on,' I said.

'A couple of years ago, Danny got connected with an organization based in London called ArtRevive. It's a group of art dealers and law enforcement people with an office in Bloomsbury, not far from the British Museum. They've been around for about ten years and by now they've collected a massive database of stolen art. The way they do it is by reaching out to places like museums, galleries, auction houses, even private individuals, and urging them to report any thefts. Conversely, they want those places to check out items that they're about to display or sell to make sure what they've got isn't stolen, that its provenance is legitimate.'

'Connecting with ArtRevive must have been a huge game-changer,' I said. 'All of a sudden, Danny's got masses of information to add to his database, which probably made it even more powerful.'

'Exactly.'

'So now he's working with ArtRevive to help them figure out where stolen items might end up?'

She nodded, but there was *another* something else.

'What?' I said.

She gave me a look as if to say, *You don't know what you're asking.* 'All right. There's this guy. Or maybe it's not a guy, maybe not even one person – maybe it's a couple of people. Danny's pretty circumspect.'

She seemed to know a lot about my half-brother.

'Before Alexandre,' I said, 'were you and Danny . . .?'

She arched an eyebrow. 'Lovers?'

I turned red and she laughed. 'It was fun, but it was over in no time. We're too different. He's so serious. I'm . . . not.' She winked at me. 'But he's great in bed. He's amazing.'

My face felt even hotter. 'That is way too much information. Which I didn't need to know.'

'Maybe so, but you *wanted* to know.' Another sly smile.

My cheeks still burned. 'On the ick spectrum, that's about eight out of ten. Tell me about this guy. Or these "people."'

'Oh. Right. He – or they – goes by Michael Angelo. Clever, huh?'

'Yup. Clever.'

'I know. Anyway, Michael – who seems to have some affiliation with ArtRevive and has access to their database – has put together this group of people he can reach out to. They're the ones who retrieve items that are stolen and return them to their owners. They're located all over the world, so it's not just a core group of people he calls on all the time with . . . special skills.'

'And Danny's part of the group?'

'He is now.'

I shuddered. 'These skills include breaking and entering?'

'Well, a painting isn't going to float out of some black-market art dealer's gallery, is it?'

'So, yes.'

'So, yes.'

I closed my eyes and imagined all the heist TV shows and movies I'd watched over the years – *The Sting*, *The Italian Job*, *Ocean's Eleven*, *The Thomas Crown Affair*, *A Fish Called Wanda*, *Sneakers*, *Leverage*, *It Takes A Thief* – where everything was so slick and effortless. *Fun*, even. Clever ex-cons and smart-aleck security wizards who could disable even the most complex security cameras with a few quick keystrokes, the gamine young thing who was going to pull off the heist by dropping through a heating vent and tumbling like a gymnast over invisible crisscrossing beams without tripping the alarm, janitors who weren't janitors talking their way past security guards and then using someone's stolen keycard or fingerprint to get access to the vault.

'It sounds dangerous,' I said.

'They're good. They've never been caught.' But Valerie flashed that worried look again. 'And until you just told me about Enrique Navarro, we didn't realize anyone had figured out they even existed. Like I said, Michael coordinates everything from wherever he's located – could be London, could be Timbuktu. And they mix it up as to who is doing each job.'

Right. They hadn't been caught. *Yet.*

It might only be a matter of time.

'Will you tell Danny I would like to be in touch with him?'

She nodded. 'It's up to him if he wants to reach out to you. Especially now. You can probably guess why.'

In other words, I might not hear from him. 'I understand.'

'Sophie.' Valerie leaned forward and placed her hand over mine. Her diamond ring sparkled in the sunlight, full of promise and hope and love. 'If Danny doesn't get in touch with you, you mustn't think it's because he doesn't want to. I can't imagine that he would want to do anything that would jeopardize your safety in any way. Especially because you *are* related. That makes him vulnerable, you know? It gives someone a way to get to him – through you. You've already got Enrique Navarro breathing down your neck. If you ask me, the best thing would be to keep some distance between Danny and you. And Navarro.'

'At least ask him, Val. Please?'

'I will,' she said, 'but you must know there are no guarantees. I'm afraid you'll just have to wait and see.'

TEN

Val left the Enid A. Haupt Garden through the Renwick Gates and climbed into a waiting Uber on Independence Avenue after promising she'd be in touch with news about Danny if she could. I knew what I'd told her about Enrique Navarro had rattled her. Once Danny learned about it, he might decide meeting me was too much of a liability and then he'd really disappear into thin air.

Maybe now I was the last person in the world he wanted to meet.

I walked back to the Mall and took the Smithsonian metro two stops to Metro Center, changing to the Red Line for another two stops to Dupont Circle. It's one of the deepest stops in the Metro system; by the time you take multiple escalators to reach the street, it's as if you've emerged from a mine shaft.

For the first time in several years, the National Park Service had turned on the water to the beautiful old fountain in the park at the center of Dupont Circle. The moment that happened, the little park returned to life as if someone had watered *it* after being all but abandoned during the pandemic. Once again lawyers and lobbyists and office workers spilled out of nearby buildings on their lunch hours to sit on the fountain steps and sun themselves or lounge on the grass with friends. Mothers and nannies came with strollers and baby carriages to while away a pleasant morning or afternoon sitting on the benches that ringed the fountain. Street musicians had returned with their trumpets and saxes and violins; so did the chess players who brought their games and groups of vocal advice-givers to the tree-shaded tables across from Mass Avenue. I made a quick detour through the park to listen to a saxophonist with long white hair play 'I Will Always Love You,' the piercing high notes soaring above the rumble of traffic. A growing crowd tossed bills and coins into his instrument case, and when I added a few dollars, he winked at me. I left the park by the crosswalk at New Hampshire Avenue, partly to get a glimpse of the chess games, but also to pass by one of the two entrances to the Dupont Underground, an avant-garde art gallery located quite literally underneath Dupont Circle in a now-defunct trolley station.

A cavernous place with passageways that led into the darkness of who-knew-where, the art gallery only took up a fraction of the trolley station. A few months ago, the Underground had held its post-pandemic grand re-opening: a retrospective of some of my late grandfather Charles Lord's never-before-seen photographs. The exhibit, which had lasted a month, brought people back in droves – my grandfather had been among the legendary photographers of the post-World War II generation and his work was well known. The Underground still hadn't returned to regular hours, which included not only viewing the latest exhibits but also tours of some of the spookier passageways. When the place was closed, a section of chain-link fence held in place by wires and chains lay across the railing to the entrances to keep people from going downstairs to sleep or pee or shoot up.

Today, the fence was gone and the gallery was open. I leaned over the railing and peered down. Landon Reed, the veterinarian from the homeless camp in front of the Church of the Epiphany, stood at the bottom of the stairs, cradling something small and furry – I could see a tail – in his hands.

He looked up, a surprised look crossing his face. 'Well, hello. I didn't expect to run into you again so soon. How are you? How's the arm?'

'I'm fine, thanks. The arm's better. I'm surprised to see you, too. Is everything all right?'

He sprinted up the graffiti-painted steps. 'I was walking back from the homeless camp at McPherson Square when I heard this little girl. So I stopped.'

He opened his hands so I could see a tiny tuxedo kitten with a sweet face. She looked as if she were wearing a black Carnivale mask that covered her eyes and ears except for the white Harry Potter scar between her eyes. White nose, mouth and whiskers. Two tiny black spots like beauty marks on either side of her nose. Only one set of eyebrow whiskers, which gave her an off-kilter look. A mostly black body except for the white tuxedo shirt and black paws with white boots. Black tail with a white tip as if she'd dipped it in paint.

'She's adorable,' I said. 'How old is she?'

'Eight weeks, give or take. And she's not feral, but she hasn't been spayed yet. Her ears aren't tipped.'

'What's that?'

'If we find feral cats, vets leave them in the wild since they won't make good house pets. But we do try to spay or neuter them so they won't have more kittens. Whoever does that tips their ears – makes a small cut – before they let them back on the street so the next vet knows the cat has already been fixed,' he said. 'It helps keep the population down – a little.'

'She's such a baby – you'd spay her this soon?'

'She may be a baby, but she could also already be a mother. I'll have to check when I get her back to the clinic.'

I reached out to stroke the kitten who started to purr, a startlingly loud, contented sound from such a tiny body. She turned big gold eyes on me, and I melted.

Landon Reed smiled. 'She likes you.'

'She's a cutie,' I said, then caught the look in his eyes. 'Wait a minute . . . you don't . . . you're not thinking . . . *no.*'

'She needs a good home. Unfortunately, I can't keep her,' he said. 'I've got two cats who are siblings and have made it clear they rule the roost. I'm not going to leave her here, put her back on the street. And I don't want to take her to the shelter if I can avoid it. It's a kill shelter.'

'You want me to take this kitten home with me?'

'Not right away. I'll take her back to the clinic, check her out for a couple of days, make sure she's OK. Hopefully, she doesn't have ringworm. Be sure to wash your hands well when you get home in case she does. And, of course, I'll spay her and give her the shots she needs,' he said. 'You'll be all set.'

'Dr Reed—'

'Landon.'

'Landon. I'm sorry, but I'm not ready to take on a pet. It's not something I expected to do right now.'

'Finn, uh, caught me up about you the other day after you left,' he said. 'I'm so sorry for your loss, Sophie – it must have been brutal losing your husband. If it's not too out of line to say this, animals are great at helping people deal with all kinds of medical issues, as well as with grief and loneliness. In some ways, they're better than humans.'

Grace Lowe, my best friend, had said almost the exact same thing to me the other day: that I needed a pet, a companion, so I didn't always come home to an empty house. It was one thing to hear it from Grace. It was another to hear it from someone who didn't know me at all but seemed to take it for granted that I must be lonely. Besides, he had already knocked me off balance by unexpectedly bringing up Nick.

'That's a pretty nervy assumption, don't you think? For you to presume . . .' I stopped before I lost my composure in front of this stranger who had just zeroed in on my vulnerability, my Achilles heel, with laser precision.

He looked as stricken as he had the other day when he knocked me over and sent me flying across the sidewalk. 'I'm so sorry. I just keep saying or doing one dumb thing after another, don't I? It was inappropriate and I apologize.' He held out the kitten. 'Peace offering? Why don't you hold her?'

I took the kitten, who began to purr loudly. She was soft as velvet. I cradled her in the crook of my arm as he'd done. 'She is awfully sweet.'

'She is. And I'd say she's definitely made up her mind about you. Now it's your turn.'

'I don't have a single thing for a kitten,' I said, but it was useless to protest because the kitten had decided she was mine and so had Landon. 'No bed, no dish, no litter box, no food.'

'Don't worry. There's a pet store in Adams Morgan on Columbia Road. It just opened. You can get everything you need there. What's your phone number? I'll call you and then you'll have my number so you can call if you've got any questions. Plus I'll text you a list of cat food brands I recommend for kittens and anything else I think you might need.'

I gave him my number, and when my phone rang, he took the kitten so I could add his name and number to my contacts. 'Are you always this pushy?' I said. 'The other day you insisted on putting cream you use on animals on a scrape I got after you and Bruiser decked me. Now you've talked me into adopting a stray kitten. And that's after knowing you for all of about twenty minutes – if that.'

He looked startled, but then his dark-blue eyes lit up and there was a glint in them. 'I work with animals all day. They're uncomplicated. No guile, no pretenses. You don't have to tiptoe around them, worry about hurting their feelings or second-guess what they're thinking. They let you know. I guess I've started talking to people the same way I talk to animals.'

'Did you just admit you're talking to me as if I'm a cat or a dog?'

He laughed. 'I'm direct, that's all. I say what I think.'

'No fooling.'

'Come on,' he said. 'Let's walk. I need to get this little one back to the clinic before she pees on me. Where do you live?'

He'd finagled my phone number and now he wanted my address. 'Eighteen-oh-nine S Street.'

'I'll walk you to your place and then I can head up Eighteenth, which is where the clinic is. By the way, what's the kitten's name?'

'Her name? You want me to name her already? We hardly know each other.' I almost said, *Just like you and me.*

'If I know her name, I can use it when she's with me and she'll start getting used to it.'

'Oh.' I thought for a moment. 'Her name is Harriet.'

'Harriet?'

'Yes. Look at her forehead. She's got a scar like Harry Potter. And she's a girl. So . . . Harriet.'

'Cute. Suits her.'

For the rest of the walk back to my apartment, our conversation shifted to the practical matter of what I needed to do and buy for the kitten. At my front gate, he said, 'I'll call you and we can figure out when I can come by with Harriet. It's going to be a few days, though. And if she's pregnant – which I don't think she is, but I need to be sure – it will be longer.'

'I'll come get her. It's no problem. Like you said, you're only just up the street.'

'If I bring her to you, I can see your place, help you figure out how to help her navigate her way around until she gets used to being indoors.'

'Are you sure that's necessary?'

'I can tell by the look on your face that I'm on my third strike before I'm out. Look, I'm not using this kitten to get to see you again. I'm not that guy. I really would like to see where you live so I can help you get Harriet settled. Especially since I gather you've never had a cat before.'

He was relentless. I gave in. Again.

'Call me and let me know when she's had her shots and I can have her.'

'I will.'

'Tell me something.'

'Sure.'

'Do you always get your way?'

For a moment, I'd caught him off-guard. But then he nodded. 'When it's something worth fighting for I do.' Harriet started to squirm. 'I'd better go. She's getting impatient. I'll call you, Sophie.'

I watched him walk down the street, head bent as he talked to the little kitten. There had most definitely been a wedding ring on his finger, and it had been there recently based on that tan line. Was he divorced? Widowed, like me? Separated? Although he claimed not to have been chatting me up, it still felt as though he'd been flirting with me. If so, he hadn't wasted any time since taking off that ring. Was he looking for a rebound relationship? Those were the worst: the rebound person still hadn't worked things out from the last relationship.

No, thanks.

Either way, I hadn't seen or heard the last of Landon Reed.

Right now, I wasn't sure how I felt about that.

For the rest of the afternoon, I read more of Danny's stories for *The Guardian* along with ICIJ's reports on looted and plundered art. My phone pinged with regular texts from Landon, recommending brands of kitten food for Harriet and telling me that her physical exam had gone well. Surgery to spay her would be tomorrow morning.

It sounded like she'd be with me sooner rather than later, so after I finished reading, I drove to the pet store he'd recommended and spent a small fortune on a tiny kitten – including going a little overboard buying her toys, just like a gaga new parent. When I got home, I carried everything upstairs and put it in the spare bedroom.

Then, since I was still punchy and restless, I walked across the alley to my studio. I'd taken on a pro bono project for a local charity that provided jobs for disabled adults, spending time taking photos at their facility and at the various job sites where their clients worked, so they could use them for their website and for fundraising. I had promised to finish them by the beginning of next week.

The moment I turned the key in the lock to the door, I knew someone was already there. Waiting quietly, patiently, in the dark. I walked in and flipped on the lights. He blinked in the sudden brightness. He'd been lying on the old Chesterfield sofa Max sold me before he moved out. He sat up and faced me.

'Danny,' I said.

ELEVEN

'Sophie.' He stood up. 'How do you do?'

And so I met my half-brother. Cultured British accent. Pleasant baritone. Black hoodie, black jeans, black sneakers. More boyish and handsome in person than the mug shots I'd seen on *The Guardian* and British Museum websites.

Gentleman burglar.

'*You broke into my studio,*' I said. Not the first thing I expected to say to him or the appropriate reply to 'How do you do?'

'It was dead easy. You could do with a better lock, you know, since you've got cameras and a computer in here. Expensive equipment.'

No apology, no remorse. Unrepentant. In fact, he seemed to enjoy my stunned, sputtering reaction to his unconventional entrance.

'Thank you very much. I'll look into that. And consider the source.' I was still standing in the doorway. We were sizing each other up, staring at each other with frank, open curiosity. Plus something else: the faintest frisson of hostility, of too much unresolved baggage, too many lost years. Too much time we couldn't get back. I looked away first, broke the spell. Then I shut the door, locked it – just for effect – and walked into the room.

'You couldn't have knocked on the door or at least let me know you were here?' I said. 'You really had to break in?'

'No one knows I'm here – in Washington,' he said, 'except for a very few people who need to know. Now you're one of them.'

And just like that I'd been dragged into whatever danger and secrets had brought him here.

'You're here because you want information,' I said. 'This isn't a get-to-know-you family visit.'

His dark eyes – which were so much like mine and Antonio's – grew even darker and more unfathomable. 'No,' he said, 'it's not a family visit.'

I was right. He was only here because he needed something from me. That was all.

'You *knew* about me.' The hurt and resentment seeped into my voice. Unintentional, because I hadn't meant to let him know, hadn't meant to let him hear how vulnerable and wounded I'd felt. 'You've known about me for years but you never tried to find me.'

'You knew about *me*, too.' He hurled my words back in my face. 'Our father wrote you letters for years and you never replied. Not once. What was he supposed to think? Was *I* supposed to think? We found out your mother married a multi-millionaire who swept you away to his estate in the Virginia countryside where he was raising Thoroughbreds. You had a new life, a brother and a sister. A new *family*.'

I wasn't prepared for the breadth and depth of *his* anger. Or that the two of us would be unraveling so quickly, unpacking so much pent-up grief and anger, and leaving it in the middle of the room where it pulsed and seethed.

'I didn't know about those letters until the other day,' I said, my voice uneven. 'I only read them the night before last. My mother kept them from me. All of them. The first I learned of you was from Enrique Navarro. Who I also never heard of until he sought me out.'

Mentioning Navarro's name seemed to jar him. 'We need to talk about him,' he said. Then, abruptly, 'I don't suppose you have anything to drink?'

'You don't suppose wrong. I've got Scotch, whiskey, gin, vodka, tequila, cognac, brandy, wine, beer.' I ticked them off on my fingers. 'I'm assuming by "drink" you meant alcohol. Not a cup of tea.'

He looked startled, possibly because I'd listed enough different kinds of booze to open my own bar instead of offering him Coke or ginger ale.

'I entertain clients here. My houseguests use this as a private apartment when they stay with me. To reply to your unanswered question about whether I'm a lush, I'm not.'

He gave me the ghost of a smile. 'Thanks for clarifying that. And I'll have a Scotch, please. Neat.'

'Of course,' I said. 'You're British. Allergic to ice cubes.'

'Funny,' he said. 'Very funny.'

The alcohol was in a cabinet in the kitchen. While I fixed two Scotches – neat for him, rocks for me – he started pacing the room, examining the photos I'd hung on the wall. Some from my days with IPS, others I'd taken since I moved home. When I walked back into the main room with our drinks, he was holding a framed photo of Nick. I'd taken it when we were on a ski holiday in Zermatt years ago, the jagged white mountain behind him sharp and spiky as if it could puncture a hole in the blindingly brilliant blue sky, Nick's handsome face, tanned, rested and oh-so-happy. It had been an idyllic vacation. We'd spent a lot of it trying to get pregnant.

Unsuccessfully, as it turned out. A few months later, a doctor told us it wasn't meant for us to become parents.

Danny looked up and his eyes locked on mine. 'I'm so sorry,' he said. 'I wish I'd known him.'

'You knew about Nick?'

'I know everything about you. I may not have been in touch, but I kept track of you.' He set the photograph back on my desk. 'I lost my fiancée six months ago. She was killed by Russian gunfire along with the curator of a small museum near Lviv while the two of them were on their way to tour the museum, which had recently been looted – by the Russians.'

I handed him his glass and our fingers touched. 'I'm sorry for your loss, too. I wish I could have been there for you.'

A muscle in his jaw twitched. 'Thanks.'

'I think we should sit down,' I said. 'Then we can talk about why you're here. I know you have questions.'

He sat on the sofa again; I took one of the pair of matching club chairs – more Max purchases – across from him.

'You didn't tell me her name,' I said, after a moment.

'Joie. J-O-I-E. Spelled the French way. She was French.'

'It's a beautiful name.'

'Everything about her was beautiful.'

We drank in silence for a minute. Then I said, 'Valerie Zhou told me what you do. She told me about the algorithm you built and how it's helped you predict where stolen or plundered art and artifacts might turn up.'

He held up his glass and looked at it as if it were a prism through which he could see things changing and refracting in the light. The room. The furniture. Me.

The truth.

'People would kill to know about that algorithm,' he said, and a shiver went through me. 'That's one of the reasons you and I can't be seen together. Especially if someone should, say, find out we're related.'

'Enrique Navarro knows.'

'Precisely.' He took a long, deep drink of his Scotch.

'Do you know him? He said you do, but he met you when you were a little kid. Supposedly, he was good friends with . . . our father. He also knew your mother.'

'I don't remember him.'

'Could you ask your mother about him?'

'I could if she were alive.'

'Oh, God. I'm sorry. I had no idea.'

'Well, you wouldn't, would you?'

'Apparently, Navarro didn't know she passed away, either.'

'Apparently not.'

'What do you want to know about Navarro?' I asked.

'I want to know how he tracked *you* down. How did he find you?'

'He saw my name on a list of photographers in the press pool for the friendly between Real Madrid and DC United here in Washington next week.'

'And he figured out that you were Antonio Medina's daughter? *That's* how he found you – a random connection? That's it?'

'Yes. He asked if I knew where you were since you'd taken a leave of absence from *The Guardian*. Obviously, I had no idea. He also told me he suspected you were involved in several high-profile art thefts.'

He swore in Spanish. 'How did he figure *that* out?'

'Easy. You left a trail of breadcrumbs. The story you wrote about the stolen tapestries turning up in Cuenca caught his eye,' I said. 'It's *Spain*, his territory. How would he *not* see that story? So all of a sudden you were on his radar. He also noticed that you wrote a couple more stories on the same subject. Art stolen from a small museum or a church or wherever. Then, bam. A few months later, the lost treasure shows up on the doorstep of said church or museum without even a note attached. Like Santa Claus at Christmas or the Tooth Fairy leaving money under your pillow. Magic.'

He swore again. 'Believe it or not, I had nothing to do with the art that was returned in those stories. I found out later that a guy affiliated with ArtRevive was responsible.'

'You mean Michael Angelo?'

He grinned. 'Yes. Corny, I know. But whoever he is, he's a wizard.'

'You don't know him?'

'I do not.'

'How did you hook up with him?'

'We found each other, or I should say, he found me. Through ArtRevive. He's the one who suggested my algorithm could be even more powerful if we input all the data from the ArtRevive database into it.'

'And is it?'

'You have no idea.'

'How does it work?' I asked. 'How do you find something that's been stolen – and then retrieve it?'

'The algorithm finds patterns, probability, a likely scenario based on past thefts. Thanks to the ArtRevive database, there are hundreds of thousands of examples. What method the burglars used – did they walk into the place in broad daylight, break in at night, were they armed – that sort of thing. What did they take and who is likely to be interested in acquiring those items, who can move them? Then we run a regression, actually multiple regressions, mathematically calculating which variables are likely to have an impact on the outcome – in other words, where we might find the stolen item – and which variables we should ignore.'

'So it's math?'

'Math and data,' he said. 'And knowing what inputs are important.'

'Then what?' I asked. 'Once you find whatever you're looking for, how do you retrieve it?'

He held up a hand. 'Hang on. The algorithm is not a treasure map. X marks the spot. What it does is tell you where you're *likely* to find something that's missing. So first you've got to find it. And there's no magic wand to wave for that.'

He looked down at his glass, which was empty. 'A refill?' I asked.

'If you don't mind.'

I refilled both our glasses and said, 'So what do you do?'

'Scut work. Michael's got people, contacts; we start asking questions, looking around.'

'What kind of people?'

'People in law enforcement, gallery owners, sources – a fence, say – who might be willing to talk for the right amount of money.' He shrugged. 'If we get lucky and find what we're looking for, then there are people who take care of getting it back to where it belongs.'

'And those are the people who "re-steal" the stolen art,' I said. 'A theft no one is going to report because if they did, they'd be admitting what was taken were items that were *already* stolen.'

'Exactly.'

'What about Enrique Navarro?' I asked. 'He figured out what you're doing or figured out *something*. He told me he wants to write a story about it. Maybe earn himself another Ortega y Gasset Award.'

'Navarro is an outlier,' he said. 'I don't know what to make of him. Yet. Or whose side he's on.'

'Do you think he might traffic in stolen art himself?'

'Plenty of stolen and looted items pass through Spain. It's a huge conduit. As a journalist, Navarro travels a lot. He could get stuff through in his luggage quite easily, believe it or not. We checked him out. He goes back and forth all the time between Washington and Madrid.'

'He told me that. He has an ex-wife who's American and his children and grandchildren live here. He also said he could help you.'

'With what?'

'I have no idea. Do you think he could be a courier bringing things into the US?'

'That's what I'd like to find out. Lately, we're seeing items coming through Washington instead of New York. Especially things from Ukraine. Religious items, antiquities, art.'

I told him about the murder of the British courier at Dulles and my hunch that what he was bringing in had come from Ukraine.

'We knew about that,' he said. 'We've got a source at the FBI. They found the guy who killed the courier, a small-time dealer from DC. And the stuff *was* from Ukraine. So you were right.'

'I hadn't heard about it or seen anything in the news.'

He gave me an ironic smile. 'You will when they're ready to make that information public. So keep it under your hat for now, OK?'

I nodded. 'If you have a source at the FBI – and it sounds like a very good source – why don't you let them handle this? Why don't you let Interpol and Scotland Yard and the FBI do their job? Why are you even getting involved?'

'Because there's *so much* being stolen and looted. Those agencies don't have the resources, the time and the money to take care of the little stuff. They go after the big fish. We try to help the small museums, the churches, the private collectors who don't have much hope of ever recovering what they've lost.'

'In other words, you're the Robin Hood of the art world,' I said. 'Or else you're sort of vigilantes, taking the law into your own hands.'

'We right wrongs,' he said in a firm voice. 'All we want is for the stolen items to be returned where they belong. No one gets hurt. We change up teams depending on where in the world we need to be. No real names used – in fact, we don't even know each other's names.'

'Who finances all this? Or do you do it out of the goodness of your heart and live on your altruism?'

'I'd like to say the latter, but of course there's money involved. There has to be, to run a network like Michael does. To recover a stolen item – extract it from, say, a vault or a building where there might be exceptional security and it's a potentially dangerous situation – requires specialized skills they don't teach you in school. You don't find those people on streetcorners.'

'Skills like breaking and entering? Disabling alarm systems? Picking locks? Using explosives to blow open a safe? *Those* kinds of skills?'

He held up his hand. 'Obviously, you've got the point. Not everyone who does this sort of thing is a former Boy Scout.'

'So, the money? Is it all on the up and up?'

'It comes from a lot of sources – off and on the books. Insurance companies who don't have to make a huge payout are happy to see something returned where it belongs. Dealers, private collectors, museums. Everyone kicks in a little something for the greater good.'

'The greater good being getting stolen art returned to its owners.'

He nodded.

'Why are you here? Now? In Washington. What are you looking for – this time?' I asked.

He got up without asking and got the bottle of Scotch, filling both our glasses with more than a couple of fingers. If I drank all that, I'd be a little drunk, but this evening seemed to call for not following the rules of good or prudent behavior. For taking a risk or two.

'A number of Ukrainian antiquities and religious artifacts have started coming into Washington, as you know about firsthand because of the dead courier at Dulles,' Danny said. 'Believe me, he was just one cog in a much bigger wheel. Except what's coming in is not being moved through the channels we know of, and things are disappearing, not turning up anywhere else. It's as if they're vanishing into thin air. Whoever is behind this is clever; they're not leaving any footprints – so far. The reason I'm here is for a reconnaissance trip.'

I sipped my Scotch and thought about what he'd said. Before I turned this carriage house into my photo studio, Max used the building as a warehouse to keep items he didn't have room for in his antique gallery.

'What if the reason you're not finding these items is because they *aren't* going anywhere? What if the buyer is keeping them, hanging on to them?'

His eyes narrowed. 'You mean waiting before putting them on the market?'

'That's one possibility. The other is what if one of the people involved is a collector?'

Someone, say, like Robson Blake who had an underground vault containing rooms I had not seen, maybe a whole maze of rooms. Two floors filled with who knew how many undisplayed paintings, sculptures, artifacts, icons.

Danny shook his head. 'Doubtful. Usually, if the stuff is hot, they want to move it as soon as possible. They want their money. Plus you are talking about items that need to be stored somewhere. It's not cryptocurrency. You need a warehouse or someplace to keep it all. And the place must be safe and secure.'

'I *know* that.'

'Then what?'

'I'm just saying you might consider the possibility that you're dealing with a collector who doesn't plan to sell what he's acquired. Maybe he wants to keep some of those beautiful things for himself.'

'*He*. Do you *know* such a collector?'

I shook my head, maybe a little too quickly. 'No,' I said.

He leaned toward me. 'I don't believe you.'

What tenuous filaments connected the two of us besides DNA and the same father? We barely knew each other, had gotten off to a rocky start, and we couldn't be more different.

Still, what he was doing . . . I admired him for it. It took courage, guts; it was a hell of a risk.

If I told him what I suspected, was I doing a good deed or betraying someone who had trusted me? All I had to go on was a hunch. Except that Robbie's caretaker, Bernard, had been so angry that I'd seen the icon room by myself. I had thought it might just be the eccentricity of an extraordinarily wealthy man who valued his privacy. But Bernard's anger had been disproportionate to the severity of my transgression. After all, he'd left the door open.

You weren't supposed to see that room.

I deleted the video.

Maybe the real reason I wasn't supposed to see what was in that room was because some of those items had been stolen, and Bernard knew it. If I told Danny that I might, just *might*, have an idea where some of the plundered art he was looking for could be located, then he and his team were going to check it out.

How, I didn't know. But if they discovered that anything had been stolen, they were almost certainly going to try to steal whatever it was back. Especially if they learned that these were beautiful items that belonged halfway around the world in a church or a museum or a monastery, not locked up in a vault in Washington, DC, for one person to worship at his own private altar.

'Sophie.' Danny's hands were clasped tight around his glass as if he were praying. When I looked more closely, his grip looked as if he wanted to strangle something. 'Please tell me.'

'If you tell me something.'

'What?'

'Are you doing this partly because of what happened to Joie? Is this some sort of retaliation or payback to the men who killed her?'

He nodded and I looked into my brother's eyes, catching a fleeting glimpse of a cold, calm fury that scared me. Three glasses of Scotch and Danny's sorrow and loss – something I understood only too well – loosened my inhibitions and my tongue.

I set my empty glass on the table between us. 'Have you ever heard of Robson Blake?'

He blinked. 'The philanthropist? Of course I have. Who hasn't? The man's given piles of money to museums and cultural institutions all over the world, not to mention the art and antiquities he's donated.' He paused. 'Wait a minute. You're not saying . . . Jesus Christ, Sophie, are you *serious*?'

I told him about Robbie's icon room, how I had accidentally seen it and how upset his caretaker had been when he discovered where I'd been. Danny nodded at my camera equipment sitting on the table I used as a desk.

'Did you take any photos?'

'No. I didn't.'

'Did you have your camera with you?'

'Yes, of course I did. I was there for a photo shoot.'

'Then why the hell—?'

'The icons were in a room in a *vault*, Danny. A room with the door accidentally left open. I wasn't supposed to see any of it. I just told you. The caretaker practically had a coronary when he found out. He said he'd be sacked if Robbie learned about it.'

'Still—'

I held up my hand to stop him. 'I have rules, a code of conduct, about what I will and won't photograph. At the time, I had no idea anything in that room might not belong – legitimately – to Robson Blake.' I eyed him. 'Besides, there were security cameras.'

'There are ways around those,' he said.

'I bet you know them.'

'You bet right,' he said. 'All right, do you remember what any of the icons you saw looked like? Could you describe them?'

'There's one I especially remember,' I said. 'It was exquisite, the Virgin of Vladimir. The frame was gold and silver – beautiful, intricate carving – encrusted with rubies and sapphires and emeralds. It was in the center of the altar he'd created on a pedestal in a carved wooden kiot.'

'What size was it?'

'Maybe twelve by sixteen inches. Maybe a bit larger.'

He pulled out his phone, found his photo app and started scrolling. After a few minutes, he handed me the phone.

'Is this it?'

I stared at the photo of the icon I'd seen in Robbie's vault. There was no doubt.

'Oh my God. Is it stolen?'

'It came from a small Orthodox church outside Kyiv,' he said. 'It's been missing since the beginning of the war. The icon probably dates to the thirteenth century. It was a gift to the church from Peter the Great, though originally it came from Constantinople. Not long after it was installed in the church, people who came to pray before it started believing the Virgin and Child were responsible for certain miracles. People were healed from life-threatening illnesses, wounds were cured, a cancer diagnosis suddenly went away.'

'You mean like the miracles attributed to the shrines at Lourdes or Fatima?'

'This place is not as big or as famous. It's more like the Holy Dirt of Chimayo in New Mexico. *El Santuario de Chimayo,*' he said pronouncing the Spanish name with a perfect Castilian accent. 'The icon was in a little chapel that had a dirt floor. When the new church was built, it was moved there, to the iconostasis. One morning, the priest discovered it was missing and found it back in the chapel. After it happened a couple more times, they figured the chapel was where the icon wanted to be. That's when people started taking a little bit of dirt with them when they left, believing it had healing powers.'

He took the phone back and stared at the image. 'No one ever expected to see that icon again. It just disappeared into thin air. A lot of people at ArtRevive thought it had been destroyed.'

I sat back in my chair and watched him. He was already planning. Thinking.

'You're going to figure out a way to steal it and return it to the church,' I said. 'Aren't you?'

'Remove it from somewhere it doesn't belong,' he said. 'Semantics, Sophie.'

'What if . . . Robbie doesn't know it's stolen? What if someone sold it to him and he didn't do due diligence?'

His look was pure scorn. 'You can't be serious. Someone with the connections he has in the art world could be that naive, that easily duped? Do you really believe that?'

'Robson Blake is a philanthropist. Everyone loves him, worships him; he's so incredibly generous and giving. He can *buy* whatever he wants. He could probably afford the whole damn Louvre,' I said. 'He doesn't *need* to steal anything.'

'Which is exactly why someone like him would do it. For the thrill. He gets a kick out of it,' Danny said. 'Come on, you know that.'

Of course I did. Robbie had used almost the identical words at Max's the other night: it was the thrill of the hunt. It wasn't about the painting or the sculpture or an antiquity. It was about having something *no one else possessed.*

Why did it seem so personal, learning what Robbie had probably done? I barely knew him. Sure, he was Max's friend, a connection through his partner Gil Tessier that had grown into a close relationship. Still, I was angry. If it was true that he knew the icon was stolen, he was a phony, a hypocrite.

I've photographed royalty, heads of state, the Pope, famous people who were leaders and trailblazers, household names. People who dazzled, intrigued, were envied and admired. The job of a photo-journalist is that we often take someone's photo on the best day of their life. Or the worst. A day marking a special achievement, the culmination of a career, a celebration. Or the spectacular, very public and often tawdry fall from grace. Charles Lord, my grandfather who was a legendary photographer and the reason I became a photographer, used to say that every saint has a past, and every sinner has a future.

Robbie Blake, who everyone believed was a saint because of his boundless generosity, now appeared to have a past he'd managed to keep hidden in a vault in his home. If that was true, I wondered what his future would look like. Danny said they were only going to steal – re-steal – the Virgin of Vladimir icon and maybe anything else in the icon room that was also stolen. Robbie would be furious when he found out, but what was he going to do?

'I'm supposed to meet him at his home tomorrow afternoon at five,' I said. 'He's hired me to take an author photo for a book he's collaborating on.'

'What are the odds you could see that icon room again?'

'Slim and none. I wasn't supposed to see it the first time. I told you. They have video cameras. A security system.'

He waved a hand with a gesture as if to say, *We could break into the Louvre or the British Museum if we needed to, so the security system in a private home is no big deal.*

'What do you need?' I asked. And just like that, I was *in*. Offering to help Danny with his audacious plan to break into the fortress-like home of Robson Blake and somehow get into his Fort Knox vault and remove a stolen icon.

'A floor plan would be extremely helpful.'

'He might give me a tour of his art collection. I'd get to see more of the house.'

'Good. Also, anything you can learn about that security system. And who else is in the house besides Blake.'

'A housekeeper and a caretaker for the art collection. His name is Bernard. I don't know anything about the housekeeper or if he has a cook or other staff.'

He was nodding as I spoke, spinning his empty Scotch glass back and forth between his hands. Planning. Strategizing.

'You don't have to get involved in this, you know? You've already helped enough by just letting us know where that icon is. That's huge.' Then he added, 'So far nothing has ever gone wrong, but there are always risks. And this would be one of the most high-profile heists we've pulled off – assuming we are successful, which we will be.'

'I know that.'

'I won't be disappointed if you want to quit now,' he said. 'If you want to back out.'

That was what he *said*. What he meant – I could tell by the way he said it, the unspoken subtext – was that he wanted, *needed*, me to stay in the game.

'Don't worry,' I said. 'I'm in.'

TWELVE

I t was dark outside by the time we finished talking and Danny was ready to leave.

'When am I going to see you again?' I said.

'I don't know.' He gave me an uneasy look and I knew I wasn't going to like what came next. 'It's not a good idea for us to keep meeting right now, Sophie. Already this visit was a risk. For both of us. The fewer people who know we're related, the better. We've got enough problems with Navarro as it is.'

'You asked me to draw you a map of Robbie's house, check out the security system, find out who else works for him. What about that?'

'You can get that information to me through Val. Or we'll figure something else out.'

'Is it always going to be like this?'

'I don't know. I hope not.' He laid his hands on my shoulders and bent down – he was a good six inches taller than me – to give me a brotherly kiss on the forehead. My arms slipped around his waist, and we stood there without speaking, his chin resting on the top of my head. In the aching silence that followed, I knew two things with absolute clarity: first, it might be a very long time before I saw him again, and second, the people he was involved with – for all his so-very-Spanish macho talk that they'd never been caught – were playing a dangerous game, stealing from thieves and then laying the stolen plunder on the doorstep of its rightful owner. Poking a rattlesnake and expecting not to get bitten because what they were doing was *right*. Justifiable. Especially because no one got hurt.

Danny found my hands, which were still around his waist, and gently placed them by my side. 'Adios,' he said. 'Be careful.'

'Vaya con Dios, Danilo.'

I turned out the lights in the studio before I opened the front door. He slipped into the alley, vanishing like smoke. After he was gone, I sat down at my computer and did an Internet search for any information I could find about the theft of the Virgin of Vladimir from the little dirt church outside Kyiv. Danny had been right: all I found was a short IPS story that had run on a back page of *The International Herald Tribune* about the murder of the pastor and how he had been savagely beaten to death with the butt end of the rifles of two soldiers while parishioners too frightened to do anything watched. A little story that didn't warrant much attention from the press, even less from the overworked and beleaguered law enforcement officers, but devastating to the members of that church and everyone who had worshipped and believed in the mystical powers of the icon.

After that, I searched for 'Joie' and 'journalist' and 'Ukraine.' Sure enough, that story popped up on multiple sites. Joie Delavigne, age twenty-four, journalist with Radio France International, was killed by Russian gunfire along with the curator of a small museum near Lviv while the two of them were on their way to tour the museum, which had recently been looted, just as Danny said. What he hadn't said was that the windshield of their Jeep had been so spattered with blood you couldn't see through it. There was a photograph. I couldn't tear my eyes away. Someone's candid photo that captured Joie smiling, relaxed, happy. Seated at an outdoor café that looked as if it was somewhere in Eastern Europe, possibly Ukraine. A glint in her eye that I recognized instantly because once upon a time that had been me: the cocky confidence of inexperience coupled with Pollyannaish ambition, that she would do – *could* do – whatever it took to get the story. Wearing an invisible suit of armor that made her invincible, or so she thought.

It was easy to see why Danny had fallen for her; she was a knockout. I thought of the bleak expression in his eyes when he had told me of her death and wondered now how much of the reason he felt so remorseless about the work he did – re-stealing looted art, giving a proverbial middle finger to the murderers and thugs who thought they'd gotten away with something – was retribution for what had happened to her.

And decided maybe the answer was that it was *all* of the reason.

By the time I walked across the alley to my apartment, I was so jittery and keyed up that everything I saw or heard had turned menacing: the eyes of a raccoon caught in the moonlight, a gust of wind snapping a tree branch somewhere, the sound of a gunshot that I realized when I finally calmed down must have been only the noise of a car backfiring.

I had just promised to help my half-brother rob the home of one of the wealthiest and most generous philanthropists in the United States, told him I'd draw a map of Robson Blake's house, explain where the lower-level vaults were located, check the location of security cameras, and learn what I could about the staff Robbie employed.

None of this was me.

Except now it *was* me. Even though I wouldn't be there when Danny's team broke in to remove the icon, I was still an accessory to a crime that could very well carry jail time for me if they got caught. Danny had said as much, but then with that irresistible smile, he'd added, 'Don't worry. We won't.'

The lights were on in Max's apartment. Another night I might have stopped by to check in on him, but he was the last person I wanted to see after what I'd just learned about his good friend Robson Blake. Because what I hoped – *prayed* – was that Max had no idea about the stolen icon. I really hoped he hadn't known about it and decided to turn a blind eye, because, well, it was *Robbie*, who was so incredibly generous and giving. Besides, Ukraine was a country at war – wasn't the icon *safer* in Robbie's vault?

But what if the icon *wasn't* the only item in his vault that had been stolen? What if there were more icons? More paintings and sculptures and fourth-century BC necklaces that belonged to Scythian women? What if Robbie's vault *was* that stopping place where stolen plunder resided like toys at Santa's workshop, waiting until Christmas to be delivered to their next owners? Then what? Was Robbie dealing directly with the Russians or using a middleman, maybe a dealer in a country where the icon had transited before coming to Washington?

The flip side of this scenario was that he wasn't aware the icon had been stolen. *He didn't know.* Didn't he deserve the benefit of the doubt? It happened all the time that people bought a work of art and had no idea of its real provenance. The papers had been faked or forged. They didn't ask.

Inside my front door, I picked up a swath of mail the mailman had pushed through the brass mail slot in the entryway earlier in the day. The spring and summer calendar for the National Gallery of Art was tucked between two bills. On the cover was a photograph of *Las Meninas*, a seventeenth-century portrait of the young daughter of the king of Spain surrounded by her entourage, a masterpiece painted by Diego Velázquez, Spain's leading artist during a period known as the Golden Age. Next to the Velázquez was one of a series of fifty-eight paintings – also called *Las Meninas* – painted three hundred years later by Pablo Picasso, deconstructed works of art that were a homage to Velazquez's portrait. Underneath the Picasso in small print was written: *On permanent loan from the collection of Robson Blake.*

I smacked the brochure against my hand. Someone else might not know the icon was stolen, but Robbie – who was incredibly well connected in the art world – had known *exactly* what he owned. He knew the icon was stolen.

He had to.

I made a salad for dinner, then fixed a mug of chamomile tea, which I took, along with my laptop, upstairs to bed. For a few hours as my tea grew cold, I searched for anything I could find about stolen Ukrainian art and artifacts and about Robson Blake. On a dedicated art news website, I read about five fragile Byzantine icons from Ukraine that were now on display in Paris, in the Louvre, after being smuggled out of the country by train in a top-secret mission to safeguard them from theft or destruction. The Ukrainian cultural minister had been on hand for the opening of the exhibition, which had been bittersweet and a bit heartbreaking. The same article went on to say that other museums in Ukraine had resorted to hiding their art – one museum had removed and hidden its entire collection: 25,000 works of art.

As for Robbie, there were plenty of articles extolling his philan-thropy and generosity as well as a couple of stories about his collaboration with Olivia Sage on her books about Byzantine art. The two of them had apparently traveled together to Turkey, Greece, Cyprus and Russia, the countries where icon painting and church architecture still followed traditions that had originated in the Byzantine Empire. I studied photographs of them on a trip to Russia taken ten years ago and wondered if there was something romantic going on between them. Max had said Olivia was married to Jerome Sage, the Broadway producer, and the Sages divided their time between New York and Washington. But that didn't mean that when Jerome was in New York for his latest play, Olivia was necessarily there with him since she taught at Georgetown.

It was nearly midnight when I finally shut down my laptop. Tomorrow afternoon I would spend a couple of hours with the homeless kids who were going to take part in the soccer camp, watch them scrimmage and run drills and generally have fun, getting ready for when the players from Real Madrid and DC United would be there for the real thing. After that, I would drive over to Robbie's house in Kalorama to take his author photo.

There are Native American tribes and other cultures that won't allow their picture to be taken because they believe a photograph – which makes an image – steals the soul, and then a shaman must go in search of that lost soul. When I looked at Robbie's portrait photos tomorrow, I wondered if I would see any trace of his soul.

And if I did, what would it look like?

I put on running clothes and jogged up 16th Street to Meridian Hill Park on Friday afternoon just before two thirty to meet Finn and the kids. The soccer field was in the upper park, so I sprinted up one of the staircases running along each side of the waterfall that connected the lower and upper parks. I heard the kids before I saw them. Lots of yelling in English and Spanish, the kind of banter and encouragement and trash talk that happens any time a bunch of guys get together for an impromptu pickup game of anything. There were about twenty of them – they looked like a mix of middle school and high school boys – kicking around a couple of soccer balls they passed back and forth with deft, agile footwork, or occasionally a header that sent a ball shooting off so someone had to go retrieve it.

I spotted Finn Hathaway dressed in an old UVA tee-shirt and running shorts. Surprisingly, no soccer socks with shin pads as I would have expected, but as I looked around, none of the kids were wearing them, either.

A few had on real soccer shirts, but many showed up in white undershirts with hand-drawn numbers and the name of a favorite player drawn on the back of the shirt with a marker. It looked like no one owned cleats; most of them wore sneakers, but several had on scuffed, battered-looking dress shoes. Ready to play.

Finn had told me it would be like this. No family member around to cheer anyone on, either. The parents, or parent, would be working or caring for other children. Maybe drunk or high. Finn told me once he'd gone to pick up a young boy to drive him to an awards ceremony at his school because no one was going to take him. When he got to the apartment where they lived, the father met him at the door. 'I'm here for Jorge,' he'd said. To which the drunk, utterly stoned father had replied, 'Who's Jorge?'

I was halfway across the field to meet up with Finn when someone called my name. I spun around. Landon Reed sprinted toward me, dressed in a white tee-shirt with what looked like the profile of the head of a unicorn encircled by a navy letter C printed across his chest. Navy running shorts with something stenciled in faded gold letters. When he reached me I saw *UC-Davis* on the shorts. And the unicorn was a horse. Maybe Davis was where he'd gone to vet school.

'I didn't know you were going to be here today,' he said, and I knew instantly he was bluffing. Finn and I had discussed this scrimmage in the park the day I'd met him. 'I thought you were just planning to take pictures of the soccer camp when the players were here next week. This is just a practice session.'

'I know it is. But I want to meet these kids, let them get to know me, see me without a camera. They're a lot more likely to act naturally the next time when I do show up with one,' I said. 'What are you doing here?'

'I offered to help out and Finn took me up on it.'

'Do you play soccer? *Did* you play soccer?' I was trying not to look him over too intently, but he was more fit than I expected and, from what I could see, it wasn't because he was a gym rat. Long, lean legs, well-muscled arms that looked as if he got a regular workout in his job wrangling dogs the size and weight of Bruiser. A few faded scars on his arms and legs, probably an occupational hazard of trying to calm a scared animal or give an injection. The remnants of a suntan, perhaps leftover from southern California.

'I grew up overseas, in Europe and the Middle East,' he said. 'All the American schools in whatever country my family lived in had soccer teams. Are you a fan?'

'Sort of.' Yet another surprise to learn he'd had a cosmopolitan childhood, but also gratitude that Finn hadn't mentioned anything to him about my connection to soccer. 'By the way, how's Harriet?'

His face lit up. 'She's a sweetheart, a little princess. She's had all her shots, and everything looks great. Weighs in at a whopping two pounds, twelve ounces – which won't be for long. Her surgery was this morning, and she came through like a champ. I'd like to keep her overnight and then I can bring her to you maybe tomorrow or Sunday if you like.'

'How about tomorrow?' I said.

'You miss her already, huh?' He sounded pleased.

'Actually, I do. And I bought everything on your list. Plus some toys and a few other things.'

He grinned. 'You'll make a great cat mom. How about tomorrow morning? Around ten?'

'Ten would be good.'

'Hey, Landon!' Finn waved him over to where the kids had gathered in a circle. 'We need you here. Stop flirting. Sophie, you come, too. I could use your help.'

Landon flashed a look at me as though he didn't mind being called out on flirting, and I felt my cheeks grow hot.

'Come on,' he said. 'We've been summoned.'

For the next forty-five minutes, Finn and Landon had the kids practice passing, dribbling, shooting goals, and running sprints. Finn had brought a whiteboard to draw on and show them tactics. Orange traffic cones for them to run between to practice dribbling. My contribution was moving the cones around as needed. And being timekeeper.

We took a break to give the boys water and pass out cut-up oranges. By then I'd learned a few names and spoke to several of the kids in Spanish. The second forty-five minutes consisted of scrimmages with breaks so Finn or Landon could explain different plays and tactics. Finn had brought the neon orange vests the Streetwise vendors wore when they sold newspapers on the DC streets, but half the kids had already stripped off their shirts, so he threw the vests on the ground, abandoning them, and the teams were Shirts and Skins.

At four o'clock, Finn announced that practice was over. The next time they would meet would be for the real thing in a week. A van with the Streetwise logo showed up to take some of the boys to a couple of central drop-off locations downtown. A few of the older ones said they'd make their own way back to where they lived. While the younger kids were getting on the van, Landon asked me out to dinner.

'I have to work,' I said. 'Thank you, but I can't.'

'Now? It's almost the end of the day on a Friday.'

'I'm taking someone's portrait for an author photo for a book,' I said.

'It won't go that late, will it? We could have dinner after you're done. I need a shower anyway – I'm all sweaty. I've also got to check on the animals – including Harriet – for the evening.'

'I'm not sure how long it will take,' I said. 'You never know with these sessions. If the client wants more pictures, I could be there for a few hours.'

'You still need to eat. What if I get takeout and bring it over to your place?'

'You don't give up, do you?'

'Is that yes?'

He looked so hopeful that I gave in. 'I'll text you when I'm leaving. The appointment is in Kalorama, so it's not far.'

'Great. Do you like Middle Eastern food?'

'I love Middle Eastern food.'

'There's a restaurant down the street from me that's supposed to be pretty good.'

'Mama Ayesha's?'

He nodded. 'I've heard it's good, but I haven't had a chance to try it yet.'

'It's a cultural landmark and it's terrific. Best restaurant in Adams Morgan, although technically, it's on the fringe of Adams Morgan.'

'Great. Since you just vetted it, I'll get us takeout and see you later.'

He had come to the park on foot as I had, but we lived in opposite directions, so we said goodbye near the waterfall. I heard him whistling as he left, something pretty and tuneless.

He seemed like a nice guy. He was kind and had a good heart. If it hadn't been obvious before, after today I knew he was interested in me. I still wasn't sure how I felt about him, especially because I didn't know the story about the wedding ring he had recently removed from his ring finger.

Tonight, before things went any further, I was going to ask him. Some things you need to know.

I showered after I got home and changed into a pair of navy trousers and a pale-blue Oxford cotton blouse. Ballet flats. I pulled my hair into a twisted knot and secured it with an oversized speckled blue butterfly hair clip. A bit of makeup, my favorite floral perfume.

Done.

The drive from my house to Robbie's home in Kalorama took

only a few minutes, even in rush-hour traffic, and I got there at exactly five o'clock. I parked the Mini in the driveway as I'd done the other day and grabbed my camera bag and tripod. I'd get the diffusers and lights on a second trip. Usually, I preferred to do formal portraits in my studio where I already had everything set up, but Robbie wasn't my usual customer. And he paid extremely well.

I rang the doorbell and waited for the housekeeper to answer. After a minute, I rang it again. Waited some more. Did I have the wrong Friday? The wrong time? The other day Robbie had given me his business card, so I had his phone number. When I called, it went to voicemail, the impersonal recording that gives you pause about whether you've dialed the correct number or you've reached someone else.

I left a message, explaining that I was at his house *right now*, trying to keep the irritation out of my voice at being stood up. Before I disconnected, I asked him to call when he got my message. I turned to leave but decided to try the front door handle – just in case.

And opened the door to Robson Blake's house just like that. A fortress with security cameras, a state-of-the-art alarm system and millions of dollars of art on the walls and hidden away in a subterranean vault, and the front door was unlocked. A quiet chime from a sensor indicated the open door, but no insistent beeping as if the alarm had been set and I had forty-five seconds to disarm it. Robbie had staff: a housekeeper and Bernard, the caretaker, for his extensive art collection. *Where were they?*

Was everyone gone for the day because it was five o'clock on Friday? Had the door been left unlocked for me because I was expected, and Robbie figured I'd let myself in once no one answered?

Was he even *here*? He hadn't answered his phone. I stepped inside and called, 'Hello, hello, is anyone home?' half a dozen times before it was clear no one was going to answer. Either I could leave right now, wait for Robbie to call and apologize for standing me up, and we could reschedule the photo shoot. Or maybe he was here after all and something had happened so he couldn't answer the door. Maybe he was on another of those private phone calls.

The logical place for him to be was in his beautiful study. I left my gear in the foyer and walked down the hallway. The house was preternaturally quiet, as if it might be waiting for something to happen. Or maybe something already had. The study door was closed as it had been before, so I knocked. No answer.

I saw him as soon as I opened the door. Lying face down on the floor in front of his enormous desk, arms splayed out as though he'd been reaching for something or someone. Dark reddish-brown blood pooled around his head, seeping into his expensive pale-blue and cream Persian carpet. I'd been in enough war zones for IPS that I'd seen blood-soaked bodies before, but some things you don't get used to. Especially when they are as startling and out of context as the scene right in front of me.

The first thing I thought was that the killer was long gone. He wasn't still here in the house. I would have felt it; the house would have warned me, let me know. Then there was the fact that Robbie's blood – that rusty reddish-brown color – was a few hours old. He was dead; he'd been dead for a while. What I had to do now was call 911.

My eyes swept the room. There was one more thing that was out of context, out of place. The kiot that held the icon of the Virgin of Vladimir was propped on its easel in a corner of the study instead of in Robbie's icon room where it had been the other day.

The door hung open. The icon was gone.

Had Robbie brought the Virgin of Vladimir upstairs to worship it in this room instead of at the altar in his vault? To show it – show it *off* – to someone? To a potential buyer? It didn't look as if he had struggled or tried to fight off his killer, so maybe whoever had been here with him was someone he knew. Had that person come up behind him, surprising and overpowering him with an unexpected blow to his head before he knew what happened? And what had his killer used to strike him? Nothing looked disturbed or out of place. No potential murder weapon had been left next to the body.

As I scanned this room filled with priceless art and tried to recall where everything had been when I'd seen it the other day, the icon was the only thing that appeared to be missing – which made no sense. Unless it was the only item someone wanted.

Danny.

He and his team wouldn't work this fast – *couldn't* work this fast. Could they?

No one gets harmed, he'd said. *We remove the stolen art, and we get out. We've never been caught . . . yet.*

What if this time they *had* been caught? Had Danny decided not to wait for me to tell him about floor plans and the security system and the underground vault? Bernard told me I wasn't supposed to see that downstairs room and what was in it because it could cost him his job. So who knew about the icon besides Robbie, Bernard and me – and my half-brother?

Were the bodies of Bernard and the housekeeper somewhere in this house, too? I shivered and decided I didn't want to find out.

I pulled my phone out of my pocket and dialed 911.

And prayed to God that my brother hadn't been here before me.

THIRTEEN

I sat on the front doorstep and waited for the police to arrive. Robbie was gone; I didn't think I could handle keeping vigil at a murder scene, especially one that had been so bloody and disturbing. Besides, I needed to calm down before a DC police officer began asking me questions that were only going to beget even more sharp, probing questions. Beginning with what I was doing here and how I had just waltzed into a home with a state-of-the-art alarm system belonging to one of the wealthiest philanthropists in America.

Kalorama is not southeast DC, not a neighborhood where shots are fired, drugs are dealt, homes are robbed or bad things happen. Police sirens may scream past Kalorama Road heading up or down nearby Connecticut Avenue, but they *do not* enter this neighborhood as a rule. Except for tonight, mere minutes after my 911 call. Probably because of the address I'd given the dispatcher . . . and the name of the homeowner. Robson Blake, deceased. The first cruiser pulled up, blue lights pulsing with a strobe-light intensity that seemed seizure-inducing if you were susceptible.

Two sturdy-looking officers got out of the car, heading straight for me. Was I the one who called 911? I said yes and told them about finding Robbie when they asked. I also said at least two other people were employed in Mr Blake's home – neither of whom I'd seen – and that the front door had been unlocked when I arrived. They exchanged the wordless glance of partners who have worked together for a long time as the younger one stepped away, speaking into a microphone that sat on his shoulder like an obedient parakeet. It didn't take long for the street to take on a carnival-like air of unreality – more cruisers, EMT vans, a firetruck, the oversized SUV of the district commander, a knot of curious, worried neighbors pushing closer to the house, voices and cellphones buzzing, pointing at the stranger's car in the driveway – mine – until someone in a uniform took over crowd control. A television van showed up from News Channel 8 with a perky blonde reporter who hopped out with her cameraman in tow. First on the scene, kudos to her. This would be a big story. Not just a local one; there would be national and international interest. *BREAKING NEWS* would flash on the Channel 8 crawl any minute, maybe in time for her report to be on the tail end of the six o'clock flagship program.

The officer who questioned me – his nametag said J. Gonzalez – moved me out of view to the front lawn and mercifully shielded me from the growing crowd of onlookers. He asked the questions I expected: what was I doing here, how did I know Robbie, how had I entered the house and known where to find him, had I touched anything, moved anything, done anything? When he was finished, he asked me to wait and had another officer babysit me.

A few minutes later, Gonzalez returned. 'Do you know if anything was missing from the room where you found Mr Blake?' he asked.

Here it was. They'd seen the empty kiot, with its door hanging open. He already knew the answer. I told him about the icon, explaining that it was a sacred image of Mary and Jesus, known as the Virgin of Vladimir.

'So it's a religious painting,' he said.

'Not exactly. It's different from a painting,' I said. 'Icons are symbolic depictions of saints or Mary and Jesus, like this one was, or scenes from the Bible and painted in a very specific two-dimensional style. They're venerated by people of the Orthodox faith the way Christians venerate a cross. This icon, the Virgin of Vladimir, is probably the most famous, most sacred icon in the Orthodox Church,' I said. 'The original came from Constantinople and ended up in Ukraine. In Kyiv, to be precise. Now it's in a museum in Moscow. Since then, there have been thousands of copies and reproductions. Millions, probably.'

Gonzalez had been making notes, his pen scratching on the pages of a small notebook, but when I said, 'Ukraine,' his head bobbed up. 'You seem to know a lot about this icon,' he said in a neutral voice.

'My late husband's grandmother was Russian Orthodox and we visited her in Moscow. I saw the original Virgin of Vladimir. Like I just said, it's in an art museum now – the Tretyakov Gallery – after it was moved from a church in the Kremlin years ago.'

'That house is full of paintings worth millions,' he said, indicating Robbie's house with the tip of his pen. 'I've been here before. Mr Blake was quite a collector. You just said that icon was the only thing that was missing. One, how do you know that, and two, why

would someone only take one small religious painting and not make
off with a Picasso or a Rembrandt or a Monet? Or all of them. I'm
thinking whoever killed him had time to yank a few paintings off
the walls. Maybe more than a few paintings.'

He knew his art.

'First of all, I have no idea if it's the only thing that's missing.
But I did see the open door to the kiot and realized the icon was
gone. It's also possible it could be somewhere else in the house and
it's just not in the kiot,' I said, keeping my voice level. 'Look,
Officer Gonzalez, are you accusing me of anything? Because I'm
the one who called nine-one-one.'

'Johnny? I have a question for Ms Medina.'

We both turned around. The officer who had arrived with Gonzalez
walked toward us after leaving the house. The sun had sunk so low
in the sky that the light had begun to drain the color from what was
left of the day. The second officer, whose nametag said P. Chen,
held a sealed bag in his hand with something inside. In the dusky
light, I couldn't make out what it was. He came over to us and
showed it to me up close.

'Do you know what this is?' he asked. 'Do you know what's
inside this bag?'

My throat went dry. 'A tripod. A desktop tripod.'

'It's something a photographer uses, right?'

'Yes.' My voice, faint.

'Does it look familiar?' For the second time this evening, a police
officer was asking me a question to which he already knew the
answer. And knew I knew the answer, too.

I nodded. 'It's mine. I must have left it here the other day when
I took some close-up photos for Mr Blake.'

Chen and Gonzalez exchanged another of their inscrutable
glances, and Gonzalez said, 'We're going to have some more questions for you, Ms Medina. There's blood on this tripod. Though
nothing has been determined with absolute certainty yet, the medical
examiner confirms that the blow or blows to Mr Blake's head were
made by a blunt object. And that the head of this tripod could have
left wounds that were consistent with the ones he found.'

'What are you saying?' I could barely breathe.

'I'm saying that it's very possible your tripod is the murder weapon.'

*   *   *

It took all my self-control and composure to stay calm. Not to panic. Even though what I really wanted to do was tell them – *shout* at them – that what they were thinking was wrong. That what they were saying was crazy. *Insist* I was innocent. Even if my tripod turned out to be the murder weapon, *that didn't mean I killed Robson Blake.*

No matter what it looked like.

Instead, what happened was this: Officers Gonzalez and Chen assured me I wasn't under arrest or being charged with anything. Instead, they asked if I'd be willing to go down to Homicide head-quarters in the Daly Building on Indiana Avenue and answer a few questions. No, I wasn't going to be put in a box and interrogated while someone watched from another room on CCTV to see whether I twitched the wrong way or sweated profusely or blinked too rapidly, behaved as if I were guilty or hiding something. It was going to be a *conversation* because they believed I could provide valuable information that might help in the search for the murderer of Robson Blake.

'Do I need a lawyer?' I asked.

'Do you *want* a lawyer?' Gonzalez shot back. 'Like I said, you don't have to do this and you're free to leave. You're not being accused of anything. If we do have more questions for you, you can absolutely retain counsel if you believe you need to. It's your right. But we'd appreciate it if you'd help us out if you can right now.'

He'd done a neat job of boxing me in. If I said, *No, thank you,* or lawyered up, was it going to look worse for me down the road? The answer to that was *Hell, yes* if my brother's name so much as wafted across their radar in any shape or form, whether he'd been involved in the theft of the icon or not. And if he was guilty of murder, or, more likely, accidental homicide – my God, he couldn't have done it, could he? – then it was all over but the crying. I'd be dragged into the middle of that for sure.

'I'll answer your questions,' I said.

'Good,' he said. 'Then let's get you out of here so you don't end up on the nightly news.'

An unmarked car idled around the corner out of view of the commotion that had kicked into overdrive out front. Another officer escorted me through a gate in the high wooden fence surrounding Robbie's house and helped me into the cruiser, which took side streets through the Kalorama neighborhood, bypassing the scrum of television vans, reporters doing their standups and a growing number of curious neighbors – all of them crowding the perimeter of police and emergency vehicles that were still there continuing to process the crime scene. They hadn't yet removed Robbie's body from the study. It would be a while before that happened. Apparently, he'd been alone in the house at the time of the murder – Gonzalez told me that just before I left. Bernard and the housekeeper hadn't been home this afternoon. Which made me wonder why.

Later, I would have to come back to retrieve my car, which I wasn't looking forward to doing. By now some intrepid reporter – or, very likely, all of them – had managed to check out my license plate, maybe through a friend at the DMV they knew to call on, and subsequently Googled me a million times. It's what I would have done. It would only be a matter of time before the press – my erstwhile colleagues – caught up with me. And pounded me with questions.

Were you and Mr Blake romantically involved? You were the one who found the body – how did you know where he was if you'd only been to his home once before? How did you get into the house – did he give you a key? Doesn't he have an alarm? Was it a murder and a robbery? Or, if none of the priceless paintings he owned were taken, what was the motive for his murder? Describe the scene you found when you walked into his study.

And the question I was really dreading if word somehow got out: *Is it true your tripod was the murder weapon?*

Yes, but I didn't do it.

The first thing DC Homicide Detective Joe Ellis did when I was shown into his office half an hour after leaving Robbie's home was to ask if I'd like something to drink. I asked for a bottle of water, and the officer who had escorted me into the building left to get it.

'Have a seat,' Ellis said, and I sat down in a chair opposite his desk, the back designed so I had to sit up ramrod straight. 'Thank you for coming in.'

'You're welcome.'

Ellis was a short, bald, compact sparkplug who looked as though he worked out in the gym most mornings. A large map of DC hung on the wall behind his desk flanked by multiple awards and framed photographs of him with people I recognized, including the current mayor, several of her predecessors and a former US president. On one end of his desk was a lineup of five Starbucks cups – presumably empty – looking as if they were waiting to be picked up by customers who had ordered online. A photo on his desk angled so I could see it of a good-looking redhead and two young children. A perfectly assembled Rubik's Cube. Papers, files, a phone with multiple lines, an overflowing inbox. Walls painted institutional dingy white, fluorescent lights, no window except one with blinds he could close if necessary that looked out on the squad room.

The officer brought my water, handed it to me, saluted the detective and left, closing the door.

'Can I ask you something?' I said to Ellis.

'I don't know. *Can* you?' He picked up the Rubik's Cube and scrambled it into six sides of mismatched colors.

One of those. 'OK. *May* I ask you something?'

'What is it?'

'The gentleman who takes care of Mr Blake's art collection – Bernard – told me there are security cameras throughout the house because the art he owns is so valuable and the insurance company requires it. What happened to them? If they were on, wouldn't you already know who killed him?'

Ellis manipulated the cube, already starting to put it back together. He glanced up and gave me a disbelieving do-you-really-think-we-didn't-check-that look.

'Don't tell me the cameras weren't working,' I said.

'They could have been working. If they'd been turned on. At least, the cameras on the main level.'

'*Nothing* was turned on?'

'The cameras on the second and third floors and the two lower levels were active, but nothing on the main level. Nor the front-door camera. Do you know anything about that?' He twisted the layers of the cube again. Lined up the yellow side. I had a feeling he did this all the time, used it as a stress buster. He'd have it reassembled before I left.

'No, I don't. How long were they turned off?'

'Aren't I supposed to be interviewing you?' he asked. The orange face was lined up, but now the yellow side was a bit scrambled. 'Since noon today. We've already spoken to Mr Carlson.' He must have seen my puzzled look because he added, 'Bernard Carlson. The caretaker. We also spoke to his housekeeper. She had a dental appointment, so she left early. Mr Blake gave Mr Carlson the afternoon off. According to Mr Carlson, it was not uncommon for Mr Blake to turn off one or more cameras if he wanted privacy when he had a visitor.'

That could mean anything. Any*one*. If Robbie had trafficked in stolen art, he certainly wouldn't want those meetings recorded.

'I see.'

'Mr Carlson also said you had been downstairs to the lower level where the vaults were located.'

'Because that's where the items Robson Blake wanted me to photograph the other day were located.'

'And what were those items?'

I told him. Robbie had asked me not to say anything about the X Patent drawings, but he probably hadn't figured he'd be dead when I broke that promise. I also told Ellis that was most definitely how and when my tripod ended up at Robbie's house: Bernard had helped me carry my equipment upstairs; obviously, it had been left behind. Neither of us had realized it at the time.

'I understand you also spent time in a room that was off-limits without Mr Blake being present,' Ellis said. 'A room where the icon that is now missing was located.'

Bernard, obviously singing like a canary, giving up secrets. He was probably also a suspect, so that's why he was trying to get his version of the story out in front, establish his innocence, before Ellis found out these things for himself.

Just like I was.

'It was an accident,' I said. 'I went to the wrong floor. Bernard had left the door to that room open. The icons that were inside were exquisite. I spent a few minutes looking at them and then took the elevator to the correct floor.'

I didn't tell Ellis that Bernard had told me he'd deleted the video because he was afraid of losing his job if Robbie found out I'd been there. Anyway, by now I'd gotten the impression that Robbie's famous security system was somewhat ad hoc. He turned it off and on at will, depending on who was in the house with him. 'Interesting coincidence you happened to see the missing icon just the other day,' Ellis said in a way that suggested he didn't believe in interesting coincidences.

Jesus, they were moving at the speed of light, almost as fast as the Rubik's Cube was starting to come together. Maybe Ellis was figuring he'd wrap up this murder investigation and reassemble the cube at the same time.

'Yes,' I said, keeping my voice calm. 'It is.'

'Officer Gonzalez said you seemed to know quite a bit about the missing icon. Can you tell me how you know this information?'

I told him about Nick, his grandmother and visiting Moscow to see her. Which was when I'd seen the original Virgin of Vladimir icon in the Tretyakov. Just like I'd told Gonzalez. Ellis probably knew that, too.

'Do you know what would have made the icon Mr Blake owned so valuable that it would be the only item a thief would choose to steal in a house filled with so many valuable works of original art?'

How long before Ellis learned the truth: that the icon was stolen? Which was what made it extraordinarily valuable – more valuable than any painting, any sculpture, any artifact in that house – to my brother, and probably to no one else with the obvious exception of the people who venerated it at the church from which it had been taken.

'I'm not an expert on icons,' I said. 'Or art, for that matter.' That much was true. If I said anything else, I'd be moving into lying territory.

'I see.' A few more twists and turns to align the colored tiles and voilà. A perfect Rubik's Cube.

'You did that very quickly,' I told him.

Ellis set the cube on his desk. 'I should hope so. It's probably the five thousandth time I've done it. You're free to go, Ms Medina. I don't have any more questions for you, but down the road, I might want to talk to you again. Thank you for coming in today. I appreciate it.'

I stood up and looked him in the eye. 'Again, you're welcome. I'm glad I was able to help. But I also want you to know I didn't kill Robson Blake. I found him. I called nine-one-one. I explained how I knew about the missing icon and how my tripod ended up being left behind when I was there taking photographs a few days ago. If there's anything else, Detective Ellis, you need to go through my lawyer. The only other thing I want to add is that I hope you find Robbie's murderer. Soon.'

'Ms Medina.' He returned my stare with a weary look. 'You have no idea how many people sit in that chair you just sat in, tell me their side of the story and say exactly what you just said. *I didn't do it.* Sometimes they're right. Sometimes they're not. Someone killed Robson Blake and I *will* find that person. *Soon.*'

'I'm glad to hear that,' I said. 'And let me repeat, *it wasn't me.*' Then I left.

I called for an Uber as soon as I was outside the building on Indiana Avenue, but my hands were shaking. I hadn't lied to Ellis, but I hadn't told him the whole truth, either. If I had, it would have meant dragging Danny into his crosshairs and as good as admitting that Robbie's murder might have been a botched robbery that also resulted in an accidental homicide and not the other way around – and that my brother was their likely suspect. The reason being that *I* had told Danny about the icon. Which, by the way, was stolen. I hadn't mentioned that, either.

But even if Danny had nothing to do with Robbie's murder, which was what I hoped and prayed was true, once Ellis got wind of his and Michael Angelo's off-the-books thefts of stolen art – and he would – even if they did the right thing and returned what they'd taken to its proper owner, the whole house of cards would come crashing down.

I rubbed my temples with my fingers trying to stave off a pounding headache until my Uber, a white Toyota Camry with license plates that matched what was on my phone, pulled up in front of me.

'Sophie?'

'Yes.'

When I got in, the driver said, 'Pardon me, but are you OK? Is everything all right?'

'Thank you, I'm fine. I'm getting a headache is all. It'll go away.'

We left the Daly Building and the driver pulled out into the evening traffic, passing the former Newseum which had become the new Johns Hopkins building as he eased on to Pennsylvania Avenue heading downtown. His eyes met mine in the rearview mirror. He wasn't going to push. He knew I'd lied. I had given an address that was a few doors away from Robbie's house so he wouldn't drop me off right in front where there might still be police vehicles, news trucks and spectators. At a minimum, there would be bright-yellow crime scene tape strung like Christmas garland and fluttering in the evening breeze. Plus he'd picked me up at DC Police Headquarters. Eventually, he was going to figure it out.

And then maybe wonder a bit more about me.

I let him drive away after dropping me off on Kalorama Road, leaving a whopping tip and a five-star review. Asking him to wait until I sussed out the situation in front of Robbie's house and maybe take me somewhere else hadn't seemed like a good idea. Yet another reporter – an older gray-haired man – was doing a standup, probably for the eleven o'clock news. A klieg light lit him like high noon. A few people – presumably Robbie's neighbors – stood in the background behind him, maybe hoping to be interviewed so they could say the usual: *this never happens in our neighborhood, it's so peaceful and quiet here, everyone loved Robbie, he was such a good person.*

The only way I wasn't going to be part of this reporter's story – if not the goddam lede – was to retreat and wait until everyone had left. Otherwise, I could just imagine his script.

I'm here with Sophie Medina, with an exclusive interview – we're the FIRST to bring this to you – with the woman who found billionaire philanthropist Robson Blake bludgeoned to death in his home earlier this evening. Ms Medina, is it true the police brought you in for questioning because you're also a possible suspect? Can you describe your relationship with Mr Blake – were you close friends? That's your car parked in his driveway, isn't it? Folks, keep it here for ALL THE LATEST in this rapidly developing story.

I turned and walked in the other direction, away from Robbie's house, and called Grace Lowe, my best friend, and the senior Metro reporter at *The Washington Tribune.*

She answered on the second ring. 'Soph,' she said. 'What's up?'

'I have a story for you,' I said. 'But first I need you to pick me up.'

'Sure.' She sounded puzzled. 'Where are you? What's wrong?'

'I'll tell you when I see you. And I'm standing in front of the French ambassador's residence on Kalorama a few houses away from Robson Blake's home.'

She was silent for a couple of beats. 'Oh, God,' she said. 'I'll be right there.'

FOURTEEN

'*W*hat *happened?*' Grace looked puzzled and concerned as she pulled up in front of the French ambassador's residence in a midnight-blue Audi and I climbed into the passenger seat. 'Sophie, what are you doing here? What's going on? And why did you bring up Robson Blake? Did you know that he was found dead in his home this afternoon? He was murdered.'

'By me. I mean, I found him. I didn't kill him.'

'What the hell? *You* found him? How come I didn't know about *that?*' As my friend, I could tell she was horrified. As a journalist, I knew she was pissed, wondering why she was only learning this *now*. 'Who else knows?'

'Gracie, my car is in his driveway. I was supposed to do a photo shoot for Robbie this afternoon; that's why I was there. By now every journalist in Washington covering that story has done their homework and my name will have popped up when they checked the car registration. Including the *Trib*, so I'm surprised you *didn't* know. I hoped I might be able to get it out of there, so I had an Uber drop me off, but the street in front of the house is still crawling with journos and neighbors. And a DC cruiser is babysitting, so I walked away. I don't want to be someone's exclusive on the eleven o'clock news.'

'Wait a minute. *Robbie?* You know Robson Blake well enough to call him Robbie – knew him, I should say? And Ubering from where?'

Wait until she heard.

'The Daly Building. Homicide Division. And I only met Robbie twice.'

'Whoa, whoa, whoa. You're gonna need to explain it all to me, sweetie. And obviously, we need a drink. Probably a couple. Ben is still on the Hill preparing for a hearing tomorrow and the kids are out with friends, so I got takeout from Lapis, the Afghan place on Columbia Road. I'm sure you haven't eaten.'

She turned off Connecticut on to Calvert Street and drove past a low ochre-colored building where golden light as soft as velvet sifted out of four filigreed doors. Plain black letters that spelled Mama Ayesha's were illuminated by underlights. My memory pricked. Takeout. Landon. Damn.

I'd completely forgotten. By now, he was probably expecting me to text him.

I pulled out my phone as Grace put on her turn signal for Mintwood Place, the pretty tree-lined street in Adams Morgan where she and her husband and two children lived in an elegant Georgian Revival. As long as I'd known her, Grace had impeccable taste: her house was perfect. Beautiful. Just like she was. She pulled into a driveway and parked the Audi in a small, detached garage, a luxury in this part of town.

'Give me a minute,' I said. 'I need to send a quick text.'

'Everything OK?'

'I just remembered I promised to have dinner with someone tonight and it's not going to work out,' I said, typing.

Hi, it's Sophie. I'm not going to get home until very late tonight; I apologize. Something came up and I've been unavoidably detained. Can we postpone for another time?

'Anyone I know?'

He had already texted back, quick as lightning. *You still need to eat. We can do this later.*

'Nope. Someone I met through Streetwise.' Hopefully, that would end the Spanish Inquisition about a possible date if she thought it was someone I met at the homeless center and therefore probably a professional connection. I didn't want to tell her about Landon. At least not yet. Grace thought I needed to *start getting out there again* and she'd been nudging. Just like Max and my mother.

I'm really sorry. It's just not going to work out. Rain check?

We were walking through the front door when three little dots did their wavy dance on my screen. His reply.

Sure. Some other time.

He didn't write after that, and I figured he was either angry or hurt. Or both. I felt bad, but he'd find out soon enough why I'd canceled. I bet he'd never heard *I was being questioned by a DC homicide detective about a murder case after I found a dead body* as an excuse to wiggle out of a dinner date before.

My name attached to Robbie's murder was going to be all over the news. By tomorrow morning at the latest, if it wasn't already trending on the Internet as a subset of #RobsonBlakeMurder right now.

'Wine or hard stuff?' Grace was asking, shedding her Burberry jacket on an antique Windsor bench in the front hall.

I took off my leather jacket and left it next to hers. 'Scotch. And Grace, if anyone is going to get my story first, it's going to be you. I'm not talking to anyone else. Not even another journalist at the *Trib*. You or no one.'

She sighed and I followed her into the dining room where she and Ben kept a well-stocked assortment of liquor on a carved oak sideboard that had belonged to her grandparents. She poured a hefty serving of Scotch into two glasses filled with ice and handed one to me, clinking hers against mine.

'I need to make a call,' she said. 'I'll be back.'

She was probably calling the *Trib*'s managing editor. She and I were too close for her to write this story: conflict of interest, inability to be objective, inherent bias, all of it. She was my oldest and dearest friend ever since we'd met on the first day of eighth grade after Harry married my mother and moved us to Middleburg. We both knew that any editor in any newsroom anywhere on the planet would automatically disqualify her and ask someone else to write the piece, but I'd laid down my conditions.

When she came back, she said, 'I won this round but just barely. Stu is going to go over the story himself with a fine-tooth comb to make sure I'm objective.'

Stu was Stuart Adelman, the managing editor of *The Washington Tribune*.

'OK,' I said. 'That's fair.' And, frankly, more than I'd expected.

Grace and I are both journalists, so we know the rules of the game. If something's off the record, you can't use it. If it's on background, you can't attribute it to the source that gave you the information. Instead, you have to describe the informant in such a way that it's clear you talked to someone who knows what's going on, but they want their name kept out of the news. Vague enough that it can't be traced back to that person who would either get their head handed to them by a superior or, worse, get them fired. Another rule is that both the journalist and the source must agree beforehand what's off the record or on background. Otherwise, the implicit assumption is that everything is *on* the record, for attribution.

We decided to eat dinner while I talked and Grace typed. Before we did that, she said she needed to reheat a couple of the dishes that had grown cold, and soon the kitchen smelled fragrantly of coriander, cumin, cinnamon, cardamom, ginger and turmeric. I closed my eyes and just like that I was back in Kabul, in Kandahar, in the foothills of the beautiful Hindu Kush mountains, taking photos for some story for IPS, a cascade of memories flooding my brain. Not the interminable war, not the killing and bloodshed, or the senseless destruction of a country and its culture and history, but meals and conversation and heart-to-heart talks with Afghans who became friends, in cozy cafés, in their homes and around their kitchen tables.

As a photographer, I'd like to believe sight is the strongest of our five senses, but it's our sense of smell, which is also the oldest in terms of human evolution. Located in a part of the brain that triggers memories and emotions, scent can bring us to a remembered time or place or person as quick as the flutter of an eyelash. The memories are so overwhelming and automatic – even physical – that every so often I have wished a 'scent button' could be embedded in one of my photographs like the scratch-and-sniff perfume ads in women's magazines, because I know it would make that photo even more powerful and evocative.

Dinner was excellent: sambosas filled with spinach, shrimp and beef to start, followed by pureed pumpkin spiced with coriander and garlic and topped with homemade yogurt, eggplant cooked with tomato and spices, and *morgh qorma* as a main dish – chicken, tomato, split peas, pitted plums, cilantro and basmati rice.

We ate in Grace's comfortable, homey kitchen, seated across from each other at the family dinner table which was tucked into a corner and surrounded by picture windows that overlooked the fenced-in backyard and garden. A necklace of fairy lights winding through the railing on the back deck and a wash of light from a gibbous moon turned plants and bushes and trees silvery white like Narnia during the reign of the White Witch.

There were some things I was willing to tell Grace off the record because writing about them would compromise the police investigation into the murder of Robson Blake; I knew she'd go along with that. There was almost nothing I could tell her on background because the trail of breadcrumbs could only lead directly back to me.

No one knew what the murder weapon was except the murderer, the police – and me. No one except the police and I knew the tripod that probably bludgeoned Robbie to death was mine. So that was off the record. I couldn't say for sure whether the Virgin of Vladimir icon had been stolen or was somewhere else in the house. For all I knew, it was in another room or back downstairs in the vault and the kiot was still in Robbie's office. And I most definitely wasn't prepared to divulge the information that it had been stolen from a church near Kyiv. Whether or not Robbie knew that detail when he acquired the icon was speculation on my part, so I wasn't going to talk about that, either. It opened a whole box of Pandoras.

I also hadn't told Grace about Danny, and right now I was going to keep it that way. Instead, I gave her the basic information about what had happened, facts she could easily corroborate with a second source: the DC police. How I'd found Robbie, what I was doing at his home at that hour and that the door had been unlocked so I had walked in. That was it.

'Why don't you spend the night here, Soph? Especially since we both know that, beginning tomorrow morning, you're going to be swarmed by our colleagues who will want you to give them chapter and verse about what happened, what you saw when you found him, all that stuff,' Grace said.

'Thanks, but I need to get my car out of Robbie's driveway, and the sooner the better. Before even more people see it and trace it to me. Then I'll go home. I can always sleep in the loft bed in my studio if I need to.'

'Are you sure?' She raised an eyebrow and I nodded. 'OK, then, after we're done here, I'll drive you back to Kalorama.'

'Thanks. Hopefully, by then the police will have put a lid on any more news for tonight and everyone will have gone home.'

'Speaking of the police, did Ellis ask you anything else besides how your tripod ended up at Robbie's? After you explained why you were there, that is.'

'He wanted to know about the missing icon. And how I knew so much about it. I told him about Nick being half-Russian and his grandmother being Orthodox.'

She brushed a strand of blonde hair out of her eyes and poised her fingers over her keyboard, eyes down. 'Did he think those were . . . coincidences?' She was treading carefully.

'You know as well as I do that no cop believes in coincidences.' I didn't mean to snap at her. Another journalist who wasn't Grace would have taken it as a possible sign of guilt. 'Honestly, I don't know what he thought. Grace, you *know* I didn't murder Robson Blake. Despite how it looks.'

'I know, I know. I'm sorry, Soph. I had to ask. Anyone else writing this piece would have – you know that.'

'I do and I'm sorry, too. It's just so . . . crazy, you know?'

'I know you didn't know him well, but do you have any idea who might have done it?'

'No,' I said, and caught her flash of surprise at how quickly I'd blurted that out. 'Since the door was unlocked, it's possible someone just walked in. Or the killer was someone he invited in, and things took a bad turn.'

Grace frowned as if she were trying to puzzle things out with what little she knew. 'If it was a bungled robbery that turned into a homicide, you'd think whoever did it would have lifted a couple of paintings while they were there.'

'Maybe they did, but the paintings they took were in other rooms – or else they managed to break into the vault downstairs. It's also possible it was a straight-up murder. Either someone showed up intending to kill Robbie or whoever it was got in a fight with him, and things got out of hand. They didn't plan to kill him, but it happened.'

'Man or woman?' she asked.

'Man. Whoever it was must have been close to him when it happened – physically close, I mean. And had a powerful swing to hit him hard enough that the blow or blows killed him. Which makes it sound like it was a guy. The more I think about it, the more I believe it had to be someone Robbie thought was a friend or someone he knew as a business associate. In other words, someone who'd been invited. Especially because the security cameras were turned off.'

Which, if I was right, made it less likely it was Danny. Please, God.

We had switched from Scotch to cardamom tea after dinner. I picked up my cup and took a sip. Grace watched me, a calm, unperturbed expression on her lovely face, but I knew she'd picked up my little equivocations, my flash of anger and frustration. We knew each other so well we could finish each other's sentences, breathe for each other. I also knew she intended to get to the bottom of why my answers and my behavior had been just a bit *off*. Why I was shutting her out.

'What is it?' she said. 'Tell me.'

'It's nothing.'

'Don't give me that. It's something. Obviously, you didn't kill him. But something else is bugging you about this.'

I still couldn't tell her about Danny. Not yet.

'I don't want to be invited back for another cozy chat with Detective Ellis, that's all,' I said. 'Once was enough. I'm not guilty, but he makes me feel like I need to be super-defensive or as if he could surprise a confession out of me for something I didn't do. It's unnerving.'

'Well, you *didn't* do it,' she said again in a matter-of-fact tone. 'So why would he invite you back? There must be hundreds of security cameras in that neighborhood, Soph, even if Robson Blake turned his off. It's Kalorama, for God's sake. Someone saw something; some camera picked up someone.'

'I'm sure you're right.'

'Of course I'm right. Look, let me finish this piece and send it to Stu before another reporter scoops me. Then let's go get your car. Do battle with whoever is still there.'

'Sure. You write and I'll clean up.'

'Leave everything. The housekeeper will be here tomorrow morning. She'll take care of it.'

'I got it.'

Because what I really wanted – *needed* – was a distraction to keep me occupied, so Grace wouldn't zero in with her laser focus that something was still on my mind. No, I didn't kill Robbie, but what if Danny had become impatient and decided he and his crew should retrieve the icon now because he'd known where to find it? What if my scenario that the killer had been someone Robbie invited to his home was wrong?

Ellis would put Danny and me together faster than he'd done that Rubik's Cube and then I *would* be back in the Daly Building for another question-and-answer session. Probably not in his office, either.

And that, frankly, terrified me.

After Grace finished her story, sent it to Stu and got his editorial stamp of approval, we drove to Robbie's house to get my car. As expected, yellow crime scene tape had been stretched across his front door in a huge X, as if it were the location of treasure on a treasure map. A DC police cruiser sat out front. Mercifully, the cameras, reporters and neighbors had called it quits for the night. I knew I wasn't going to be able to just waltz up and get in my car without first explaining myself to the occupant of the cruiser and probably having him vet my story with Ellis, which was exactly what happened.

It took a few minutes, but finally, after a conversation with someone whose voice squawked through his phone that I was legit, he said to me, 'OK, you can take your car. Your story checks out.'

Grace waited until I backed the Mini out of the driveway and followed me to the light on Connecticut Avenue. When it changed, she turned left and I turned right. I wondered how long it would be before she did some more digging and then called me again, asking me to fill in gaps wide enough to drive a truck through the things I hadn't told her. Wondered how long I could hold out. We had never kept anything from each other, especially nothing this big.

Until now.

A red-and-white-striped Mini Cooper sticks out wherever it's parked as though the paint is neon and the car glows in the dark. I'd already decided I wasn't going to leave my car on the street in front of my house for every journalist who wanted to find me to see as confirmation they had the right address. When I first moved into my apartment and before I bought the Mini, India Ferrer, my landlady, had let me borrow Niles, a vintage racing-green Rolls Royce that had been the pride and joy of her late husband. I'd only driven Niles a few times and only when I desperately needed a car because I also owned a mint-green Vespa on which I could zip around the city with speed, ease and efficiency. Parking the Vespa was a breeze – an empty patch of sidewalk with a streetlamp or something to which I could attach a chain and I was done. No meter to feed, either. Trying to park Niles in one of DC's cramped street parking places was like trying to dock the *Queen Mary*, especially because I'd been terrified I'd scratch or dent his beautiful exterior. Lately, with the skyrocketing number of carjackings after the pandemic, Niles had been whiling away most of his retirement days in a garage next door to my studio. There was just enough room to squeeze the Mini next to the Rolls and I still had my garage key, so tonight Niles would have the pleasure of a little companion. By tomorrow I'd hear from India anyway – she lived on cable news, so I'd get a breathless, excited call and she'd expect me to tell her *everything*. When India talked, you could just about see the exclamation marks at the end of every sentence in the speech bubbles above her head. I could explain then about the Mini's temporary parking place. She wouldn't mind, in return for an inside scoop – firsthand knowledge – sharing details about the murder of a local celebrity, which she would then pass on to a coterie of like-minded gossips, er, friends.

After I locked the garage, I headed straight for the studio. I didn't need to think twice about not sleeping in my apartment tonight. Even if no one was sitting in a parked car waiting for me to get home, there'd be someone – maybe even a scrum of people – waiting to ambush me tomorrow the first time I set foot outside my front door.

I'd never put a television in the studio, but I could livestream the eleven o'clock news – which would be on in ten minutes – on my computer. I got an opened bottle of brandy and a glass from the kitchen and brought them back to my desk. I'd shut off my phone after my exchange with Landon, so while I was waiting, I turned it back on and watched the little red counter go crazy as each new text came in. Plus, I had fifteen phone messages. I jabbed my finger on the on/off button and powered the phone off again. Tomorrow I'd deal with all of it. Not tonight. Besides, now I knew for sure: with that many messages and texts, my name had to be out there attached to the news of Robbie's death.

At eleven, I tuned in to News Channel 8. Surprisingly – or maybe *not* surprisingly because this was Washington, after all – the lead story was the cherry blossoms. Today, the National Park Service had officially declared that it was 'peak bloom,' meaning the whole city would go a little crazy for a few days. During that time, there would be a general stampede to the Tidal Basin to catch a glimpse of the beautiful, ethereal pink flowers, Washington's lovely grace note for a city that had lately become known for its ugly political discord and disharmony – and its skyrocketing crime. Peak bloom, which was an official proclamation, was a big deal.

The second story – *and now more breaking news* – was Robbie's murder. The two news anchors took turns describing what had happened, none of which was anything I didn't know. Next up was the perky blonde who'd been the first to arrive at Robbie's house earlier today, reporting from police headquarters on a press conference the DC Chief of Police had held this evening. The chief had delivered a short, terse statement that they were actively looking for the murderer of Robson Blake. Also, that they had set up a tip line with a 25,000-dollar reward for the person or persons who provided information that led to the arrest and conviction of Robbie's killer. After his statement, the Chief turned the podium over to Detective Joseph Ellis, who was overseeing the investigation. Ellis said he would take questions. *Who found Robbie?* Ellis tiptoed around that, leaving out my name and explaining that Robbie's body had been discovered by an individual who showed up for a scheduled appointment with Mr Blake and had found him inside the house, already deceased.

Then from Ms News Channel 8: *Was that person the individual whose car was in Mr Blake's driveway? According to DMV records, the car is registered to a Ms Sophie Medina, whose website says she is a freelance photographer from Washington, DC. Is that also correct?*

Well, yes.

Is Ms Medina a person of interest in this investigation?

She is not.

Was anything missing or stolen? Mr Blake owned a lot of valuable art.

We're continuing our inventory of Mr Blake's home and his art collection with the help of his staff. At the moment, we're not prepared to discuss that subject.

After that question, he shut down the press conference. 'If we have any developments or breakthroughs,' he said, 'we'll let you know if and when we can.'

And that was that.

Mercifully, no one appeared to have seen me leave Robbie's house in a police cruiser, and Ellis didn't mention our little tete-à-tete in his office. But until there were other leads and more information, I was the bright shiny object, the mystery woman no one had spoken to yet – except Grace. The rest of the Channel 8 report was background stuff, highlighting Robbie's generosity and philanthropy, along with shocked, horrified comments from people who knew him and had been beneficiaries of his patronage.

I clicked off the news and did a quick Internet search for Robson Blake plus murder. Pictures of me – from my website, from social media, from IPS – were already popping up like weeds after rain. I shut the computer down, knocked back my brandy and let it burn

my throat. I poured another glass and then I climbed the stairs to
the loft and threw myself on the bed.

The last thing I thought of before I fell asleep was that I had no
way of getting in touch with Danny, who by now must know my
name was tangled up in the investigation into the murder of Robson
Blake – unless he'd moved into a cave recently. Had he been to
Robbie's house just before I had? And this time things hadn't gone
according to plan?

No one gets hurt.

He'd been so cocky, so sure of himself. He worked with the
A-Team. Experts at what they did. They never screwed up.

But what if they had gotten it horribly, comprehensively wrong
this time?

Then what?

It probably wouldn't take long for Ellis to put two and two
together, and Danny's name would show up on his radar as a person
of interest – at a minimum. And Ellis would find him, too.

I had no doubt about that.

FIFTEEN

A shaft of morning sunshine streaming through a tiny window in the loft of my studio woke me just after seven on Saturday morning. I sat up, still dressed in the clothes I'd been wearing since yesterday, which were now rumpled and disheveled. My head pounded after too much brandy – the empty glass sitting on the bedside table, a silent admonishment even though I had no recollection of drinking it. My tongue felt as though it had been coated in fur, and if I looked in a mirror, I imagined I probably looked like roadkill.

I splashed water on my face in the downstairs bathroom and walked into the little kitchenette to make coffee. While it brewed, I turned my phone back on and it rang in my hand.

Mom.

We hadn't spoken since the other day when she gave me my father's letters. This call was going to be about me finding Robbie and her finding out about it on television.

'Sophie, where have you *been*? Harry and I have been *beside* ourselves with worry. After we heard the news yesterday, Tommy stopped by your apartment last night around eleven after his shift at the hospital was over and said you weren't *there*. What *happened*? Are you in trouble?'

She sounded distraught. Harry probably had had to give her a Valium to calm her down last night. I could see her wringing her hands, giving me the *How-could-you-do-this-to-me?* look.

'Mom. I'm OK. I'm not in trouble and I decided to sleep in my studio last night because I figured there might be reporters camped out on my doorstep once it leaked out that I was the one who found Robson Blake.'

'Oh. Well, all right. But you might have called. You should have known we'd be worried about you, thought about how upset we'd be. I couldn't sleep a wink last night.'

Right. Because, of course, this is about you, Mom.

'I was with Grace. There'll be a story in the *Trib* this morning if you haven't already seen it.'

I heard papers rustling in the background and then Harry's deep voice, murmuring, 'Here it is.'

A moment later, he came on the phone. 'Sweetheart, is there anything we can do? Would you like to come home for a few days, get away from DC? If any reporter shows up out here, we can have a little conversation about their First Amendment rights as well as *our* Second Amendment rights, should we find it necessary to exercise them. You're entitled to your privacy.'

Jesus. Freedom of speech and the right to bear arms. Harry didn't mean, of course, that he'd greet any journalist who drove all the way out to Mayfield with his shotgun. At least, I hoped he didn't. Virginia was the number-three state for gun ownership in the country – only Florida and Texas were ahead of us, and nearly half of all adults in the beautiful, bucolic Commonwealth of Virginia had guns in their homes. Not to mention the headquarters of the NRA was here, tucked away in a quiet, affluent northern Virginia suburb. No, Harry was just talking, he wasn't really serious, even though he was my much-beloved stepfather, who would do anything – *anything* – to protect me, make sure no harm befell me.

'It's OK, Harry. If I had to cover this story and I was still working for IPS, I'd do the exact same thing. Track me down and get a statement. Or, in my case, a photo.'

'I think we should get Sam involved in this, honey. It's Saturday, but I can make a call. Sam owes me a favor over some land I helped him buy. A couple of favors.'

Sam Constantine was our family lawyer, practically an uncle to me. I'd already thought about contacting him because I'd meant what I said to Detective Ellis. The next time he wanted to talk to me, I wanted to have legal representation.

'Thanks, Harry, but I should be the one to call him. I can handle this.'

'Sophie, you need to let Harry—' my mother broke in.

'Caroline.' Harry, cutting Mom off. 'Sophie said she can handle it. She's right. Let her do this. And sweetheart,' he said to me, 'if you need anything, you know you only have to call, right?'

'I do. Thanks, Harry.'

'Is there anything we can do for you now?' he asked.

'Could you call Tommy and Lexie for me, please? I got voice-mails from both of them. Thank them for calling and thank Tommy for stopping by. Tell them I love them and I'm OK.'

'I'll call them,' my mother said. 'You know, sweetie, the *neighbors* have been calling as well.'

'*Mom*. I didn't kill Robson Blake. He hired me to take author photos for a book he was collaborating on with a professor from Georgetown. I showed up at his home for my appointment, and he was dead when I found him. That's *all*.'

No point telling her about the murder weapon being my tripod. Or the slow-drip poisonous fear in my veins that Danny might be involved. Harry would need to give her an elephant tranquilizer to calm her down.

'I need to go,' I added. 'I've got another call. It's Max. Love you.'

I hit *end call* and accepted Max's.

'*Where. Are. You?*'

'In my studio.'

'Good, because there's a gaggle of reporters – or is it a murder? No, wait, that's crows. A murder of crows. Whatever it is, they're outside the house, milling around on the sidewalk. And my guess is that they're not going anywhere until they have a word with you.'

I groaned, and he said, 'I'm coming over there right now. Gil is with me. There's no one in the alley, so that's the good news. No one seems to know about the carriage house.'

Thirty seconds later, there was a knock on the door. I opened it and Max and Gil Tessier spilled into the studio. Max looked as if he hadn't slept any better than I had; there were deep circles under his eyes. Gil shot a concerned look at me, his eyes traveling over my wrinkled clothes, my bedhead hair, the two streaks of yesterday's mascara under my eyes that looked like a couple of bruises. My slightly hungover general state of exhaustion. His jaw tightened and he shook his head, as if he still couldn't believe the surreal news about Robbie.

'I made coffee,' I said. 'It's pretty strong.'

'Good,' Max said.

They sat on the Chesterfield sofa where Danny had been sitting what seemed like a lifetime ago. I took the club chair facing them, all of us nursing a mug of coffee.

'I found out last night when I turned on the eleven o'clock news,' Max said.

'I found out when Max called me,' Gil added.

'Your lights weren't on, so I knew you weren't home,' Max said.

'I should have realized you'd be here. Sophie, I've been so worried about you. *What happened?*'

I gave them the official version, leaving out my little Q&A session with Detective Joe Ellis. Also, the fact that my tripod was probably the murder weapon. And I deliberately didn't say anything about the icon, although I did wonder if Max or Gil had any idea Robbie owned it. And if they did, if they knew whether Robbie believed he'd bought it from an honest dealer – or had he known it was stolen?

I almost didn't want to know if the answer to that last question was yes, because it also meant that, by default, Max and Gil knew it was stolen as well. And traveling a little further down that rutted, potholed road, if they did know the icon was stolen, did it mean they condoned what Robbie had done, or had they just turned a blind eye? Excused him? Most of all, did they know whether this was a one-off thing or had Robbie been involved in buying or trafficking stolen art on a regular basis?

I thought of my brother sitting on the same sofa three days ago, the anger and passion in his voice as he told me what it was like to be the victim dealing with the weary indifference of authorities who said there was little chance of catching the thieves and even less of recovering what had been stolen – especially if it was a small or not very artistically important item. How easy it was to strip a work of art or an artifact of its provenance and give it a shiny new identity for the next owner – a gallery, an individual, a museum that didn't do due diligence for whatever reason. How many hundreds, thousands of items were stolen, plundered *every day*, the obscene amount of money that changed hands, the greed and avarice that oiled the machine so it would never stop. All because someone loved a thing of beauty so much or wanted an item they alone possessed that they didn't care that it had come wrapped in a shroud of lies and thuggery, maybe even stained by blood.

'There's a crowd of people, including a couple of guys with cameras and recording equipment, standing on the sidewalk outside your front door,' Gil said.

'Define "crowd."' I said.

'Fifteen, maybe.'

Fifteen wasn't a crowd. It bordered on being a small mob.

'Where's your car?' Max asked. 'I didn't see it on the street and it's not here in the alley.'

I told him about leaving it in the garage with Niles.

He smiled. 'What a good idea. It's also the only car I can think of that would have fit in there next to that Rolls.'

'You two knew Robbie,' I said. 'Do you have any idea who might have done it? Did he have any enemies?'

In the awkward silence that followed, I had a feeling that each of them was waiting for the other to be the first one to answer my question.

'Robbie was a friend,' Max said at last, 'but I didn't know everyone in the rarefied circles someone with his kind of wealth moved in. If he had any enemies, I never heard about it. But it doesn't mean he didn't.'

'Gil?' I asked.

'The same,' he said. 'I can't imagine anyone who would have done it.'

'Sophie, love,' Max said, 'do you want company when you face those reporters? You shouldn't have to do that alone, and I don't think they're going anywhere until they talk to you.'

'I might as well get it over with,' I said, 'and I'd appreciate an escort. But look, I'm a journalist, too. They want a story and I'm part of it. I'll give them a statement and answer their questions and that will be the end of it.'

At least I hoped it would.

Facing the press was harder than I expected with everyone jockeying for position and cameras and microphones thrust in my face from all sides. Before Max, Gil and I left the studio, I had written down what I intended to say and no more. I'd been to too many press conferences where someone showed up unprepared or got caught off guard. What happened was they ended up babbling and saying far more than they intended to because they panicked and couldn't figure how to shut up and quit talking. I read my few lines while I was standing on the front steps, flanked by Max and Gil who I introduced simply as 'friends.' When I was done, I said, 'Look, guys, I'm a journalist like you all are. I know you need something to write, but this is all I've got. Anything else and I refer you to Detective Joe Ellis who is running this investigation.'

It still didn't stop the questions from being pelted at me like balls from a tennis ball machine on the fastest setting. *What did he look like? Can you describe his injuries? How did you know where to find him? What do you know about the murder weapon? Were there any signs of a struggle? How did you feel when you saw him? Were you romantically involved?*

'The answer to the last question is a most definite *no*. I was there to take his photograph – it was a business appointment. For answers to all your other questions,' I said in a firm voice, 'once again, I refer you to Detective Ellis with the DC Police Department. I have nothing more to say.'

'She's *done*, folks,' Max said. 'You heard her. You're free to go.'

He unlocked the front door, opened it wide enough for me to escape inside, then closed it behind me. I locked it and blew him a grateful kiss through the sidelight. The first thing I did when I got upstairs to my apartment was strip off my clothes and take a long, hot shower until I could no longer smell the sour odor that clung to me. I had thought it was the scent of Robbie's death that lingered on my skin. But the more I thought about it, the more I wondered if maybe it wasn't fear.

SIXTEEN

The list of people I needed to talk to was long and it began with Danny. He hadn't reached out or tried to contact me since the news about Robbie's murder went viral on the Internet. There were a couple of possible reasons for that.

My least favorite was that he was on the run.

Valerie Zhou might know where he was or how to get in touch with him. But *if* he had disappeared because he had been at Robbie's house the day he died, I needed to call Sam Constantine, and the sooner the better. Because if Detective Ellis wanted to talk to me again, he would have a good, solid reason this time. He wouldn't be on a fishing expedition. He'd *know* something. And sitting across from Ellis as I stammered answers to his questions, while he re-assembled a perfect Rubik's Cube for the five thousand and first time and watched me with stone-faced calm, would be a bad idea.

I called Sam's private number while I was clearing up my breakfast dishes.

He answered on the third ring, pre-empting me before I could get a word out. 'Sophie. What's going on? I've been worried about you, darlin'. In fact, I very nearly phoned Harry and your momma to ask if I could do anything, if you might need legal counsel. I'm glad to hear from you. Your name is all over the news.'

I slumped into a kitchen chair, relief flooding through me, grateful for this good man who had just folded me in his big protective embrace, no questions asked. Sam would handle everything, take over, fix all the problems.

'That's why I'm calling. I spent an hour last night being questioned by a detective who is leading the investigation into Robson Blake's murder. The last thing he said was that he might want to talk to me again. I told him if that happens, I'd do it with my attorney present. Will you help me, please, Sam? I can drive out to Middleburg and meet you whenever it's convenient.'

'First, you never should have talked to that detective without counsel present.' He sounded mad. Not the best way to start this conversation. 'I don't care if you're as innocent as the driven snow.'

'I'm sorry.' Penitent. 'Really.'

'What's done is done. Second, I'm in town today. Doesn't happen often anymore, but I'm at the office on K Street. Packing my things. I'm done with DC, ready to be a country lawyer and work part-time from here on out. Why don't you drop by, in, say, half an hour and we'll have a little chat?'

'I'll be there,' I said.

I took the Vespa to Sam's office on K Street, also known as Lawyers Row in downtown Washington. K Street – in fact, all of DC's business district – on a Saturday morning is a ghost town of empty high-rises and quiet streets. There is little traffic and even fewer pedestrians. The small businesses that exist to serve the people who work in those buildings wither and fade on weekends. Many are closed. Sam's building, one of the newer ones, was all soulless steel and mirrored glass. A marble lobby, a uniformed guard watching something on his computer, a directory of who worked here and in what suite – all of it interchangeable with every other building on the street. My footfalls echoed as I walked across the floor to tell the guard I was expected on the fourteenth floor in the offices of Boyd, Hamilton, O'Donnell, Crane, and Constantine, LLC. He made a call and told me I could go up.

My phone buzzed with a text message as I stepped into the elevator.

At your place with Harriet at ten as requested. There was no answer when I rang your bell just now.

Landon.

I called him.

'Where are you?' He sounded just a little irked.

'Do you read the paper? Check the Internet? Watch the local news?' *Live in a cave?*

'Uh, no. Not really. Why?'

'I'm so sorry, but I'm not home. I'm downtown getting ready to meet my lawyer.'

'Why do you need a lawyer?'

'You really don't follow the news, do you? The client I was supposed to meet last night – Robson Blake – was dead when I got to his house. The police are looking for his murderer.'

His silence went on for a few beats. Then he said. 'Murderer. They think *you* did it?'

'No. Maybe. I don't know. It's complicated. And I didn't do it. I also completely forgot about you coming by this morning with Harriet, plus I owe you an apology for last night. I was detained for a while by a detective from the DC police department who had a few questions for me. Then I was with a journalist from *The Washington Tribune*.'

'You had quite a night.'

'I did.'

'You know what?'

'What?'

'You're nothing like I expected.'

'What *did* you expect?' The elevator had whirred to the fourteenth floor and stopped. I stepped out, leaned against the wall, my head tipped back, my eyes closed. Waiting for his answer.

'Not this.'

I didn't want to ask what 'this' was. 'I'd better go. Can you keep Harriet a little longer?'

'Look, she's going to need someone who can be with her, help her get settled, adjust to being indoors. Can you do that?'

At this moment in time, I couldn't. 'I don't know. I'm sorry. Right now, I don't know.'

'I can keep her for a few more days. Call me then and give me your answer. If it doesn't work for you, I'm sure I can find her another home. She's a real sweet kitten.'

'Thank you for the reprieve.'

'You're welcome.' He was still miffed. 'I think you and Harriet would be good for each other, but if you can't make up your mind, I want her to go to someone who is ready to love her and care for her. No offense, but she's my priority.'

Left unsaid: *you can take care of yourself.*

'Of course. I understand.'

'Good. And good luck with your lawyer,' he said, a brusque dismissal before he disconnected.

I shoved my phone in my pocket, my face burning after having been schooled and come up short with Dr Landon Reed and a tiny bit of fluff named Harriet. Although I was irked, too. He had a right to be upset, but the reason I'd stood him up – twice – had hardly been frivolous. Maybe I wouldn't be such a good cat mom after all. Maybe he and I would be better off calling it quits before we even got started. Not that we had much of a relationship anyway.

I walked down the corridor to the glass-fronted office of Sam's law firm and rang the doorbell. Sam himself came to let me in.

It had been a while since I'd seen him. He looked a little more stooped than I remembered, bent forward as if leaning into the wind, hair tussled, wrinkled khakis, a blue-and-white pin-striped shirt, a pair of Nikes. His smile was tired, but he gave me a warm hug.

'It's good to see you, Sophie,' he said. 'It's been a while. Too long, in fact.'

The last time was Nick's funeral. Two years ago. I know he remembered. He just wasn't going to bring up Nick.

'Thanks, Sam, for doing this on a Saturday.'

'Nonsense, you know you're practically family. I've known you since the day you and your momma moved to Middleburg.'

'I remember.'

'Come on,' he said. 'We'll talk in the conference room. My office is full of moving boxes and it's a mess.'

The conference room was windowless, paneled, shelves lined with burgundy and moss-green law books, a mahogany conference table, leather chairs, plush enough that you could sink into them but not enough to get too comfortable. It was a room that reinforced your understanding that every minute you spent in here cost somewhere between ten and twelve dollars – maybe more – so you didn't want to draw an unneeded breath or waste a millisecond of anyone's time. Sam sat at the head of the table; I took the first seat next to him. He was old school: a legal pad and a Mont Blanc pen.

He took his reading glasses off the top of his head and put them on. 'OK,' he said. 'Start at the beginning.'

I told him about arriving at Robbie's house yesterday and what had happened. When I told him I'd accidentally left a tripod behind that turned out to be the murder weapon, he set his pen down and folded his hands together as if he were praying.

'Who knows about that?' he asked.

'The police, me and now you. The murderer. Of course.'

Sam gave me a sharp look. 'Anyone else?'

'Possibly Bernard Carlson, the caretaker of Robbie's art collection. He helped me the other day by carrying some of my equipment out to my car. He must have left the tripod downstairs, and obviously, I forgot about it, too.'

'Let's keep it that way, shall we? Don't discuss that piece of information with anyone. I'm serious. Not a single soul.'

'Yes, sir.'

I took a deep breath. Wait until he heard what else I had to tell him. My tripod being the murder weapon was the least of it.

'There are some other things you should know. Mom and Harry have no idea. Mom would totally flip out. Harry . . . I don't know what he'd do.'

'Lawyer–client confidentiality,' Sam said. 'You know I can't discuss private matters with anyone else.'

I told him about Danny. Everything, from the beginning.

When I got to the part about Danny's restitution art squad and what he'd said about intending to steal back the icon, Sam set his pen down and ran his hands over his craggy face.

'Jesus, Mary and Joseph. You offered to *help* him with a floor plan of the house and the security system?' His voice went up half an octave.

'It never came to that. But, yes, I did. Sam, that icon was stolen from a little church in Ukraine where people came to pray to it because they believed in miracles, that the Virgin had the power to heal or cure illnesses. It was sitting in a vault in Robson Blake's home, part of an iconostasis on a private altar, where no one could see it, where he alone could worship it.'

'And your brother was going to take the law into his own hands and steal it back. Sophie, this way comes anarchy, lawlessness. We don't need citizen vigilantes.'

'I know. I know. But it's stealing from thieves and returning the stolen items to their rightful owners.'

'Breaking and entering – and robbery – is *against the law*. That's why there are people who *enforce* it. It's their *job*. They have accountability for their actions as well, though don't get me started down that road. But my point is that we're a society that lives by, is governed by, the rule of law.'

'OK,' I said. 'I understand, I do. Now what?'

'How certain are you that the icon is missing and maybe not back in the vault or somewhere else in the house?'

'I don't know. I suppose the answer is "not certain at all." I suspect Detective Ellis knows by now, but that's not information they'd release to the public or the press.'

'All right,' Sam said. 'Say it's gone. How likely do you think it is that your brother stole it like he said he would?'

'I don't know the answer to that, either. Danny wanted floor plans, knowledge of the security system. My gut reaction is that he didn't steal it, but I can't say for sure that he didn't jump the gun and decide to show up early. I know it sounds incredibly unlikely, but what if Robbie was already dead when Danny and his crew arrived? Also, what was the icon doing in his library instead of in the vault?'

'You're asking me?'

'No, not really. What I am asking is what do I do now?'

'Nothing. There's nothing for you to do. Even if your brother or one of his cohorts did take the icon, you weren't involved. You *did* tell him where it was but that's not the same as being an accessory. So I think we're going to be OK,' he said. 'But if that detective – or anyone else – wants to talk to you, you do *nothing* without me by your side. And you're going to let me do the talking. Are we clear?' He looked at me over the top of his glasses. Using the courtroom voice that made my nerves skitter.

'Yes, sir. As crystal.'

'Good.' He capped his pen and set it on top of his legal pad. 'Anything else before I get back to this damned packing? I swear, it's taking forever.'

I opened my mouth to say something, then thought better of it.

'Sophie,' he said, and for a moment I thought he was going to shake his finger at me, 'you know I need to know everything if I'm going to be your attorney, so you'd better not hold anything back. I mean it. I can't have you surprising me with something at the last minute. Do you understand?'

'I do.'

'Then what is it?'

'What if . . .?' I stopped.

'What if what?'

'What if I'm indirectly responsible for Robbie's death because I offered to help Danny and everything went wrong so Robbie ended up dead?'

Sam shook his head and stood up. I stood, too. He put an arm around my shoulder and gave it a squeeze. 'Darlin', I can help you with your legal problems. As for clearing your conscience, that's way out of my realm of expertise.'

He walked me back to the reception area and unlocked the door.

'Be in touch if you need me,' he said.

'I will. Thank you. And about your fee . . .'

'We'll work something out. Don't worry about it.'

I hugged him and he bussed me on the cheek. 'Stay out of trouble,' he said. 'I mean, don't get in any *more* trouble.'

'I won't. I promise.'

I heard the metallic click as he locked the door behind me. The elevator was still on the fourteenth floor, so I stepped in and pushed the button for the lobby. Sam couldn't help me with my guilty conscience, but I knew someone who could. As soon as I was outside on K Street, I called Jack O'Hara.

'Do you have time to see me today?' I asked. 'Please?'

'I'm saying the five at the house tonight,' he said. 'Do you want to come? After Mass, we could get takeout for dinner and talk in my suite. Or maybe sit in Stanton Park for a bit. The cherry blossoms are spectacular this year. It's peak bloom this weekend.'

'I know. That sounds great. I'll bring the dinner wine.'

'Are you all right?'

'Jack, you watch the news and follow what's happening on the Internet,' I said. 'You must have heard.'

'I did. Besides, I read Grace's article in the *Trib*. Then she called me this morning and filled me in on the rest of it. I wondered if you might be sleeping in after everything you had to deal with yesterday, so I figured I'd call you later.'

'I was up early. There was a scrum of reporters outside my front door who wouldn't leave until I talked to them. And I just hired Sam Constantine.'

He let out an explosive breath. 'Good Lord. You really need a lawyer? I thought you were the one who found Robson Blake.'

'I was, but it's complicated. I'll tell you tonight. And Jack, I need you to wear your purple stole because of what I have to tell you. Even if it's just virtual.'

The one he wore when he heard confessions that meant he could never, ever reveal what I told him, or his soul would fry in hell for all eternity. Or so he said.

'I figured as much. You've been in my prayers all day, Soph. I'll see you at Mass.'

My next call was Valerie Zhou who answered on the first ring. She asked the two questions everybody had been asking. *Are you all right? What happened?*

'I need to talk to you,' I said. 'In person. As soon as possible.'

'Where do you want to meet?'

'In front of Ginevra de' Benci.'

The only painting by Leonardo da Vinci in the Western hemisphere. It was set off by itself in a room at the far end of the Old Masters wing of the National Gallery of Art. Valerie would know exactly what I was talking about.

'I can be there in half an hour,' she said, and I heard the little hitch of apprehension in her voice.

'Good,' I said. 'See you then.'

The National Gallery of Art would have been a lot more crowded if it had been raining outside or any other weekend but peak bloom for the cherry blossoms. Still, Ginevra de' Benci had visitors as she always did. Valerie found me studying the painting of the delicate Florentine girl Leonardo had painted in the mid-1400s to commemorate her engagement at the age of sixteen. He hadn't been much older himself. Ginevra was a beauty. Pale porcelain skin, austere expression, eyes cast away from the artist as if she were indifferent to having her portrait painted. Not elegantly dressed, though, nor wearing a single piece of jewelry. Leonardo had been experimenting with a new medium: painting with oils. The setting had also been innovative because he had placed Ginevra outdoors instead of sheltered inside in her family's home, which had been the tradition. Always an iconoclast, always experimenting.

'She's beautiful, isn't she?' Val said.

'Yes.'

'Are you OK, Sophie?'

I wasn't. But I wasn't going to tell her that because there were too many secrets I had to keep bottled inside me. 'Why don't we walk down to the West Garden Court and see if one of the benches is free? We can talk there.'

'Sure,' she said. 'My turn to ask. Why did you pick this place to meet?'

'Because it's easier to see if anyone is following me. I had to face what seemed like the entire Washington press corps this morning on the front steps of my home. I'm not answering any more questions and I don't want to be ambushed again.' It wasn't an entirely honest answer.

The real reason was that meeting Val in front of this painting seemed only right. What had brought me into Robson Blake's world was something else created by Leonardo da Vinci: a tall case clock that was as different from the painting of Ginevra de' Benci as it

could possibly be. A reminder of what an incredible genius he had
been, someone who saw the world through a lens he deliberately
tilted and made connections no one else had thought of before. And
somehow, he always found one. Unlike me. What I couldn't figure
out was whether there was a connection between Danny and Robbie's
death. Until I had an answer to that, I was flying blind.

'Why did you want to see me?' Val asked.

'Val, really?'

We found a bench tucked into a corner and sat. Val looked down
at her hands, which were folded in her lap, and fiddled with the
large diamond on her ring finger. 'You talked to him, didn't you?'
she said. It was a statement, not a question. She knew.

'He came to see me the day after you and I talked. Obviously,
you told him how to find me. He broke into my studio and was
waiting there for me. That's how we met.'

'*He's in town?*' Her eyes, outlined as usual in heavy black eyeliner
so they looked bigger and even more exotic, grew wide.

'He was. For all I know, he could be on his way to Ukraine by
now.'

'What are you talking about?'

She really didn't seem to know, which was a surprise because
she was the one who had told me about Danny's art restitution squad
and what they did. And about Michael Angelo, the maestro who
orchestrated these kamikaze smash-and-grab thefts.

'Robson Blake had an icon in his home that was stolen by the
Russians from a church outside Kyiv. I happened to see it – by
accident – in a vault in his home. When I found Robbie the other
night, the icon was in his study – actually, it *wasn't*. The kiot the
icon had been in was there, but the icon was gone,' I said.

'Let me guess. You told Danny about it.'

'Well done. A-plus. I haven't heard from him since that night,
so now I'm wondering where he is. Whether he and his "team," as
he calls them, paid a visit to Robson Blake's house and took the
icon. And maybe now Danny's trying to get it out of the country
and back to Kyiv.'

She turned pale. 'I have no idea. Sophie, Robson Blake is *dead*.'

As if she was telling me something I didn't know.

She went on. 'Danny wouldn't . . . *do* anything like that. All they
want when they plan one of their break-ins is to take what is stolen.
That's all.'

'Maybe so, but what if this time his plan didn't work out the way he thought it would? What if Robbie Blake surprised him, or the other way around? How can you be so sure Danny didn't kill him, Val? Have you spoken to him? Did he *tell* you he didn't do it?' There was a little bubble of hysteria in my voice, which had grown louder and now echoed off the courtyard walls. Val laid a finger over her lips: a warning. Already, the heads of a couple entering the garden courtyard to examine the fountain more closely had swiveled in our direction.

Sam had given me strict instructions to tell no one about my tripod being used as the murder weapon, so Valerie had no idea just how much trouble I might be in. Especially if Ellis learned about Danny *and* the fact that we were related. Put it together with the murder weapon being mine and you had a real ugly stew of coincidence and circumstantial evidence that looked bad for me.

'Look,' I said, 'I spent an hour being questioned by the detective from the Homicide Division who is in charge of finding Robbie's killer. If Danny was at that house before I was or someone working with him was there, I need to know about it. I'm sure you understand why.'

She looked panicked. 'I don't know. Honest, Sophie. I have no idea.'

I believed her. She wasn't making it up. She didn't know.

'Can't you find some way to get in touch with him? I have to talk to him. I have to know what happened. Even if he was there. *Especially* if he was there.'

'I'll try,' she said. 'I'll do what I can.'

Not encouraging but better than nothing. Especially if Danny didn't want to be found.

By anyone.

Because now what I was wondering was this: would my brother let me take the blame for something he did if it would save the project he believed in, so he and Michael Angelo could continue the work they considered so necessary and important? He was already adept at bending the law until it just about snapped in two because the ends justified the means. Would he sacrifice me for something he believed was the greater good? Figuring that ultimately I wouldn't be punished because I wasn't guilty, although I might have a hell of a time trying to prove it.

I had no idea what the answer was.

Right now, I figured it could go either way.

SEVENTEEN

The parking lot behind Gloria House, the Jesuit residence where Jack O'Hara lived on Capitol Hill, was full of cars, which meant there would be a crowd at the five o'clock Mass. The priests and seminarians who lived there had always opened the doors of their big, rambling Victorian house of studies to the local community, to anyone who wanted to attend Saturday evening or Sunday morning Mass. People came because the weekly homilies were down-to-earth, compassionate, humorous, and sprinkled with the erudition the Jesuits were known for as scholars and thinkers. Plus, they wove faith into something you wanted to listen to, realized you needed to hear. When you left, you felt better.

The chapel was nearly full when I got there so I slipped into a spot in the last pew. It was Lent, the season of atonement, a month before Easter. Jack would be wearing purple vestments, and he would light two candles on a wreath lying on a stand on the altar for the Second Sunday of Lent. When he stepped on to the altar and turned around to face the congregation, he cast a quick look around and I knew he was looking for me. My old friend, my confidante, my ex-boyfriend. Our eyes met briefly, then he was all business again, Father O'Hara saying Mass.

The first reading from the Old Testament must have been chosen expressly for me, from Leviticus, the story of the people of Israel straying from God's commandments; despite not realizing they'd done anything wrong, they were guilty anyway. To atone for their sins, they were required to sacrifice a bull.

I'd told Danny about the icon in Robbie's home and then offered to help him with information about the layout of the house and the security system so he could steal the Virgin of Vladimir and return it to the church in Kyiv. I still didn't know if he or someone from his crew had shown up on Friday before I got there. And now Robbie was dead.

Was it my fault? Was *I* unintentionally guilty? Sam said I hadn't *done* anything, so the legal answer was no. But morally or ethically?

If that answer was also no, why had my conscience been pricking me for the last twenty-four hours? Why did I *feel* so guilty?

Because Robbie might still be alive if I hadn't said anything to Danny, that's why.

The line to greet Jack and chat with him after Mass usually went on longer than Mass itself, partly because he was what Grace and I called 'Father What-a-Waste' since he was so damned good-looking it was almost a sin he had to be celibate. The little old ladies – also known as 'the Holy Harem' – especially wanted to stop and chat. I sat where I could watch him with each person who grasped his hand, wished him a good week, shared a problem, sought his advice. He was endlessly patient, refusing to rush anyone, urging a few people to make an appointment to see him privately so they could talk at length.

When the last person had left, he came over to where I was waiting for him. 'Let me change and then why don't we go over to Stanton Park and talk there for a while? There's a new Italian place on Barracks Row that someone told me has great pizza and they deliver. We can call them afterwards and eat in my suite.'

'I'd like that. And I brought wine for dinner.' I held up a carrier bag.

'Thanks.' He took it from me. 'I'll stash it in the sacristy. Give me a few minutes.'

We made small talk on the walk to the park across the street until we were sitting on a bench under a canopy of cherry trees, the pale-pink flowers packed so tightly together on the branches they could have been a lacy pink umbrella sheltering us. Most people think of the Tidal Basin when they think of Washington's cherry blossoms, but there are other places in the city – like Stanton Park – where they are abundant and equally breathtaking. This evening, as Jack had said, the park was especially beautiful. In a week or so when the blossoms finally began to drop off the branches to make room for the new leaves, the sky would look as though it were blizzarding flowers and the ground would look like pink snow.

Jack picked up a cherry blossom that had fallen on the bench and twirled it between his index finger and his thumb. 'Figuratively speaking, I've got my stole on,' he said, 'and your secrets are safe with me. You can tell me whatever you want.'

A few of the benches in the park were occupied, people walked past us heading up to the Hill or down to Union Station, the usual dog-walkers were out for the evening stroll, cars zoomed around the square pinwheeling off on to one of the streets that intersected the park. No one was paying the slightest bit of attention to Jack and me. Here I could confess anything. Everything.

'There's a lot to tell.'

'I expected there would be.'

'There's no way you could expect what I'm going to tell you.'

Jack heard people's confessions for a living. He taught ethics at Georgetown Law School, and I knew for a fact that he often received phone calls or text messages from cabinet secretaries, diplomats, military commanders, the city's power brokers and, on occasion, the White House. He talked with anyone who sought his counsel, regardless of their faith – even if they had none. What everyone wanted from him – *needed* – was his help to work through the difficult and occasionally bleak issues they wrestled with that some-times required choosing between what was bad and what was worse. Navigating the amoral and often immoral world of politics without selling out. Keeping secrets that threatened to eat a person's soul alive and make them wonder whatever had happened to their conscience.

When I'd asked him what hearing so many confessions was like – people telling him their deepest, darkest secrets, which he then had to hold inside himself – he'd laughed and said, 'Oh, Soph, it's nothing like you're thinking. Sins are really boring.'

'Well,' he said to me now, 'maybe you should just start talking.'

I had told Sam Constantine all the facts about Danny, our rela-tionship, our conversation in my studio when I'd agreed to help by providing information about floor plans and the security system to facilitate his team breaking in and taking – or 're-stealing' – the Virgin of Vladimir icon. With Jack, it was different. We'd known each other since we were kids. We'd dated through high school and off and on in college. We'd even had sex. Once. Long before he'd ever thought about becoming a priest.

He knew me so well.

I told Jack everything about Danny, my anguish when I found out he'd known about me but never reached out. About my father's letters, my anger at my mother for keeping them from me. He listened and let me talk as darkness fell around us, soft and gentle, and the park grew quieter, voices receding.

Soon it was just the two of us as Stanton Park emptied out, with only the faint sounds of the city – a bus revving its engine, a car horn, someone's high-pitched laughter – in the background. Even the birds were silent.

'That's a lot to process, Soph,' he said after I told him about reading my father's letters, my voice more raggedy than I had intended it to be. He laid an arm lightly across my shoulders, giving me a brotherly squeeze. 'You're going to be OK. I *know* you. You'll get through this.'

'There's more. And it's not very good.'

He withdrew his arm and turned so he was facing me. 'Does it have to do with why you ended up at police headquarters being interrogated by a homicide detective last night?'

'Grace told you.'

He'd already told me they'd been talking. I'd figured Grace had called him the moment she got back from taking me to Robbie's house to pick up my car.

'She did. She's worried about you. So am I, for that matter.'

I told him then what Danny did, about his algorithm to track stolen art, the team he and Michael Angelo assembled to steal certain items and return them to their original owners. Jack nodded without interrupting; I couldn't tell if he was horrified or fascinated. Or both.

'The first time I was at Robbie's to take photos, I accidentally ended up in a room where there were dozens of icons, including an especially beautiful jewel-encrusted icon of the Virgin of Vladimir. I found out from Danny that it had been stolen from a small church outside Kyiv,' I said. 'It was pretty special – people believed the Virgin had mystical healing powers, that she could perform miracles. I figured Robbie had to have known it was stolen. I was so angry about it that's when I told Danny I'd draw a floor plan of Robbie's house and pass on any information I could find out about the security system.'

'Does Sam know about this?'

'He does. Detective Ellis, on the other hand, does *not* know any of it because I would have had to drag Danny into the middle of it, and right now I have no idea if he was the one who broke into Robbie's house or not. As for Grace, she knows *nothing*. She doesn't even know about Danny.'

'So let me guess,' he said. 'Now you feel guilty – maybe even responsible – because Danny might have broken into Robson Blake's house after you told him about the icon and now Robbie is dead?'

'Yes, but it's worse.'

'You already told me what you had to say wasn't going to be very good.'

'Yeah, well, the murder weapon was my tripod. So it is worse. Apparently, I left it behind the last time I was at Robbie's. Sam told me not to tell a living soul about that. So besides Sam, the police, me and the murderer, you're the only other person who knows. *Grace does not know about that, either.*'

I caught the startled look that flashed across his face in the glow of a streetlamp that had just flicked on. 'Holy Mother, Soph. What did your detective friend have to say about *that*?'

'Well, he let me go – right? So obviously he believed what I told him, though he said he might have more questions later. But at least right now he's not accusing me of anything.' I touched his arm. 'Jack, *I didn't do it.* You *know* I didn't do it.'

'Of course you didn't.' He sounded calm, reassuring. He *believed* me. But still. The torrent of words that had tumbled out, my confession filled with admissions of deeds that were so, so unlike me. I had crossed a line and another and another . . . until they had all blurred together. Jack must have been thinking the same thing I was: *if Danny had killed Robbie – even if it was accidental homicide – then I would be the one who was right in the middle of it.*

Ellis would haul me in to answer more questions.

He stood up. 'Come on. Let's go inside. It's getting chilly. Besides, I think we could both use a drink and something to eat.'

He called for the pizza as we were walking back to Gloria House, but I insisted he use my credit card to pay for it. Once we were in his suite, he said, 'I know you brought wine, but someone I helped with a . . . problem . . . recently gave me a bottle of Chianti Classico and told me it's ready to drink now. I looked it up. It's a one-hundred-and-fifty-dollar bottle of wine. I think tonight would be the perfect night to drink it under the circumstances.'

'Don't you want to save it for a special occasion?'

'I think everything you've just told me counts as a special occasion.'

'Are you sure?'

'*Very* sure,' he said and got the wine and two glasses out of a small mid-century modern cabinet where he kept dishes, glassware and a few nonperishable items. 'It's probably sacrilege that I'm not allowing this to breathe, but it will evolve the longer it's open. And right now I really need a drink.'

I took my usual seat, taking off my shoes and sitting cross-legged in the middle of his sofa while he poured our wine. He handed me a glass and plopped down in his favorite recliner.

'To . . . a good outcome,' he said.

'To a good outcome.'

He drank some wine, savoring it.

'This wine is gorgeous,' I said. 'It tastes like liquid velvet.'

'My . . . client . . . knows his wines.' He set his glass on a small side table. The floor lamp he used for reading was turned down to its lowest setting, so his face was partially in shadow. I could feel the room shift as we slowly circled back to the loaded conversation we'd been having in the park.

He started it. 'Does the reason you were brought in to talk to Detective Ellis have to do with your tripod?'

I nodded. 'Partly.'

'What's the other part?'

'Ellis thought I knew a lot about the missing icon even though I told him that Nick was half-Russian and that his grandmother was Orthodox and lived in Moscow. I think he thought I knew a little too much.'

'You didn't do anything, Soph.'

'That's what Sam said. He also said he could help me with my legal problems, but my moral and ethical qualms were way out of his league.'

He smiled. 'Sounds like Sam.'

'The icon wasn't there when I found Robbie, but I have no idea where it is now. It could still be in the house,' I said. 'Or whoever killed Robbie took it.'

'Is the icon the only thing that's missing?'

'I don't know.'

'I read an article about Robson Blake's private art collection in *The New York Times Magazine* a while back. He lives in a small museum. Wouldn't the killer take one of his Monets or Picassos? Doesn't he own a Rembrandt? Why take a fairly insignificant icon – if it *is* missing?'

'I know. It doesn't make sense. Unless it *was* Danny. Because the icon is the only thing he wanted. And that's what haunts me.'

Actually, that's what *terrified* me.

Jack's phone buzzed and he picked it up. 'Sit tight for a minute, OK? Our pizza guy is at the front door. I'll be right back.'

'Wait.' I got my wallet and pulled out a ten. 'For the tip. I'll get out the dishes and silverware and set the table.'

Jack ate almost all his meals downstairs in the refectory with the seminarians and fellow Jesuits who taught at Georgetown as he did. If he ate in his suite, it was breakfast – coffee and a bagel or toast – before dashing out the door to the law school. The 'table' I was setting for dinner was his coffee table, and we would eat sitting on the floor across from each other. I found plates, knives, forks and paper napkins in the cabinet next to his bookcase where he'd gotten the wine glasses. Our Lady of Kazan, the icon he'd inherited that had been restored by Olivia Sage's friend at the National Gallery of Art, hung above the cabinet. The same icon I'd seen in Robbie's study, though painted by a different artist with a different interpretation.

Like Robbie's, it was simple and primitive. Mary's head tilted sharply at an almost unnatural angle toward Jesus, who looked nothing like an infant and more like a miniature version of an adult. It was the same flat, sad-eyed depiction that had characterized Robbie's icon, but what made this one so startlingly beautiful was the burnished gold background that gleamed as if the painting was lit from within.

Two of Olivia Sage's oversized coffee-table books on Byzantine art lay on their side and stuck out on a bookcase shelf that was next to the icon. I pulled them out. Olivia's name was the largest and most prominent under the title. Robbie was listed as 'in collaboration with' rather than as a co-author, just as he'd explained the other evening at Max's. I flipped to the title page. Olivia had signed both books to Jack. *With warmest regards to a dear colleague and friend.*

The door to the suite opened and Jack walked in with our pizza. His eyes went immediately to the books I held in my hands, and for a moment I felt as if he'd caught me prying into something intensely personal.

'I'm starved and this smells fantastic,' he said. 'Ready to eat?'

'Yes.' I set the books on an end table. 'Do you mind if I borrow these for a few days?'

'Olivia's books? Sure. Help yourself. May I ask why?' A casual question but I detected a bit of an edge in his voice. He put two slices of pizza with feta, black olives, mushrooms and onion on the plates I'd set out.

'It's their Greek pizza. It's supposed to be amazing. More wine?'

'Yes, please.'

He filled our glasses, and we sat down across from each other. After he said grace, I gestured to the books.

'The reason I was at Robbie's house on Friday was because he'd hired me to take a new author photo for the latest book he collaborated on with Olivia Sage. Obviously, I never got to take the photo, but now I'm curious how their relationship worked, what "collaborating" meant, rather than being a co-author. The two of them were also very good friends, I gather.'

Jack eyed me as he bit into his pizza and read my subtext perfectly as he always did. I was fishing. When he finished chewing, he said in a bland voice, 'I know they were.'

'Do you think she was interested in him romantically?'

He licked tomato sauce off his thumb. 'She's married.'

'And your point would be?'

'I've never seen her with Robson Blake, but she and Jerome don't seem to be particularly close. They spend a lot of time apart – him in New York and her in DC.'

'I've seen pictures of her with Robbie when I was doing some Internet research on him. My opinion as a woman? She had a crush on him. Maybe more than a crush.'

He gave a half-hearted shrug, and I knew he wasn't going to weigh in with his opinion on whether Olivia was having an extramarital affair. 'I haven't had a chance to talk to her yet,' he said, 'but I imagine she's taking his death pretty hard.'

'Olivia was the reason Robbie needed a new author photo,' I said. 'She told him the old one was outdated. The first time I was at his house, I persuaded him to let me take a couple of candids of him in his library. He reminded me he wanted a formal portrait, but I thought the candids turned out to be quite good. He never saw them, but if Olivia would like to take a look at them, she's welcome to use one of them for her book. All I'd want is a photo credit.'

'That's very generous of you,' Jack said. 'But as we both know, the photos are an excuse. The real reason is that you want to talk to her, don't you?'

I turned red. 'That's not a very charitable thing to say, Father O'Hara.'

'But I *am* right, Ms Medina.'

'OK, so what if you are? You could mention the photos to her when you talk to her, couldn't you?' I said. 'Please?'

Jack set another slice of pizza on my plate and took one for himself. 'Say I did, and she agreed to see you. What are you planning to talk to her about? You're not going to ask her point-blank if she knew Robson Blake owned an icon he knew was stolen, are you?'

'Well, not directly.' I picked up my pizza. 'But honestly, Jack. How could she *not* know? As close as they were.'

'Olivia is a good person. She's also one of the world's top scholars on Byzantine art.'

'Neither of which means she might not also have been in love with Robbie Blake. People do crazy things for love. You know that better than anyone with all the secrets you know and the confessions you hear.'

'Olivia is not some sex-starved, love-crazed teenager, Soph. She's smart, level-headed. Like I said, a scholar.'

'Oh, come on, Jack. Maybe that's her public persona. But you don't know what she's like in private. Do you?'

'Look, I like Livvie. She's a good person – grounded and down to earth. She's a colleague and a friend. I wouldn't like to believe she's caught up in whatever Robbie Blake was doing.'

'But she might be.'

After a long moment, he said, 'OK. Maybe. She might be.' And sounded as if he resented admitting it.

'I'm sorry, Jack. I hope for your sake she's not, but I have a feeling once everything is out in the open, a lot of people are going to be dragged into this. If Danny was involved, I bear some responsibility for what happened as well.'

Jack poured the last of the wine into our glasses. 'The damage Catholic guilt has done to generations of the faithful. You feel responsible for *everything*.' He shook his head. 'You're wrong, Sophie. You're not responsible for something someone else did. You're only responsible for yourself, for your own actions. Don't lay that guilt trip on yourself.'

'I didn't tell Ellis about Danny.'

'What was there to tell? *Maybe* my brother was at Robbie Blake's house? *You don't know*. You just told me that. Sam told you you're not legally responsible for what happened and I'm telling you you're not morally or ethically responsible, either.'

We had come full circle.

It's not your fault.

OK. But it didn't mean I was in the clear. Yet. And that, it seemed to me, depended on Danny.

Wherever he was.

EIGHTEEN

Jack walked me to the parking lot behind Gloria House after dinner. When we got to my car, I said, 'Will you please tell Olivia Sage about the photos I took of Robbie when you talk to her?'

Last fall, I had asked him to talk to a friend of his about whether her husband had staged his own death and she had been complicit in the plot. He had been adamant that she would never do something so egregiously wrong and he refused to talk to her.

I had been right. He had been wrong. It nearly ended our friendship. He'd taken a sabbatical afterwards that included a brutal self-examination into why he had protected someone who'd been in a position of influence in his life, someone who had connections that went all the way to the Vatican and understood Jack's ambitiousness.

We were still finding our way back to our old relationship, except here we were again. I wanted to know if Olivia Sage knew that Robbie owned an icon that had been stolen – and whether that was the only item of plundered art in his possession. Jack's mouth was set in a firm, hard line because he liked and respected Olivia.

I half expected him to turn me down. Again.

'All right. I'll do it. I'll ask her,' he said in a tight, controlled voice that made me wonder whether he was still wrestling with those same demons. 'You know, don't you, that she's not going to incriminate herself? Olivia's a brilliant woman, an internationally known scholar. If she knows anything, you're just going to tip her off that *you* know what was going on as well. And Robbie's dead. Be careful, Sophie. You could be playing a dangerous game.'

Warning me, maybe hoping I'd back off. That I'd let sleeping dogs lie. After all, Robbie *was* dead, right?

'I'll be careful.' Because to be honest, I wasn't worried about Olivia Sage. I *knew* she'd been in love with Robbie and that was her Achilles' heel. Maybe it made her dangerous, but it also made her vulnerable. I'd been the one to find her lover. There would be things she would want to know from *me*. I had something to trade when we talked.

'I'm already involved in this, Jack, whether I like it or not,' I said. 'Right now, Olivia is the only person who can answer my questions. Ellis won't talk to me. And Danny's gone.'

'I hope I don't regret this,' he said. 'Goodbye, Sophie.'

When I got home, I made myself a cup of tea and curled up in my favorite chair in the living room with Olivia Sage's coffee-table books: *Byzantine Art in the Modern World* and *Sacred Beauty: The Icons of the Orthodox Church.* She was the author. Robbie was listed as 'in collaboration with' her. What exactly did that mean? Halfway through *Sacred Beauty*, I'd figured it out. A surprising number of photos were credited as being *From the collection of Robson Blake.*

Clearly, Olivia had access to Robbie's art collection. So, by way of thanks, had she included some of those works of art in her books? Wouldn't that burnish them, give them even more cachet, further establish their provenance? Make them more valuable if he ever decided to sell them? I flipped to the index and looked for the list of credits. Yup, she had relied on art and antiquities Robbie owned nearly a dozen times. Their relationship had to be pretty tight.

If Olivia agreed to see me to look at the photos I'd taken of Robbie as I hoped she would, there was no way she was going to admit she knew Robbie owned stolen art or tell me how he'd acquired it. At a minimum, she might be willing to say whether the Virgin of Vladimir was gone – or whether it was still in his home, locked up in the vault for safekeeping. If the icon was at Robbie's, it seemed much less likely that Danny or someone from his team had been there the day Robbie was murdered. If it was in his house, then someone else had been the killer.

If it was gone, well . . . I didn't really want to think about that. Among other reasons, it would explain why I hadn't heard from my brother.

Because he was on the run.

I no longer seemed to be a person of interest to the press in the murder of Robson Blake because no one waited to ambush me on Sunday morning when I left my apartment to go for a run.

This early, much of the city would be quiet, and traffic would be practically non-existent. I could either head downtown and run all the way to the White House, which was mostly flat, or head up to

Meridian Hill Park, which would be a climb. I wimped out and did the easy run.

When I got to McPherson Square, the tent city that had been cleared out by DC authorities the day before yesterday had already re-established itself, though it wasn't nearly as populated as it had been. Located in the shadow of the White House, it had also been the city's largest homeless encampment – a fact the press frequently hammered at – as in *how can a place of so much despair and poverty exist within shouting distance of the home of the President of the United States in such an affluent and notoriously generous country?* Grace, who had covered the story of the latest clearing out for the *Trib*, told me that even though many of the people who had camped there were supposed to be offered some sort of housing or shelter, most of them were still homeless and moving from place to place, looking for another patch of land where they could put up their tent or lay their sleeping bag. Trying to outrun a new policy called 'immediate disposition' which allowed authorities to evict someone from wherever he or she was camped without notification or warning. Right now, the authorities were winning.

On a weekend, almost everyone who lived in the camp would be here rather than at their day jobs. I slowed my pace to a jog and made my way among the tents, sleeping bags and shopping carts packed with an entire life's possessions, looking for people I knew and asking if they were all right. I'd brought a backpack filled with small Ziplock bags containing a few supplies: granola bars, a pair of warm socks, a Starbucks card with ten dollars on it, sanitary products for the women, lip balm, deodorant. I handed out everything I had and finished my run to Lafayette Park.

My phone rang as I was almost back home. I pulled it out of my pocket. A DC area code and a number that looked familiar. *Danny?* I slowed my pace and answered.

Not Danny. Enrique Navarro. *Damn.*

'Sophie,' he said. 'I'm glad I reached you. I've been worried about you.'

'I'm OK. I'm fine.' There was no way I was going to start a conversation about my involvement with Robson Blake with Navarro. Because obviously that was what he was referring to, why he was worried.

'I do follow the news, you know.' Chiding. Reproachful.

'Well, you would. You're a journalist.'

'I think we should meet.'

He wanted to ask me about Danny, and he was the last person I wanted to talk to just now.

'I don't think—'

He cut me off. 'There's something you should know. I told you I could help. I know you don't trust me, but you should.'

I slowed my pace. All right, I was intrigued. He had my attention. What did he think I should know? 'Does this have anything to do with the murder of Robson Blake?'

What I really wanted to know was whether it had anything to do with Danny.

'I'd rather not discuss it over the phone,' he said. 'Do you know the carousel on the Mall by the Arts and Industries Building?'

'Of course.'

'Meet me there in an hour.'

The only place he could have chosen that would be even more crowded on a spectacular spring Sunday morning in Washington, DC, was the Tidal Basin where people would be shoulder to shoulder jockeying for position to see the cherry blossoms in peak bloom.

'I can be there.'

'Good,' he said and disconnected.

I showered and changed, and an hour later I was chaining the Vespa to a bike rack near the Smithsonian metro station. Enrique Navarro was standing next to the entrance to the Arts and Industries Building, debonair and dapper in pressed jeans, a button-down shirt with the cuffs rolled up, a cashmere sweater thrown over his shoulders. Aviator sunglasses.

He removed the sunglasses when he saw me. 'You came.'

'I said I would.'

'Let's walk.' He pointed in the direction of the Hirshhorn Museum. We crossed Jefferson Drive, dodging tour buses and cars looking for a place to park among the clogged traffic until we reached the gravel path of the Mall itself. Which was just as crowded as the sidewalk had been.

'If you wanted to have a private conversation, this isn't a very private place to do it.'

'Who said I wanted a private conversation? I just didn't want to talk over the phone.'

What *did* he want? Why did he call me?

'I wasn't aware you were friends with Robson Blake,' he went on in a conversational tone.

We shouldered our way around a knot of people poring over a map and trying to decide which museum to visit next.

'He hired me to take photographs for him,' I said. 'It was a professional relationship.'

'Did you ever go to his home?'

'Why do you want to know?' *What business was it of his anyway?*

'I knew Robbie as well,' he said. 'We were . . . well, more than acquaintances, I'd say. We also had a sort of professional relationship.'

Now he'd aroused my curiosity. Again. 'I've been to his house. Twice. The second time was the day he was murdered. The first time was a few days before that.'

'Then you no doubt saw for yourself what an incredible art collection he had.'

'I saw some of it. What was in his foyer and his library.' I left out the vault.

'I've seen quite a lot of it,' he said. 'Robbie and I met in Madrid several years ago when he was at an exhibition that I was attending because I was writing about it for *El País*. He seemed to think I knew a lot about art – especially Spanish art – because of my profession, so we struck up a friendship. When I came to Washington, he used to invite me to his home to see some new acquisition, something he wanted to show off. He also got in the habit of consulting me about a work of art he was considering purchasing when the artist was a Spaniard.'

'Do you also collect art?'

He nodded. 'Mostly modern Spanish art.'

Navarro seemed to be taking the long way around to get to whatever point it was he wanted to make.

'So,' he said in that same easygoing way, 'tell me about your meeting with Danilo.'

'What meeting with Danilo?'

'Oh, come on.' He sounded disappointed. 'Please don't play games. Of course you met.'

I didn't like *don't play games* much. So I said in a cool voice, 'I never said we did.'

'You didn't need to. I am certain you met.'

'And why is that?'

'Because of your connection to Robbie's death.'

I needed to put a stop to the direction of this conversation *now*.

'*I found Robbie*. There is *no* connection. I showed up for an appointment. He was dead when I got there.' Strictly speaking, all of that was true.

'Look,' he said, 'I . . . knew . . . Robbie owned items he acquired from individuals who trafficked in stolen or looted art. Art he obtained illegally.'

I stopped walking and stared at him. A couple with two small children who had taken over a nearby bench got up and left. Enrique steered me over to it before someone else could claim it.

'Let's sit,' he said.

Enrique knew Robbie dealt in stolen art. And he wanted to talk to Danny. He had just answered one of my biggest questions – actually, two of them. The first was whether the icon was the only item Robbie owned that had been stolen and the second was whether Robbie knew it was stolen. I now knew the correct answers thanks to him: one, no, and two, yes.

'Why are you telling me this?' I said. 'And how did you know Robbie owned stolen art?'

'To answer your second question, one day when I was visiting him, I recognized a painting that had been stolen from a small museum in Bilbao. I'd written a story about it. At first, I was certain he had no idea of the painting's provenance, but I saw more of his collection. He trusted me, so he showed me many of his acquisitions, plus he was proud of what he owned and wanted to show items off. So I started doing more research. There were other paintings, sculptures, a collection of Roman jewelry from the third century BC. Icons, a number of icons. Items that came from small museums, private collections, churches. Nothing big or flashy, you understand. Not the missing Vermeer or the Rembrandt stolen from the Isabella Stuart Gardner Museum or Van Gogh's poppy flowers, which was taken from the Mohamed Mahmoud Khalil Museum in Cairo.'

I shivered. 'All those items you just mentioned that were in Robbie's art collection were stolen?'

'Yes. And I saw only a portion of what he owned.'

'Did you ever confront him about it?'

'No.'

'*Why not?*'

'I wasn't ready. There was one piece of the puzzle that was still missing, and I needed some help.'

'Let me guess. You think Danny knew what that puzzle piece was?'

'Ah. Danny. Not Danilo. So you did meet with him.'

Dammit. I'd let that slip. I folded my arm across my chest and waited him out. *What puzzle piece?*

'All right,' he said. 'What I *think* is that Danilo and I can help each other. I *think* Robbie is exactly the sort of person Danilo – or Danny – would target if I am correct that he is part of a sort of art restitution squad that returns stolen art to its owners.' He waited, but when I was still silent, he added, 'And now Robbie is dead, and your name comes up in the middle of his murder investigation. To be frank, Sophie, you weren't surprised when I told you Robbie dealt in stolen art. So I suspect you already knew – and there's only one person who could have told you. Of course, now I also know I'm right about my supposition because you *did* meet.'

'Why does any of this matter *now*?' Was he manipulating me again? I stood up. 'Robbie is *dead*, Enrique. I should go.'

He laid a hand on my arm. 'Please sit down. I'm not finished. I have firsthand knowledge about many of the works of art and antiquities Robbie owns – owned – that were stolen. It's information I am willing to share with Danilo that I believe he will be interested to have.'

'In return for?'

He gave me a half-mocking smile. 'Oh, come on. Isn't it obvious to a fellow journalist? I want to write this story. It would be sensational, don't you agree? Billionaire philanthropist and art collector is also a dealer in stolen and plundered art. And the group of vigilantes who are committed to returning those items to their owners. It would also make a fascinating book, a bestseller, even – considering the subject.'

'Danny would never agree to talk to you if you wanted to expose what you believe he is doing.' *Plus he doesn't think of himself as a vigilante.* But I wasn't going to say that to Navarro.

He clicked his tongue against his teeth, tsk-tsking me. 'I am more and more certain I am right about what Danilo does. To be honest, I approve. So I would never do anything to jeopardize what I'm sure is a very risky and dangerous business. But I do want to know *how* he does it.'

'I can't help you with that, Enrique. I don't know where Danny is or how to reach him.' Which was one hundred percent true.

'Maybe you can answer this, then. Did Danilo know Robbie trafficked in stolen art?'

If we'd been in a room together, his stare would have pinned me to a wall. And if I answered him, Navarro's next question was going to be the burning question to which I also wanted the answer: was Danny at Robbie's house the day he was murdered?

Danny knew about the stolen icon because of me. Because I'd told him I'd seen it. Right now, there was no way in hell I wanted to let Enrique Navarro into the small, charmed circle of people who knew that piece of information, which consisted of Sam, Jack and Valerie Zhou. Sam was fanatical about attorney–client privilege, and Jack would go to his grave keeping my secret. Valerie was involved in this up to her eyebrows. There was no way she was going to talk, either.

'Danny came to Washington because he was aware that DC had become a new waypoint for plundered art to enter the US,' I said.

'You didn't answer my question.' He sounded pissed off. 'Or maybe you did. Either Danny knew about Robbie or he suspected him. As I said, I'd like to know *how* he figured that out.'

'You'd have to ask him.'

'Sophie,' he said, 'you and I, we are on the same side. I'm not the enemy. I have valuable information that Danilo needs – information he can use – that I will give him willingly. Help me out.'

'I'm sorry,' I said. 'I've told you everything I know. There's nothing else I have to say.' I got up.

'Don't underestimate me,' he said, and for the first time, I heard a hint of menace in his voice. 'I have excellent contacts and connections. If you won't help me, I'll find someone else. But then things might not go the best way for Danilo. Because, after all, even though what he's doing is commendable for those who harbor romantic fantasies about Robin Hood types, breaking and entering – and stealing – are illegal. Think about that, Sophie. You have my number. I'll give you time, but I don't have unlimited patience.'

I hate ultimatums. I hate being backed into corners. I hate being bullied.

I looked down at him. 'You do what you have to do,' I said and hoped I'd called his bluff. 'Because we're done here.'

I felt his dark eyes boring a hole into me as I threaded my way through the crowd, trying to lose myself as quickly as possible in a sea of tourists and locals enjoying a beautiful spring Sunday on the National Mall.

And wondered how much time Danny and I had before Navarro made good on his threat.

NINETEEN

I rode the Vespa up Connecticut Avenue, pushing it for all the speed it would give me – which wasn't a lot since it was a scooter, after all – but I needed to purge the anger that still burned in my throat after my meeting with Enrique Navarro. He'd asked me to trust him. I had no idea if I could, or even if I should. When I wouldn't help him, he'd threatened me.

So he knew about Robbie dealing in stolen art. *That* had been a surprise. A bigger surprise had been that he wanted to capitalize on that knowledge and write a tell-all exposé that was sure to make him a candidate for another Ortega y Gasset Award. Then turn it into a bestselling book.

I rode partway around Dupont Circle and signaled to turn off at New Hampshire Avenue, passing the entrance to the Dupont Underground. The chain-link barricade covered the stairwell today, so the gallery was closed. Darius Zahiri, its director, was a good friend. After my grandfather passed away, Darius and I had worked together to set up a retrospective of some of his edgy, previously unknown photos of the celebrities, world leaders, and sports legends he had photographed. The show, which had been the Underground's first post-pandemic event, had been a huge success. Darius had pushed me hard to give the talk my grandfather would have given at the opening. For someone like me, an introvert who was infinitely more comfortable behind the camera than in front of it, speaking to a large audience had been a challenge. But it had gone so well that the calls and emails from people who wanted to hire me had nearly quadrupled since then. After the exhibit was over, Darius continued to stay in touch and our friendship had blossomed.

In addition to managing the Underground, he also owned a small publishing company specializing in high-end coffee-table art books. What were the odds Darius knew Olivia Sage who *wrote* high-end coffee-table art books? It had to be a small world.

I called him when I got home and reached his voicemail. Darius could be anywhere in the world – literally. I still didn't know much about his personal life except that his grandparents had fled Iran during the ouster of the Shah in the late 1970s and the family settled in London where Darius grew up. He came to the US ten years ago, but he was constantly traveling abroad: jetting off to someone's private island in the Caribbean, a ski holiday in Gstaad, an ex-lover's birthday party in Paris, a few weeks at a current paramour's villa in Cap d'Antibes.

He called me back an hour later. He was in town.

'Sophie, love. I've been worried about you. I've been meaning to call. How are you?' Darius had a voice like honey over gravel, a low, sexy growl. And a cut-glass British accent.

Of course he knew about me finding Robbie the day he was murdered. The whole world knew.

'I'm OK,' I said. 'But I have a favor to ask. Any chance you might be free for dinner tonight?'

'I've been trying to get you to go out with me for months,' he said. 'You know how I feel about you. So now are *you* asking me on a date?'

'Darius, you have so many girlfriends that I couldn't possibly ask you on a date and get involved with you. I couldn't handle all the competition. You'd just break my heart.'

He roared with laughter. 'I'm supposed to meet someone for drinks tonight, but for you, my darling, I'll postpone. I'll make reservations for the two of us and text you the link, OK?'

'Thank you,' I said. 'And I hope she won't be too devastated when you postpone.'

More laughter, then he disconnected.

He'd made reservations for us at Zaytinya, José Andrés' Mediterranean tapas restaurant in Penn Quarter, a place that was so popular you usually needed to book weeks in advance. If I asked him how he'd managed to conjure a reservation in a couple of hours, he'd just wink at me and laugh.

He was waiting when I got there, devastatingly handsome as usual in a navy blazer, open-neck dress shirt, and jeans. Longish wavy jet-black hair, dark eyes, dark-complexioned, hawk-like nose, the noble features of a Persian warrior. He *would* be easy to fall for. Darius collected girlfriends like he collected art for the Dupont Underground, with an experienced, sophisticated eye. Beautiful gazelle-like creatures, each one more stunning than the last, until someone else caught his attention and he moved on to his next love. Or else he just juggled multiple affairs.

He slipped an arm around my waist and kissed me on the cheek, deliberately eyeing the way my long-sleeved black dress hugged me like a second skin. A deep V-neck and a lace cutout at the hem, black stiletto heels, my hair pulled back in a French braid, gold hoop earrings and a braided chain of yellow, white and rose gold Nick had given me that I rarely took off.

'You look gorgeous, darling,' he said. 'As always. I've asked for a table outside under one of the tents. I hope that's OK?'

'Perfect,' I said.

The maître d' led us to our table and passed us menus, murmuring *bon appetit* before he left. As he did, a waiter glided over and lit the candle in the hurricane lamp before filling our water glasses and asking if we wanted a cocktail or a glass of wine. Darius didn't drink alcohol, but he talked me into having champagne and ordered sparkling water with lime for himself.

'I read about you finding Robbie Blake,' he said. 'That must have been awful.'

'It was.'

'Are you OK?'

I shrugged. 'I don't know if anyone's ever OK after seeing someone who has been killed so brutally. I saw enough death and killing when I worked for IPS and I was sent to war zones. I think the day you get used to it is the day you lose some of your humanity, you know? Especially when it's something like this – someone you know who was murdered in their own home, a place that's supposed to be safe. A sanctuary.'

'I'm so sorry, love. I knew him, too. He was a friend.' He raised an eyebrow. 'You . . . obviously . . . were, too?'

His subtle way of probing. He wasn't asking about friendship: he wanted to know whether Robbie and I had been romantically involved.

'It was a business relationship, Darius. I had an appointment to take an author photo for a book he was collaborating on with Olivia Sage. You must know her, too?'

'I do. Interesting woman. Very bright. She and Robbie were close.'

'I saw pictures of the two of them together. Feminine intuition says she had quite a crush on him. Maybe she was even in love with him.'

'Their relationship was an open secret among their friends, though they never spoke about it.' He leaned closer to me, dropping his voice as if we were conspirators. 'Jerome spent so much time in New York. He had his dalliances up there, actresses who appeared in his shows. She had Robbie.'

'Was he smitten as well?'

'Robbie had . . . other women. Olivia pretended not to know, but, of course, she did. He wasn't always subtle.'

'That must have been hard on her. I imagine it would be difficult not to be jealous. Or even angry.'

'Like I said, she kept how she felt to herself. And she *was* married. He was not – he was free to see whomever he liked out in the open. It was different for her.'

Our waiter arrived with my flute of champagne and a bottle of San Pellegrino and a glass of ice with a lime for Darius. He also told us about the specials that weren't on the menu and said he'd give us a few minutes before returning for our dinner order.

When he was gone, Darius said, 'From what I heard and read, it sounded as if Robbie might have surprised someone who had broken into his home, an intruder. Though I would have thought with the security system he had, it would have been almost impossible for an alarm not to go off or someone not to know about it.'

I intended to ask him more questions about Olivia, so fair play to him that he was probing for information that wasn't in the news about what had happened.

'It's also possible the killer was someone he knew,' I said, leaving out the fact that the alarm and the security cameras had been deliberately turned off. 'Someone Robbie invited to his house. Maybe they got into an argument and it turned violent. When I found him, it didn't look as if he'd tried to fight back.'

'Wait. You're *not* suggesting Olivia might have been there and she killed him?' Darius raised his voice in surprise and a few heads turned in our direction.

I put my finger to my lips. 'Shhh. I wasn't suggesting anything. But since you mention it – and you *do* know her – what do you think? *Could* she have done it? Jealousy is a powerful motivator.'

'I don't think she's the type.'

I sipped my champagne and shook my head. 'Nick used to say *everyone* is the type. He always told me that we never know what any of us is capable of doing in the middle of a white-hot argument, that moment of complete fury when we just *lose* it, forget who we are as rational, sane, normal people and do something in a fit of rage that changes the trajectory of our lives forever. You're capable of murder, Darius, and so am I.'

The waiter appeared again. Darius held up a finger, a request for more time, and he retreated.

'I think we should look at the menu. And I wonder if our waiter didn't overhear our conversation, or at least part of it. He looked as if he might be considering removing the knives and any other sharp objects from our table.'

We decided to share the mezze plates, so we agreed on smoked mushrooms, crispy Brussels sprouts, and kofte kabobs. Pita and hummus as a starter. I asked for something called *imam bayldi* – eggplant, onions and tomato slow-cooked in olive oil with aromatic spices and pine nuts – because the description said it was inspired by the legendary preparation from the Ottoman era. A Byzantine dish that sounded exotic.

Darius asked for the wine menu and handed it to me. I chose a glass of dry white wine from Cyprus. He chose something called lemontha – lemon, sparkling water and orange blossom.

After the waiter left, he touched his glass to mine. 'To what do I really owe the pleasure of your company this evening, Sophie? Why do I think it has something to do with Robbie?'

Darius was shrewd, smart. He was also discreet. I had already decided I was going to tell him I'd found out Robbie trafficked in stolen art. If he didn't know already, he was well connected to the art world, not only in DC but also in New York and abroad. He'd ask questions. Get answers. *Find out.*

'You'd be right,' I said, smiling at him to take the sting out of it. 'As you usually are. Not that I didn't want to see you, of course.'

'But you want something.' A statement.

My turn to lean close to him. 'I want to *tell* you something. Did you know that Robbie was dealing in stolen art?'

He didn't have to answer.

He did not know. The look he gave me was as if I'd just rolled a grenade with the pin pulled into the middle of our table.

I touched his sleeve and said in a voice so soft that he had to lean even closer to catch my words, 'It's true, Darius. You're the fourth person I've told. My lawyer and a priest who is an old friend know. So does a woman who is . . . involved . . . in this. A journalist

I spoke to confirmed it today – he saw a painting in Robbie's collection that he recognized as having been stolen from a museum in Spain because he had written the news story about the break-in and the burglary. I'm not the only one who knows.'

Our pita, hummus and drinks arrived. The waiter, who still looked a bit ill at ease around us, departed quickly.

'Sophie, are you *sure*?'

'Very.'

'You told me you just met Robbie. That's a hell of an accusation. Robson Blake is – *was* – an incredibly generous and much-beloved philanthropist. Do you have any idea how many works of art he's donated to museums and cultural institutions all over the world? The *value* of what he's donated?'

'I imagine it's in the millions, if not billions.'

'You'd imagine right. How do you know this, anyway? Who told *you*?'

'A good journalist never burns a source. You know that.'

'Then *why* are you telling me this? You haven't answered that question yet.'

Our tapas arrived. We hadn't touched the pita or hummus because our conversation had been so intense. The waiter moved the plates off to one side so he could set down our dinner dishes, explaining each one and wishing us *bon appetit* once again. The two of us silently traded plates back and forth – a temporary truce in our heated discussion – until we had sampled everything.

I dug a fork into the imam bayldi. 'I told you because I thought you might know or maybe you'd heard rumors about stolen art coming through DC even if you didn't know who was involved.'

'Darling, so much stolen art enters this country that you just *assume* it's happening here as well. The borders for that kind of thing are porous, nearly non-existent in some instances. Most people can't tell the difference between the real thing and a fake or a copy, anyway.'

'The thief knows it's the real thing,' I said. 'That's what makes it so valuable.'

'Not necessarily. Even if the thief does know a stolen item is genuine, it's not always as valuable as you might think,' he said. 'Here's the thing. Most art thieves aren't that bright. They steal a work of art – sometimes they just walk into a museum, a small one with poor security, a single guard who needs to take the occasional bathroom break, and literally take a painting off the wall. Then they run out the door and, honest to God, get away. So now our thief's got a painting worth, say, a million dollars. He figured out how to steal it but forgot to think about what's next. How's he going to get his money for it because no one will touch it? It's too hot. So the million-dollar painting ends up being sold for nearly nothing to someone who'll just take it off his hands. It happens all the time.'

Our waiter came by to ask how our meal was and seemed pleased that we had finally begun eating, especially because Darius was already helping himself to seconds.

'Everything is outstanding,' Darius said. 'As always.'

After he left, I said, 'I suppose that explains why you read about someone buying a painting in a dusty old shop and it's a long-lost Rembrandt. It's the reason Robbie said he got into collecting. He found a couple of drawings in a bookstore in Marseilles years ago that turned out to belong to Eugène Delacroix. He bought them for nothing, discovered their provenance and sold them for a lot of money.'

Darius tore off a piece of pita bread and scooped up some hummus. 'That happens all the time, too,' he said. 'I don't know if you remember a story about the mayor of a French town who happened to read about an interview with Madonna – the actress and singer, *not* Jesus' mother – that happened to also have a photograph taken in her home in London. Behind her was – supposedly – a painting that Louis XVIII had commissioned for Versailles and which the Louvre later loaned to a museum in that town. Except the town had been bombed at the end of World War I and the painting was presumed to have been destroyed.'

'I did read about that,' I said. 'Madonna said she bought a copy of the painting from Sotheby's, knowing the original had been destroyed.'

'There's still a controversy over it. Including between the mayor and the director of the museum. Who knows how it will end up?' he said. 'But that kind of thing happens when there's a break in the link tracing the provenance of a piece of art.'

'So how does it get fixed?'

'Sometimes it doesn't. Sometimes what happens if the object is stolen is the thieves or the corrupt dealer establish a false trail of ownership so they can sell whatever it is,' he said. 'Perhaps it belonged to someone who is dead and can't verify provenance.

That's one way. Or the item appears in an auction catalog or some-where else in print. That's another way of conferring legitimacy. You establish a new trail of provenance that doesn't get discovered for years until someone spots it by accident, by chance, like the mayor of that French town did.'

I nodded and Darius gave me a shrewd look. 'There's something you're *not* telling me, Sophie. Another piece of art that Robbie owned – besides that Spanish painting – that you *know* is stolen. And I'm assuming you believe *he* knew it was stolen as well.' He set his fork down and waited.

'You . . . are right. About everything. But if I told you, it might accidentally incriminate someone who is innocent.'

'Don't you think you can trust me, darling?'

'Of course I do. But this is complicated and it's . . . personal. I'm sorry, Darius. This time I can't say anything.'

'You can't? Or you won't?'

Sam knew about Danny because he was my lawyer. Jack knew because he wouldn't tell a soul. Valerie Zhou knew because she was involved with what Danny did, and right now she was my only conduit to reach him. The list of people I could discuss this with ended with those three.

'I can't,' I told him in a firm voice. 'Believe me, I'm already in this deeper than I want to be.'

Plus, what Darius had said made me wonder about the icon if, in fact, it was missing from Robbie's house. Besides Danny, who else would take it? What could they do with it? Where could they sell it?

It seemed to me that all roads led back to Danny. If he had the icon, I had a pretty good idea of what he would do with it: see that it made its way back to Ukraine and to the little church in Kyiv. But that also tied him to being at Robbie's home the day he was murdered. And to the question that terrified me: had he killed Robson Blake, even if it had been unintentional?

Darius was watching me, his handsome face impassive in the flickering candlelight, his eyes opaque and dark. 'If that's true, you'd better be careful, Sophie,' he said, and the warning in his voice gave me the shivers. 'Get too close to the fire and you know what happens. And by the look on your face, I'm guessing you already feel the heat.'

I met his eyes and said, 'I do.'

TWENTY

After dessert and Turkish coffee during which we both had been unusually quiet, we shared an Uber that first took me to my house; then Darius was going on to an address I knew wasn't his.

'A double date tonight? Me for dinner and your drinks friend for an after-dinner drink instead?' I teased him gently. And Darius being Darius, probably a sleepover.

He flashed a wicked grin. 'Darling, you know I never kiss and tell.'

He asked the driver to wait while he walked me to my front door. I got a brotherly kiss on the cheek – and another warning. This one even more sternly delivered.

'You had very specific questions for me tonight about stolen art and false provenance. I hope you aren't protecting someone who is guilty of either of those because you're talking about conspiracy and criminal possession of stolen property. Serious crimes. People go to jail when they're caught. For *decades*.'

'No, I'm not. It's not that at all,' I said, my voice breathless. 'It's something else.'

A brother I scarcely know who might have committed unintentional homicide but whom I'm protecting anyway.

'You're going to ask around, see what you can find out about what Robbie was involved in, maybe who his dealer was,' I said. 'And if you learn anything, will you please let me know what you find out?'

'What makes you so sure that's what I'm going to do?'

'Because I know you. Because you're so well connected. *Because you want to know, too.* Don't you? Was one of the wealthiest and most generous philanthropists in America dealing in stolen and plundered art? How deeply was he involved? How long had it been going on?'

'You ask a lot, darling. You want to hold back information, but you also expect me to tell all.'

'Darius,' I said. 'You don't *want* to know what I know. You're better off not knowing.'

He leaned forward and his lips touched my forehead. 'My God, Sophie,' he murmured in my ear. 'Now I'm really worried about you.'

Upstairs in my bedroom, I slipped out of my dress and kicked off the heels, changing into workout clothes and sneakers. Then I made my usual evening cup of tea, poured it into an insulated mug and took it and Olivia's two books on Byzantine art across the alley to my studio. Darius had explained how it was possible to reinvent the provenance of a stolen or looted piece of art and, voilà, suddenly it had a legitimate pedigree. Maybe a few pesky gaps in ownership, if we were talking about centuries, but still. One way of doing that was to tie it to someone who was dead and couldn't refute or validate ownership. Another was for the item to appear in print somewhere.

What were the odds Olivia Sage had been brazen and audacious enough to use photos of items from Robbie's collection that had been stolen and print them in those beautiful coffee-table books Jack had loaned me? Maybe those odds were pretty damn good. Who would dream that a respected scholar, one of the world's experts on Byzantine art, and an incredibly generous billionaire philanthropist would be collectors – knowingly – of looted and stolen art and artifacts? No one, that's who. Robbie could buy anything he wanted; he had all the money in the world. Olivia's reputation was pure gold.

Why would they do it? Risk everything?

Because, as Danny had said to me the other night, *they could get away with it.* It was a vicarious, adrenalin-fueled thrill. Dangerous. A temptation to flirt with the dark side and not get caught.

Danny had also explained where I could go to find out if that's exactly what Olivia had done: to the ArtRevive database. I sat down at my computer, booted it up and did a search for ArtRevive. When I clicked on the link, it became clear this wasn't going to be as easy as I thought. First, I needed an account, so I created one. Then I needed to fill out a lengthy form containing detailed information about the item I believed had been stolen. Last of all, I had to hand over 300 euros. For each search. Searches didn't come cheap, and my requests would be forwarded to the ArtRevive experts who would then comb the 700,000-plus items registered with their database to see if they got a hit and found a match. It would take time and then I'd get my reply.

Either I was going to do this or I wasn't. There were two particularly beautiful icons in Olivia's book on Russian and Ukrainian icons that belonged to Robbie; the book had been published only last year. The first was called the Holy Trinity – the original and most famous icon had been painted in the fifteenth century by Russia's greatest icon painter, Andrei Rublev. It was a serene portrait of three angels seated at a table, representing the Father, Son and Holy Spirit. The second was a copy of another famous icon, also of Mary, the Mother of God, and was called the Theotokos of Smolensk. The original, which was believed to have been painted by St Luke the Evangelist and ended up in Russia when it was given as a wedding present in the eleventh century, had been lost during World War II when the Germans occupied the city of Smolensk where the icon had been kept. A copy was now in the church in Smolensk, and it was almost as beautiful as the original painted by St Luke.

Both of Robbie's icons were exquisite; both were magnificent copies. Had he acquired them legitimately or had they been stolen, like the Virgin of Vladimir? I filled out two sets of paperwork, added my credit card information and hit the *search* button. Done. Locked up the studio and walked back to my apartment. I was lying in bed watching the patterns of the tree branches and their tiny new leaves move and shimmer on my bedroom wall when I wondered – as Darius had said – whether I had only thought through the first step of my possibly foolish attempt to find out if Robson Blake dealt in stolen art abetted by Olivia Sage. But if the ArtRevive searches revealed that the other icons had been stolen – the ones in Olivia's book – that changed everything. They were in this together.

Still, it was probably a long shot.

And what was I going to do with that information if I found out I was right, that those icons *were* stolen?

My phone rang early the next morning. I reached over and picked it up off my bedside table.

Jack.

'I've got news,' he said. 'I saw Olivia yesterday when I was over on the main campus. She's taking Robbie's death hard.'

'I'm so sorry.'

'She also said she would like to meet you. And she was touched by your generous offer to let her use one of the photographs you took of him the other day.' There was a hint of reproach in his voice.

I cringed. 'Thank you for doing that.'

He ignored my thanks and said, 'Olivia asked whether you'd like to come by her apartment this afternoon. She's planning to take a few days of personal leave from the university so she can plan Robbie's funeral.'

'She's planning his funeral?'

'Yup.'

'They really were close, weren't they?'

'Very,' he said. 'She says she wants to make sure he gets the tribute he deserves. Unquote. It's going to be at National Cathedral. The church will probably be packed.'

It probably would be. Robbie had touched the lives of so many people with his generosity. His funeral at National Cathedral would be a big deal.

I closed my eyes. 'Can you tell her that, yes, I'd like to see her this afternoon? Just let me know what time and where.'

'Sure,' he said. 'I'll get back in touch with her and text you the information. And Sophie?'

'What?'

'This . . . thing . . . is way beyond you – you know that, don't you? The police are looking for whoever murdered Robson Blake. If he was involved in trafficking stolen art, it's going to come out like I told you. Maybe not right away, but sooner or later. You don't have to be involved anymore. Give Olivia the photos and then you're done.'

'Right. Thanks, Jack. Bye.'

'Let me know how it goes with Olivia,' he said and disconnected.

He was wrong. I wasn't done once I gave Olivia the photos. I was still very, very involved.

Olivia Sage lived in The Westchester, a complex of cooperative apartments that was located on one of the highest points in the city on upper Connecticut Avenue. Built in the 1930s in the Art Deco style, five buildings sprawled across ten acres, the centerpiece of which was a beautiful three-tier sunken garden with a fountain at its center. I drove through the magnificent entrance – wrought-iron

gates and pillars that had been brought over from an English estate
that had been destroyed in World War II – and squeezed the Mini
into a parking spot near her building.

Olivia's apartment was on the seventh floor of the main building.
She opened the door when I rang the bell and looked nothing like
any photo I'd seen of her. Robbie's death had obviously devastated
her; she was dressed in black, and although she'd made an effort to
put on makeup, her face was so pale that her red lipstick looked like
a slash of blood, and the two streaks of blush on her cheeks could
have been bruises that were healing. I guessed she was in her late
fifties or early sixties, despite the dark-brown shoulder-length hair.

She opened the door wider and said, 'Sophie? Won't you come
in?'

'Thank you.' I stepped inside and found myself in a dining area
that gave way to a sun-drenched living room.

'We can talk in the living room,' she said. 'Take care. There are
two steps down.'

There were three large windows that looked out on National
Cathedral and walls lined with overflowing bookcases and art.
A grand piano – a Steinway – near the windows dominated the
room, which was an eclectic amalgamation of Broadway-meets-
Byzantine scholarship that, surprisingly, worked. Framed posters
of Jerome Sage's shows starring some of the biggest names on
Broadway and Hollywood were juxtaposed with rich saturated
paintings and numerous icons: the angel visiting the Virgin Mary
in the Annunciation, the twelve Apostles standing side by side, the
Archangel Gabriel. Framed pages from a very old, very beautiful,
illuminated manuscript. Books were piled on the coffee table, on
end tables, and stacked on the floor next to a comfortable-looking
recliner that reminded me of Jack's and where, I guessed, Olivia
spent most of her time reading.

'Please, have a seat.' She gestured to the sofa and sat down next
to me.

'I'm very sorry for your loss,' I said.

'You found him.' Her voice ached with sadness and grief.

'I did,' I said. 'It looked as if whoever hit him came up from
behind him and he wasn't aware of what was happening. I don't
think he suffered.'

I had no way of knowing whether that was true or not, but her
eyes flickered and she looked a bit less haunted.

'He was struck with a tripod,' she said. 'That's what killed him
– the blow to his head.'

I caught my breath. Ellis must have told her that, so the word
was out. I wondered who else knew that fact, whether it had been
leaked to the press.

Grace? She would have called. Instantly. Worried *and* mad that
she hadn't learned about it from me.

Navarro, with his gold-plated contacts? That would be all I needed
– more ammunition for him.

I nodded to Olivia. 'Yes. That's right.'

'The tripod belonged to you,' she said, and I couldn't tell if that
was an accusation or a question.

'I left it by accident when I was there a few days earlier. Bernard,
the gentleman who takes care of Mr Blake's . . . Robbie's . . . art
collection – as, of course, you know – helped me carry my equipment upstairs. The tripod got left behind and I didn't realize it at
the time.'

Her eyes flickered again. My explanation made sense. She nodded.

'You knew him well,' I said. 'Did he have any enemies? Anyone
who was angry enough to want to kill him?'

Her head snapped back, and she gave me a cold look. '*No one*
wanted to kill him. Robbie didn't have any enemies.'

Sorry, but that was flat-out *wrong*. You didn't get to be as
successful a businessman as Robbie had been without alienating a
few people along the way. Plus, what about whoever he dealt with
who had sold him stolen art? They weren't model citizens who
played nice.

Surely that thought had occurred to her as well. Especially because
she *had* to know some of his partners in crime, didn't she? I'd just
bet 600 euros that she did.

Maybe she thought I was naive. She certainly didn't realize I
knew about the stolen icon.

'Then what do you think happened?' I asked her.

'Obviously, it was a burglary that went wrong.'

'The security cameras were turned off. The staff was gone. The
door was unlocked. That's how I got in. I walked in. It doesn't
sound like a burglary to me. Like I said, it didn't appear that he
tried to fight his attacker off.'

'He was struck from behind. The thief surprised him. You just
told me that.'

'I did. But it also could have been someone he let in. Someone he knew,' I said. 'Do you know what happened to the icon that was in the kiot? The door was open and the kiot was empty.'

She looked startled and her eyes hardened. Our conversation shifted to a whole new level of who knew what.

'How do you know about the icon?' Suspicion with an edge of anger.

'The Virgin of Vladimir? I saw it. Unintentionally. Bernard left the door to the icon room in the vault open. I took the elevator to the wrong floor. When I got there on Friday, the kiot was in his study and it was empty.'

'I don't know what happened to it,' she said. 'It's *gone*.'

'So whoever killed him took the icon.' Jesus, Lord. Please don't let it be Danny.

'It would seem so.'

'Meaning it *was* a burglary,' I said.

'That's what I said, didn't I?'

'Why would Robbie have moved it from the vault downstairs to the library upstairs?'

'He often did things like that. Especially if he had something he wanted to show off.'

We were back where we started. 'If that's why he did it, then he was expecting someone,' I said.

'He was expecting *you*. You had an appointment with him.'

She was right. Maybe it *was* me. Maybe Robbie found out I'd seen the icon room on my first visit and decided to bring the Virgin of Vladimir upstairs where I could examine it more closely.

I nodded. 'I did have an appointment with him. OK, maybe it was in the library so he could show it to me.'

She shrugged and I could tell she wanted to end this conversation.

'Was anything else stolen?' I asked.

'Why do you want to know?'

'I . . . was there. His collection was so magnificent. I hope the answer is no.'

'It is no.'

'Then why did the thief choose *only* that icon?'

She gave me a cool look and said, with some frost in her voice, 'I have absolutely no idea. I'm sure once the police catch his killer, they'll learn all the answers. As for you, Ms Medina, you are asking a lot of questions. Now it's my turn: why do you want to know all these things? You're a journalist. Is this some kind of interview and you're grilling me without being upfront about it?'

'I'm a photographer,' I said. 'And I no longer work for International Press Service if that's what you're referring to. I haven't worked for them for years.'

'Then what is it? Because you clearly have an agenda.'

I want to know if you and Robbie dealt in stolen art. I'm worried my brother might have been at Robbie's house before I was, and either Robbie surprised him or the other way around – and things went very wrong.

'I'm the one who found him. He was killed with my tripod. I'm a possible suspect, Doctor Sage. The lead detective on the investigation sat me down and questioned me the night Robbie was killed. So, yes, I'm curious. You're right about that.'

My backpack was on the carpet next to me. I picked it up, unzipped it and took out a large envelope, which I set on the sofa between us.

'As Jack O'Hara might have told you, I took some photos of Robbie in his study the first time I was at his home. My appointment on Friday was to take proper author photos for a book he was collaborating on with you, but obviously that never happened. I thought you might like these; maybe you could use one of them since they're more recent.'

She slid the photos out of the envelope and looked at them for a long time. When she looked up, her eyes were moist, and she was trying not to cry. 'These are wonderful,' she said. 'You captured him so well.'

'Thank you.'

'May I keep them?'

'Of course. They're for you. If there's one in particular that you would like to use as an author photo, please let me know and I'll send you an electronic image. The information for each photo and my contact information are on the back, so I'll know which one you choose. I only ask that you give me photo credit.'

'Of course.'

'Jack O'Hara had copies of a couple of your books which Robbie collaborated on with you,' I said. 'How did your collaboration . . . work?'

Olivia Sage was no one's fool. She knew exactly what I was asking. 'It worked very well.'

Game, set and match to her. She was done with this conversation.
'What happens to his collection now?' I asked.

'I am the executrix of his estate,' she said, which answered any more unasked questions I might have had about the nature of their relationship: she was in charge of *everything*. 'So I happen to know exactly what happens to it. He's donating it to various museums around the world, though the lion's share goes to the National Gallery in Washington. He's made a few bequests, of course. But he's donating almost everything he owned.'

'That's very generous,' I said.

'*Robbie* was very generous,' she said. 'He was a wonderful man. A *good* man.' She stood up. 'Thank you for the photos, Ms Medina. I'll be in touch.'

I was dismissed.

I drove home sifting through what she had said and what questions she'd dodged. Did she really believe Robbie was killed during a burglary? That it was totally random, and he didn't know his murderer?

If that was true, Danny fit the description of who killed Robson Blake to a T.

If it wasn't true, it seemed more likely Robbie knew his killer. He had invited him or her to his home, turned off his security cameras and met whoever it was when his staff was away. Plus, he expected that meeting to be over before I showed up at five o'clock. If that was what had happened, I wondered if his visitor had been someone he dealt with to acquire his stolen or looted art. Which might explain why the icon was in his study.

It wasn't there so I could have a closer look at it. Robbie brought it upstairs from the vault to show someone else – Olivia was right about that – perhaps a potential buyer. So either that individual killed him and then walked out of his house with the icon or Danny got there first. And he took it.

After he killed Robbie.

TWENTY-ONE

I t was just after four when I parked the Mini in the alley behind the house and in front of a black Audi that belonged to Gil Tessier. I heard their voices as soon as I got out of the car – Gil's distinctive French accent and Max's aristocratic Charleston drawl – floating over the backyard fence, a heated discussion ensuing between the two of them. I slammed the car door and the conversation stopped abruptly.

A moment later, Max called out. 'Sophie? Up here.'

I shielded my eyes from the late-afternoon sunshine and looked up. He was standing at the railing of his deck, holding a glass of wine.

'I thought I heard a car door. Gil's here.' He hoisted his glass. 'We're having a drink on the deck. Come up and join us, won't you? The patio door is open.'

My head was still swimming with theories about Olivia Sage and how deeply she'd been involved with Robbie. She'd told me as much as she was going to share. But Max and Gil knew her, too. They had to, since they'd been good friends with Robbie. Hadn't Darius said Robbie's relationship with Olivia had been an open secret among their friends? Maybe Max and Gil knew something. Maybe they'd be willing to talk, say more than they had the other day now that more time had passed.

'I'll be right up.'

Max's spacious deck was furnished with his usual good taste, as if it were an extra room in his eclectic apartment. A black wrought-iron table and four matching chairs where he dined outdoors with friends in good weather. A wicker love seat with oversized cushions upholstered in masculine shades of brown and beige, a pair of matching chairs, a glass-and-wicker coffee table. Hanging baskets with the last of the yellow and orange winter pansies and large ceramic planters that were empty until the danger of frost had passed, which would be in the next few weeks.

Gil lay sprawled on the sofa, holding his wine glass so it rested on his chest, shirt untucked in faded jeans and expensive-looking leather shoes that I knew were Italian because he bought all his shoes in Italy, the no-socks look that was fashionable just now. Max sat on one of the chairs opposite him, well-pressed khakis, pale-pink dress shirt open at the neck, loosened blue paisley tie, papers fanned out on the coffee table, what looked like spreadsheets with columns of numbers. He scooped up the papers, shoving everything in a file folder as I stepped on to the deck. A bottle of white wine sat in a silver ice bucket next to the folder.

Gil raised his wine glass as if he were saluting me. 'Good to see you, Sophie. Have some wine and catch up with us.'

His gaze was a bit unfocused. Max caught my eye with a look that said, *He's had a few.*

'It's good to see you, too, Gil.'

'Can I get you a glass of wine?' Max asked me. 'We're drinking Sauvignon Blanc.'

He started to reach for the bottle, but Gil pre-empted him. 'I've got it. Looks like we need another. This one's almost empty.'

'Please don't bother,' I said. 'If I have a drink now, I'll fall asleep, and I've still got some work to do this evening.'

'In that case I don't think we need another bottle, Gil, if Sophie's not drinking,' Max said in a mild tone. 'We're good.' Which translated into *You've had enough, my friend.*

Gil deliberately poured the last of the bottle into his glass, sloshing a little on the table, and gave Max a sullen look. 'If you say so.'

Whatever tension had been simmering between them before I arrived seemed to seep back into the air. If it had something to do with the papers in that folder, it was probably business-related.

'Have a seat, Sophie,' Max was saying. 'At least, stay for a bit. I've been meaning to stop by and check on you, see how you're doing.'

I took the other wicker chair next to him. 'I'm doing OK, thanks.'

'You've been working late,' he said. 'I've seen the lights in your studio.'

'Thanks, Mom.'

He grinned. 'Sorry. You know I keep an eye on you.'

'Have you heard anything new about the investigation into Robbie's death?' Gil asked, sitting up.

'Me? No. Nothing. Why do you ask?'

'Well, because you're the one who found him. I wondered if maybe you'd talked to the police again.'

He meant *Or they've talked to you.* I forced a smile. 'No, I haven't heard anything or talked to anyone.'

At least, not yet.

Gil sounded solicitous, concerned. But there was an element of the macabre pleasure and fascination of a voyeur. He wanted to *know.*

'I imagine there'll be an announcement about a funeral or a memorial service soon,' Max said, changing the subject as he sat back in his chair and crossed one long leg over the other.

'It's going to be at National Cathedral,' I said. 'Olivia Sage is planning it. She says it's going to be a big deal. That's a quote.'

'How do *you* know that?' Gil gave me a sharp-eyed look.

'Olivia told me. I was with her at her apartment just now.'

'*Livvie.* Good Lord. I haven't called her since it happened. She must be devastated.' Max threw an anguished glance at Gil. 'Have you spoken to her?'

'Of course, I have. I called her as soon as I heard it on the news, then I stopped by her apartment to check on her.' He sounded reproachful, chiding Max for his thoughtlessness. To me, he said, 'How do you know Olivia?'

'Through a Jesuit friend who teaches at Georgetown Law School.'

'Jack O'Hara,' Max said and I nodded.

'Why were you visiting her?' Gil asked. 'If I may ask.'

Well, you did ask. He had a lot of questions for me today. I would tell him, but then I had a few questions of my own.

'Robbie hired me to take some formal headshots because he needed an updated author photo for the latest book he was working on with Olivia. It was her idea – apparently, it was a demand.' I explained about the candids I'd taken and bringing them over to show Olivia.

'How was she when you saw her?' Max asked.

'I'd say she's still in shock. I think planning his funeral is helping her, giving her a purpose, something to do other than grieve. She's convinced Robbie surprised a burglar who got into the house, that it was a random thing.'

'How'd somebody get past that Fort Knox security system he has?' Max said. 'In broad daylight, no less?'

'The security system was turned off.'

The two of them exchanged knowing glances.

'He did that from time to time,' Gil said. 'Robbie could be a

little paranoid about privacy, especially when he had certain . . .
visitors.'

Was Gil talking about the people Robbie dealt with who trafficked
in stolen art? *Those* visitors? Did *he* know about them, too? Did *Max*?

'What kind of visitors?' I asked.

'*Female* visitors,' Gil said in a way that I wouldn't mistake what
he meant. 'Robbie had quite an active . . . social life.'

Escorts. Companions. Darius had mentioned other women. Was
that why the alarm had been turned off? He'd been having sex, and
he didn't want the identity of his guest revealed on a security video?

'So that would mean that whoever was with him was someone
he knew,' I said.

Which brought me back to Olivia. Maybe she had walked in and
discovered Robbie *in flagrante delicto*. Maybe she just lost it.

'If that's true, then why did Olivia think it was a burglary?' Max
asked. 'What was taken?'

'An icon. There was an empty kiot in the library. I'd seen it the
last time I was there with the icon in it. The Virgin of Vladimir. I
don't think the police have released that information yet, by the
way, so please keep it to yourselves.'

'That doesn't make sense,' Max said. 'That's *all* that was taken
– a single icon?'

'Apparently.' Now it was my turn to ask questions. 'Olivia said
Robbie didn't have any enemies, at least no one who hated him
enough to commit murder. But someone did. What about you two?
Don't you have *any* ideas who might have done it?'

Max straightened the edges of the papers in the file folder, even
though they were perfectly aligned, a time-wasting distraction. 'You
said Livvie believes Robbie surprised someone who walked into his
house. She's probably in the best position to know,' he said.
Equivocating. Was that because he *did* have an idea who Robbie's
killer might be?

'He didn't fight back,' I said. 'It was the middle of the day, as
you just said. You really don't think it could have been whoever
was with him – either a female guest or someone else? Maybe even
Olivia?'

Max's jaw tightened. 'No, *definitely* not Livvie.'

'What about you, Gil?'

'I agree it was someone he knew. Someone he let in or invited
to his home.'

'So why not Olivia?' I asked.

'Because she *loved* Robbie.' Max said.

'There's a fine line between love and jealousy, especially obsessive love,' I said. 'From what you just said, Robbie gave Olivia plenty of reasons to be jealous of the other women he saw.'

'She would do anything *for* him,' he said. 'But she would never, ever be so enraged she'd do something *to* him.'

Gil cast a sideways glance at me, just a quick flick of his eyes. I couldn't tell if he agreed or disagreed with Max. But something Max just said seemed to irritate him. I wondered what it was.

Which begat the question I'd been wondering about since I first learned Robbie trafficked in stolen art: did Gil know what Robbie was involved in? Did *Max*? Maybe that's why they were being so cagey right now, because they knew some of the players Robbie dealt with, had suspicions they didn't want to share.

Jesus. What a mess.

'I think I should go,' I said.

My doorbell rang just after seven. Max had been urging me to get one of those new intercom/video systems so you could see who was at your door – especially with the skyrocketing post-pandemic crime rate in Washington and all the ugly headlines it had generated. I'd told him if someone wanted to do me harm or intended to break in, they wouldn't ring the doorbell first. Still, he had a point.

Just now, I wasn't dressed to receive guests, wearing one of Nick's old Harvard tee-shirts and a pair of yoga pants. Barefoot. No bra. The doorbell rang a second time, too late for me to grab something more decent from my bedroom. I ran down the stairs to the front door, mentally going through the list of who it could be and why. Grace would have called or texted first. Same with Jack. The other choices were Landon, who just might have the audacity to show up unannounced, with or without Harriet, or Detective Ellis, who would not be paying a social call.

I looked through the peephole.

Perry.

I opened the door. 'I happened to be in the neighborhood,' he said, 'so I thought I'd stop by and see how you were doing.'

'You came all the way from London?'

He shook his head, his eyes devouring mine. 'I figured out some business I needed to take care of in New York, but I came to Washington first,' he said. 'I came here for you.'

'You didn't need to . . .' I began and he stepped inside, kicking the door shut behind him.

'I wanted to.'

I'm not sure which of us moved first, but the next thing I knew, my arms were around his neck and his were under my tee-shirt as we kissed like two people who were drowning.

'I missed you,' he whispered, his breath hot and fierce in my ear. 'I've been so worried about you.'

'I'm OK,' I whispered back. And then because I knew it was true, I said what I hadn't told him before, 'I missed you, too.'

He groaned softly, pulling me closer. 'I'm glad. Because I wasn't sure.'

And then his mouth came down on mine again and I was lost.

When I could catch my breath, I said, 'Where's your suitcase? Where are you staying?'

'At the Tabard Inn,' he said. 'I didn't want to presume.'

The Tabard Inn was where he'd taken me the first time we made love.

I took his hand. 'Come with me.'

He'd never seen my apartment before because we'd always met somewhere else when he was in town. When we climbed the stairs and we were in my foyer, he looked around, peeking into the living room and the dining room beyond it.

'I like your place. It's got you written all over it,' he said, his voice soft with surprise. 'I don't remember any of this furniture from the cottage you and Nick rented in Hampstead.'

'Because I left everything in London, remember? Everything except the grandfather clock. Shipping all that furniture would have cost a king's ransom, so I sold or gave away all of it and figured I'd start over again back home. Max took me shopping, gave me advice and made sure I got his discount. I lucked out with a professional of his caliber guiding me.'

'So it *is* all you,' he said. 'It's nice, Sophie.'

Usually, he didn't pay attention to this kind of stuff. His apartment in London had all the charm and appeal of a motel room off a highway. His office in the bureau was just as sterile.

I took his hand. 'Come with me. There's more.'

We climbed the stairs to the second floor, and I led him into my bedroom.

'It's round,' he said.

'Well, only part of it. It's in a tower so it would be round.'

'Suits you. Just like the rest of your place.' He ran a finger down my cheek, and I shivered. 'Look, I didn't . . . I shouldn't . . . I just wanted . . .'

I moved into his arms and kissed him. 'I'm glad you did.'

I had told him making love again was a bad idea. I had told him I didn't think this was going to work because it had already changed our friendship. I had told him that I wasn't going to London, even for a quick trip, because I knew he'd expect me to stay with him and I knew where that would lead. I had told him I wasn't ready.

But now he was here and all of that fell away. He had traversed an ocean for me, and now his presence seemed to sweep away all my worries and fears, turning them to dust that would blow away harmlessly in the night air. In London, he had been my safe harbor, my confidante, a boss who fought for me and defended me, a friend who would do anything, say anything, *be* anything I needed.

I tugged him and we fell on to my bed together, wordlessly undressing each other as we kissed. After that, I forgot everything except how good he felt inside me, what he tasted like, how he explored every inch of me with his hands and his tongue, what a skilled and passionate lover he was. I had left the window partially open to let in a gentle breeze and left the curtains open because tonight there would be a full moon. As it rose in the sky, it filled the bedroom, washing us both with silver light as if we were two otherworldly beings that shimmered and shifted in the dark. I wrapped my legs around his waist and pulled him deeper inside me until we found our rhythm together again and again.

Later, when he was sitting up in bed, propped against the head-board with our pillows as a cushion, and I was facing him, straddled across his legs, I told him everything. Left out nothing. Including my 600-euro searches on ArtRevive to find out whether the icons from Robbie's collection that appeared in Olivia's books had been stolen – something neither Sam nor Jack knew about.

He fiddled with a lock of my hair as I talked, twirling it around and around on his finger. Even in the pale moonlight, I could see the furrows on his forehead and knew he was worried.

When I was done, he said, 'Do you think your brother killed Robson Blake?'

'No. God, I hope not. I don't know. What worries me – and scares me, too – is that I haven't heard from him. If he was innocent, he would have contacted me by now.'

'If it *was* Danny,' he said, 'why would he ask you for a floor plan and information about the security system and then show up before you got a chance to tell him anything? Plus, he knew you'd be there that day as well. Why would he pre-empt the plans he made with you and break into Robbie's house in the middle of the day right before you were supposed to be there?'

'I know. It doesn't make sense. Unless something happened that I didn't know about.'

'Like what?'

'Like, what was the icon doing in Robbie's study when he usually kept it in his vault?'

He kissed the tip of my nose. 'As somebody said, maybe he wanted to show it to someone.'

'Or maybe . . . he wanted to sell it?'

'Possibly. That would accelerate the timeline,' he said. 'How long until you get an answer from your ArtRevive searches?'

'Beats me. However long it takes them to go through their database. It's a long shot, anyway.'

'What made you decide to do it?'

'Something Darius Zahiri said about publishing a photo of a stolen item being a way to make it appear legitimate, respectable. Part of the process of laundering it. He was talking about an auction catalog as an example, but it made me wonder why the photo and description couldn't also be in a book,' I said. 'When I talked to Olivia this afternoon, she told me she gave Robbie credit as a collaborator because he made introductions for her in the art world, opened doors for her because of his money and connections, and gave her access to his collection. *She* wrote the book. *She* did all the work.'

'And?'

'So, in return, maybe she included photos of some of the items he owned that were stolen or plundered. To help him out. Confer legitimacy. *Maybe*.'

'If you're right,' he said, 'Robson Blake loaned or gave works of art to some of the world's major art museums. If it turns out that items in his collection were stolen, can you imagine what a bombshell that would be? The worldwide scramble to do searches on the provenance of every item he donated?'

I shivered and moved closer into his arms. 'And if Danny gets caught up in Robbie's death for any reason, I'm going to be dragged into it as well. My tripod was the murder weapon, after all.'

'You didn't do anything.'

'No, but I knew the icon was stolen.'

'Only because Danny told you. Did you check that out?'

'As you would say, "Have I taught you nothing? Second sources, Medina. Second sources." Of course I checked.'

He laughed. 'Good. Although by now Blake's caretaker must have told your detective all about it. He'd have to come clean. So my guess is that your detective friend knows it's stolen as well.'

'You're probably right.'

'I wonder where it is now?'

'That's easy,' I said. 'The killer has it. How's he or she going to get rid of it? It's too hot. No one's going to take it. Find the icon and you'll find Robson Blake's killer.'

Perry took me by the shoulders and gently laid me on my back. 'Do you think we can take a break from this rather heavy, intense conversation for a while?'

'Sure. Except if I go to jail, will you visit me?'

'You're not gonna go to jail. But if you do, yes, I'll visit you. Every week without fail.'

'You're a good friend.'

'I'm good at other things, too,' he said.

'Show me,' I said, and he did.

TWENTY-TWO

Perry and I made love again in the morning when the light was soft and we were still drowsy with sleep. Afterwards, we showered together and then I fixed him breakfast before he had to leave since his luggage was still at the Tabard Inn. He would only be in New York for two days, then he'd come back to DC before flying to London out of Dulles the following day. When he came back this time, he would stay at my place.

After that, then what? I knew he wanted to talk about us, about our relationship, but he knew I wasn't ready to make a commitment, so he didn't push me. London was home for him; he was never returning to the US. He'd been away too long. As for me, there was a time I would have packed my bag and moved back to England in a heartbeat, to return to a city I loved, but lately, I wasn't so sure. I'd started creating a life for myself here surrounded by family and friends now that Nick was gone. I was slowly finding my way again, making a new beginning.

Nick had set me up with his CIA pension and a hefty life insurance policy I hadn't known about, plus our savings, so I could do whatever I wanted, meaning I didn't need to take another job for the money unless I wanted it. I didn't need to work ever again.

But as for Perry and me: I just wasn't sure we would be compatible long-term. He'd already been through three marriages and three divorces, and had countless girlfriends. I liked him, cared for him, we got along well, best of friends. The sex was great; actually, it was amazing. I loved him but that wasn't the same as being *in love* with him. Besides, he was nearly twenty years older than I was; we were in different places in our lives.

Maybe what we had *now* could be enough for him.

It was enough for me.

He asked me what my plans were while we were sitting at the dining-room table finishing breakfast.

'You don't miss work, Medina?' he said, digging into a spinach and feta omelet I'd made for the two of us.

'Sometimes,' I said. 'But a few months ago, I started a non-profit called ViewFinder. I haven't had a chance to tell you about it.'

I'd talked it over with Jack and Grace, gotten their input, plus I got business advice from Harry. Otherwise, I'd kept quiet about it while it was a startup. In the old days, I would have told Perry. But I was afraid he'd try to talk me out of it, tell me I needed to go back to work at IPS instead of doing volunteer work.

'I take pictures pro-bono for small charities that don't have money – or much money – that they can use to advertise or fundraise. The word has been getting out and now I'm starting to get calls from people who ask if I can help them. I like doing it, Perry. After Nick died, I decided I wanted to use my photography to do something good, something meaningful that could make a difference, especially after I got involved with Streetwise.'

He was surprised as I knew he would be. 'You'll be good at that. You're good with people, great at putting someone at ease. That's why you're such a terrific photographer.' Then, predictably, he added, 'But I don't think it's going to be enough for you. Not long-term, anyway. You live on adrenalin, Sophie. *Thrive* on it. You don't want to be on the outside looking in. You want to be at the goddamn *center*.'

He could still read me so well. 'I'm OK with where I am now. Back home in Washington, near enough to Middleburg to see my mom and Harry, to the place where I grew up. Washington's pretty central, you know. Some people would say more so than London. I didn't move to a farm in Iowa, you know.'

He reached out and stroked my cheek with the back of his hand. 'I know you didn't. And we should probably stop this conversation right here, because you know what I want and it's just going to get me in trouble.'

His smile was sad, and it broke my heart. I leaned over and kissed him, grateful he'd slammed on the brakes before we started down that road again: what about our future? Because it never ended well.

We needed to change the subject. 'Are you referring to more coffee – is that what you want? I can make another pot. And it's no trouble.'

His laugh was bittersweet. 'Sure, more coffee would be great.'

He followed me into the kitchen and leaned against the counter. 'Not that I can't imagine you haven't been thinking about it your-self,' he said, 'but what the hell happened to Danny? Do you think he killed Blake? Because if he didn't, I don't know why he wouldn't get back in touch with you.'

I set the coffee pot down on the counter and faced him. 'I barely know him. I met him once when he broke into my studio. Despite that little transgression, I liked him. Now, I just don't know. If his name shows up in Ellis's search for Robbie's killer, Danny has to know I'll be dragged into the middle of things. Ellis will never believe it's just a coincidence. So when it comes right down to it, he's left me sort of twisting in the wind, hasn't he?'

'When you put it like that.'

'Plus, one of these days Enrique Navarro is going to crawl out from whatever rock he hides under and ask me about Danny again. He wants to blow up everything with Robbie and he wants Danny to work with him, which I doubt is going to happen.'

'How much time do you think you have with Navarro before he goes to someone else for help?'

'I don't know.' I filled the pot with water, dumped it into the coffee maker and added the dark French roast that I'd ground earlier to the filter. 'What I do know is that I don't think I trust him either.'

'I've got some friends in the Spanish press,' Perry said. 'I'll put out a few feelers when I'm in New York and see what I can find out. I'll let you know.'

Perry called from New York around four when I'd just gotten back to the apartment after a run.

'I miss you. And I've got news about Enrique Navarro.'

'What's the news about Navarro?'

'Hey, don't you miss me, too?'

'Of course I do. Tell me about Navarro. Please.'

'It's good to know where your priorities are, Medina.'

'Sorry. I do miss you. You know I do. But you were saying?'

He sighed. 'OK, I talked to an old friend who knew Navarro back in the day when he was the most elevated journalist in the pantheon of *El País*'s great reporters. Wrote like a poet. Everyone thought he walked on water, his stories were always so damn good – impeccable sources, stuff no one else could touch.'

'You're using the past tense. He's not so hot anymore?'

'Not by a long shot. He might even be on the way out. He's well past retirement age, for one thing. So they could ease him out that way.'

'If he feels his bosses are breathing down his neck to push him to retire, he's probably pretty desperate to write this story and he doesn't want to wait around.'

'You're probably right,' he said. 'We can talk about it when I'm back in DC. I might find out more between now and then. I'm having lunch tomorrow with an old friend who used to be at the UN in Geneva. Now he's at headquarters in New York. He's a Spaniard and he's been around, so he probably knows Navarro as well. I'm trying to be discreet when I ask about him because I don't want Navarro to find out. I don't want anything to boomerang back on you.'

Neither did I. Because I had no idea how much Detective Joseph Ellis of the Homicide Division of the DC Police Department knew at this moment in time about Robbie trafficking in stolen art. And if it had somehow led him to Danny.

But Ellis was a smart cookie, and my guess was that he knew plenty.

What I didn't know was whether I was still on his radar or not.

I was restless after dinner and decided to go over to the studio to get some editing done on a photo shoot I'd done for a non-profit that provided weekend lunches for kids from poor neighborhoods who normally ate at school Monday through Friday. It was gradually growing lighter later at night, but it was still March and daylight-saving time wouldn't start until the weekend, so it was dark when I left the apartment.

Halfway across the alley, the hair on the back of my neck stood up and I stopped walking. Someone was waiting in the shadows. Years ago, Perry had sent me on a course in Scotland for a week of hostile environment training for journalists who were going to be sent to war zones or other dangerous places. We were trained by British ex-Special Forces soldiers, and they were relentless in telling us to keep our guard up, not to get careless, to always be alert.

So now I *knew* someone was in the alley. The crime rate in DC had soared since the pandemic, especially robberies and carjackings, but also homicides. All I had was my phone, nothing useful if I needed to defend myself. Turn and run? Call out and see if that spooked whoever was there?

I sprinted toward the studio, hoping I could outrun him and get inside before he reached me. The sound of a car engine starting up in the alley along with the flash of bright white headlights made me turn instinctively, shielding my eyes against the glare. Whoever it was seemed to come from *inside* the studio while I was distracted by the car. Before I could run or cry out, I felt a blow to the side of my head. Searing pain and a blinding headache as I fell to the ground.

After that, nothing.

TWENTY-THREE

When I woke up, I was lying on my side where I had crumpled to the ground. My attacker had fled, probably in the car with the blinding headlights. I tried to sit up as a stabbing pain shot through my head, which now felt as if it had become unhinged from the rest of my body. I lay down again before I threw up. My phone had been in my hand before he hit me. Now it was gone. I reached out and groped around me, hoping my fingers would touch it. Nothing but gravel and dead leaves. It had to be somewhere close by, unless my attacker had taken it. But either way, that eliminated the possibility of calling for help. Now my best option was making it across the alley to my apartment.

By the time I reached the front steps, I was exhausted, and my head throbbed wickedly. I slumped on the bottom step, feeling like the ground was tilting away from me. I lay my head down on my arms and closed my eyes, hoping the spinning would stop.

'Sophie? Are you OK?'

With an effort, I raised my head. Landon Reed stood at the gate, dressed in a tee-shirt and running shorts. He was already opening the gate, not waiting for my response, scooping me up in his arms as if I were a child's doll.

'What happened? Don't pass out on me, OK? Stay with me.' His voice, calm but urgent-sounding, was reassuring.

I might have told him someone attacked me or maybe I just imagined I said something because no words seemed to come out of my mouth.

Through my fog, I heard him say, 'You need to get to a hospital. I'm calling nine-one-one.'

I think I told him I'd be OK if he just got me inside, but I don't remember much except the vague slamming of a car door a few minutes later, me still in Landon's arms, his voice, still urgent, telling the driver to get to the hospital *now*.

The next time I opened my eyes, I was lying in a bed in a small, darkened room, quiet except for the steady sound of something beeping. My head still felt as if it was in a vise. I started to raise my hand to touch it when I realized a blood pressure cuff was attached to my left arm and an IV had been inserted in my right hand. A motherly-looking woman, glasses halfway down her nose, walked into the room.

'You're awake,' she said. 'Welcome back.'

'Where am I?'

'GW Hospital. The ER. Do you know your name, hon?'

'Sophie. Sophie Medina.'

'Good. Do you know what day it is?'

I closed my eyes and thought for a moment. 'Is it still Thursday?'

'It is,' she said. 'Do you remember what happened to you?'

I started to nod, but a wicked lightning bolt shot through my head, and I winced. She laid her hand on my arm. 'Take it easy, hon. You've got a concussion. Luckily no fractures. But you sustained quite a blow.'

I winced and said, 'Someone hit me on the head in the alley behind my house when I was about to open the door to my studio.'

She nodded. 'That sounds about right. I gather you didn't see who it was?'

'No.'

'We're going to keep you here a little longer. Then your brother can take you home and keep an eye on you there. He'll need to wake you up every few hours to make sure you're OK, that your pupils are still properly dilated.'

'My . . . brother?'

Which one? Tommy, who worked as an ER doctor here at George Washington? *Danny?*

No way in hell.

'Are you talking about Doctor Wyatt?'

'Doctor Wyatt is your brother, too?' she asked. 'Doctor Tommy Wyatt? You have two brothers who are doctors?'

Now I was really confused. 'Is Tommy here?'

'It's his night off,' she said. 'He'll be in tomorrow. No, I meant Landon.'

'Oh,' I said. '*That* brother.'

'He is your brother, isn't he? He brought you in. Came in an Uber, said it took too long for the ambulance to get there.'

'That sounds like Landon. Can I see him, please?'

'Of course.'

She left, and a moment later, Landon pulled aside the privacy

curtain that surrounded my bed and walked into the room, still
dressed in the running shorts and tee-shirt. He came over and stood
next to me, his eyes glancing at the readout on the computer monitor
above my head. 'You're doing better. You look better.'

'Thank you. You told them you're my brother? Does she know
you're a vet?'

'They wouldn't have let me in to see you otherwise and no, I
didn't enlighten her that my specialty is animals. Is there, uh,
anybody I should notify?'

'I do have a brother who works here. He's an ER doc, but tonight
is his night off. If he'd been here, you would have been found out
pretty fast,' I said. 'And no, thanks, if you tell anyone – my mother,
my stepfather, Tommy or my sister – they're going to go nuts. My
stepfather will personally drive to DC and bring me home to look
after me because both he and my mother think Washington has
become more dangerous than a war zone.'

'Well, you did get attacked in an alley,' he said. 'You were
babbling about it in the Uber on the way to the hospital. Something
about your studio and a guy and car headlights. Did you get a look
at him? See the car? Color, make, license plates?'

'I heard a car. An engine starting not far from where I was, so I
turned to look and make sure it wasn't coming toward me. The
headlights blinded me, and someone coshed me hard on the head
from behind and knocked me out.' I shivered. 'I seem to think he
was coming from *inside* my studio. All my equipment is in there,
my computer, my cameras, lenses – everything. I need to get home
and check it out. The nurse said I could leave soon.'

'The nurse said you could leave when they felt you were stable
and had someone to keep an eye on you all night and wake you up
every couple of hours,' he said. 'Is there someone you want to call
to do that? Or you could just ask me. I'm right here.'

'You would stay and wake me up all night?'

'I would,' he said. 'Besides, you have a lot of explaining to do.
You stand me up for dinner the other night, and the next morning
I find out the client you were going to meet was dead when you
got there, so then you end up being questioned by a homicide
detective. Plus, this guy's a pretty famous and extremely wealthy
philanthropist and your name's all over the place in the news.'

'Sorry, but it's all true.'

'Do you think whoever attacked you tonight had something to

do with the murder of Robson Blake? Or was it just a random attack because DC *is* becoming more and more violent since the pandemic?'

I hadn't thought about whether my attacker had anything to do with Robbie's death – but what possible reason would he have for going after me?

None.

Which meant it had been a random attacker. A man who had been leaving my studio, where I kept my cameras, my equipment, my computer, my files worth several hundred thousand dollars and years of work. The equipment was insured but replacing everything would be an absolute headache. Especially the prime lenses and the equipment my grandfather had left me. *Those* were irreplaceable, in no small part because they had belonged to him. Priceless.

Except . . . I'd had a feeling he'd been leaving empty-handed.

Then what had he been doing there? Had he made multiple trips to that car in the alley and already cleaned me out when I found him?

'I need to get out of here,' I said. 'I need to go home.'

It was one in the morning when the hospital finally released me after I assured my doctor and the nurses I'd be better off in my own bed than in a hospital bed and my brother would be there to keep an eye on me all night. Landon backed me up. It helped that he was a doctor, even if they didn't know he was a vet. He called another Uber which swept up to the entry to the ER and deposited us at my house fifteen minutes later, driving quickly through the quiet, empty streets of Washington.

As soon as the Uber pulled away, I said to Landon, 'There's no way in hell I'm going inside my apartment before I see my studio, concussion or no concussion. Besides, my phone is missing. I think he knocked it out of my hand so it's probably somewhere in the alley. Hopefully, he didn't take it and it's still working.'

'That isn't a good idea.'

'If it were your clinic that someone broke into, would you go home and wait until morning to check it out?'

He didn't hesitate. 'All right, let's go.'

The lights were out in Max's apartment as I would have expected. Landon used the flashlight on his phone to light the way from the house through the alley to the studio.

'My phone ought to be here somewhere,' I said. 'It was knocked out of my hand when I got hit.'

'Why don't I call your number?' Landon said.

It rang, thankfully. He retrieved it in a thicket of ivy that grew up the side of the carriage house and handed it to me. A nice long crack across the face, but at least it still worked.

He shone the flashlight on the front door, and I tried the doorknob. Dammit, unlocked.

Danny.

But if he had been here, would he really have knocked me out with that blow? *My brother?*

'Maybe we shouldn't go inside,' Landon said. 'Maybe we should call the police first.'

'He was *leaving* the studio when I showed up. He's long gone,' I said and opened the door.

I walked in and started flicking on lights. Landon followed. Everything was where I'd left it. Nothing was disturbed. My equipment. My computer. My cameras and lenses. All the cases were locked, and everything was where I usually kept it.

'What's wrong?' Landon asked.

'*Nothing's* wrong,' I said. 'That's the thing.'

'Then what happened?'

'I don't know,' I said. 'But I'm going to have a look around. Because something's not right.'

'Mind if I tag along?'

'Of course not.'

'Nice place,' he said.

'Thanks. It's also a guest house when friends or family come to stay. There's a bedroom upstairs in the loft, plus the kitchenette and the bathroom down here.'

Landon watched while I opened cabinets and drawers in the kitchen, checked the bathroom, pulled up cushions from the sofa and the upholstered chairs, and finally stood in the middle of the room and threw my hands up in the air.

'I give up.'

'You didn't check the bedroom,' he said.

'You're right.'

I climbed the stairs. Landon was right behind me.

Whoever had broken into my apartment hadn't taken anything. They'd left something.

Propped up against the headboard of the bed was the jewel-encrusted Virgin of Vladimir icon.

Someone had brought Robbie's icon to my studio and there could be only one reason for that. My tripod had been the murder weapon. Now the missing icon had turned up here.

Whoever had done it was trying to set me up for the murder of Robson Blake.

TWENTY-FOUR

'**W**hat is that?' Landon asked.

'It's the icon that was stolen from Robson Blake's home the day he was murdered,' I said.

'What's it doing here?'

'Whoever hit me over the head brought it as a house present.'

'Funny,' he said. 'Real funny. Why would he . . . wait. Is someone trying to make it look like you murdered Robson Blake, Sophie?'

My head hurt. Processing this made it hurt even more. 'Apparently.'

'Jesus. *Why?*'

'I'm not sure.' He didn't know about the tripod, and I wasn't about to tell him. It only made a bad situation much, much worse. 'This icon belongs in a church in Kyiv. It was stolen by the Russians and ended up in Robbie's house – I don't know how. You can't repeat any of this, Landon, OK? *You can't.*'

He had to be wondering what he'd gotten himself into, agreeing to babysit me tonight. Because now it was plain as day the attack hadn't been random. Someone had deliberately come after me, and whoever it was had been connected to Robbie's murder. Landon's tanned face, in the dim light of the bedside table lamp, was as pale as a sheet.

'What are you going to do?' he asked.

'I don't know.'

But I *did* know this: whoever killed Robbie knew the tripod belonged to me. And that narrowed the list of suspects considerably.

If I called Ellis and told him I had the icon, it would be like turning myself in. Would he believe me when I told him someone planted it here? *Would he?* It didn't matter because it was a Hobson's choice, and I knew it. No choice at all.

'I need to call Detective Ellis and take my chances he believes me about how the icon ended up here,' I said, trying not to sound as worried and panicked as I felt. 'It's evidence in a murder investigation. And it's stolen.'

I flopped down on the end of the bed, accidentally jostling the icon. Landon reached out to steady it and seemed to make up his mind about something.

'You can call that detective, but tonight you're not going to do anything except follow the doctor's orders,' he said in a firm take-charge voice. 'Someone hit you over the head as they were leaving here. You were in the hospital tonight with a concussion. Call Ellis tomorrow. He can vet your story with the GW Emergency Room. With me. Nothing's going to change tonight. It's nearly two a.m. and you need to get some sleep. I'll check in on you, make sure you're OK. I presume you've got a couch where I can crash?'

I threw him a grateful look. 'I do. And thank you.'

I locked up, and we left and went back to the house. He followed me upstairs to my bedroom and, like Perry, I caught him looking around as if he was intrigued by the idea of a round room. I lay down on my bed dressed in the clothes I'd had on all evening. Landon put a quilt from the bottom of the bed over me and wished me goodnight.

'I'll be downstairs. Holler if you need me. I've set my phone alarm for every hour so I can come up and wake you up, check your pupils, make sure you're still lucid.'

I propped myself up on my elbows. 'You could just . . . sleep here instead of running up and down the stairs. If you want to, that is. You might get a little more rest and it's already so late.'

Our eyes met. 'If you're OK with that . . .'

'It's the least I can do.' This was awkward. Inviting him to sleep with me. Two nights in a row, two different men in my bed. Two totally different circumstances.

'OK, then.' He lay on his back on the other side of the bed and folded his hands together across his chest. 'Get some sleep, Sophie.'

'You, too, Landon. Good night.'

I closed my eyes, but I knew I wasn't going to fall asleep anytime soon. There weren't too many possibilities to consider as to who had broken into the studio. Danny had already proven that he could easily pick my lock. Maybe he'd done it again. I had the only key to the place, as well as another copy I gave to guests to use while they were staying there. I had taken a quick look at where I kept the keys – a little key holder next to the antique hall rack Max had helped me find. Nothing was missing, every key was on its usual hook.

If Danny had come back and left the icon, it meant he'd been at Robbie's. It meant he was the one who had killed him.

And now my brother – whom I barely knew – was trying to pin the murder on me.

I have a hazy recollection of Landon waking me to check on me during what was left of the night, rolling over in bed and shining his phone flashlight on my eyes to make sure they still dilated properly, murmuring that I should go back to sleep. When I woke up, it was light outside and he was gone. I heard water running in the bathroom and then eventually his footsteps clomping down the stairs.

I needed a shower and a change of clothes. I got up and walked into the bathroom, staring at myself in the mirror. I looked just like I felt. As if I'd been run over by a truck which then backed up and ran over me again. I put my hands down on the sink counter and bumped something. Condoms. Perry had left a package of condoms lying there, either forgotten to take them with him or else figured he didn't need to as he'd be using them when he returned.

And Landon had just been in here. Damn.

I showered, changed and went downstairs. He'd made coffee.

'Good morning,' he said, his voice a bit cool. 'I hope you don't mind that I found your coffee and made a pot. I tend to drink my coffee strong, so I hope that's not a problem.'

'No, of course not. Thank you.'

He handed me a mug. 'I don't know how you take your coffee.'

'Milk and sugar,' I said. 'Thanks. I'll get them. What about you?'

'I drink it black.'

He leaned against the counter and watched me take a carton of milk out of the refrigerator.

'I can't thank you enough for last night,' I said, pouring milk into my mug. 'For what you did for me and for getting what was probably a very lousy night's sleep, if any at all.'

'Why didn't you suggest calling your boyfriend?' he said. 'I'm sure he would have come right over.'

'I don't have a boyfriend.' I took the sugar bowl out of a cabinet. 'And it's not what you're thinking.'

'How do you know what I'm thinking?'

I could feel my face burning. 'This is awkward. My ex-boss from London was in town the day before yesterday. I had no idea he was going to be here. He's in New York now and he'll fly back to London – where he lives – on Saturday morning. That's it.'

'You don't owe me an explanation.'

'You asked about my boyfriend. I don't have one. I'm not seeing anybody, and I haven't been in a relationship since my husband died two years ago,' I said. 'Since we're on the subject of relationships, what about you?' I stared at his left hand and the visible line of a wedding ring against his suntan.

His face turned red and his mouth tightened.

'My wife of sixteen years is a professor of microbiology at Stanford,' he said. 'She's brilliant. Eight months ago, she came to me and said she met someone else. Another Stanford professor. I think we're probably going to end up getting a divorce.'

'I'm sorry. Though it sounds as if you'd like to reconcile.'

'It only works if both of us want to reconcile.'

'And she doesn't?'

'She doesn't.'

'I'm sorry,' I said again. 'What made you decide to move here?'

'I thought it would be easier to get over her, to move on, if I were far away. Plus, I wouldn't have to see them . . . together.'

'And is it easier?'

'I don't know.'

'You're still in love with her,' I said.

'I don't know that anymore, either.' Which meant that he was.

'I found out after Nick died that he'd been involved with someone else. I had no idea. It was a complete shock. Now he's gone and there's nothing I can do about it.'

I have no idea why I blurted that out. The air between us practically vibrated with electricity and the subtext of things we weren't telling each other that had nothing to do with the words we were saying.

It was his turn to say he was sorry. He added, 'That had to be rough.'

'For me, there's no closure – there never will be – no face-to-face talk so I could ask him why, argue with him and get it out of my system. Tell him how badly he'd hurt me and what he'd done to our marriage. Find out if it was over for us. You, on the other hand, can still talk to your wife. Maybe you can reconcile, work things out.'

'I don't know. It might be too late for that. But you're right. At least I'll eventually get closure. One way or the other.' He set down his mug. 'I should go and check on the animals. I've got appointments in an hour and a half, and I need a shower.'

I nodded. 'Thank you again. As for Perry . . . I don't know. Things happen, you know?'

'I do know.' He walked over and kissed me on the forehead. 'OK if I check in on you later?'

'Yes. I'd like that. And I still owe you an answer about Harriet. Though my life needs to be a bit more stable before I take on a kitten.'

'After what happened last night, "stable" is not a word I would associate with you at the moment.' I think he was trying to make a joke and I managed a feeble smile. 'I'll keep her for a few more days. Then you can let me know.'

'That's fair. And generous of you. Thank you.'

He smiled half-heartedly and left the kitchen. A moment later, I heard his footsteps on the stairs and the front door opening and closing.

I rested my elbows on the counter and held my head with my hands, wondering what the hell to do next.

The doorbell rang as I finished cleaning up the breakfast dishes and my heart skittered wildly. *Now who was it?* My head still hurt, even when I closed my eyes and shut out everything around me. My brain still didn't feel completely connected with my mouth and I knew my thinking was fuzzy.

Whoever it was rang again before I could get downstairs.

'I'm coming.'

I looked through the peephole. Detective Joe Ellis and a female companion stood side by side in the vestibule. The carved-in-stone expression on Ellis's face made my heart pound even harder.

I sucked in a deep breath and opened the door. 'Good morning,' I said and hoped I sounded calm, even a bit curious as to why they were paying me a visit.

'Ms Medina, this is my colleague, Detective Castillo. May we come in? We have a few questions for you.'

I figured Ellis might show up but not this soon. I wasn't ready for him, but I needed to hold my ground. 'Do you have a warrant, Detectives?' I hoped it sounded conversational and not combative.

Ellis's face was impassive, and his eyes turned into depthless

dark pools. 'We do not.' Each word carefully and precisely enun-
ciated, letting me know he was pissed off that I was shutting him
out. And that I'd probably regret it the next time I saw him.

'Then, I'm sorry, the answer is no. On the advice of my lawyer,
I don't have anything to say to you without him being present.' I
was gripping the doorknob so hard to keep my hand from shaking
that my knuckles were white. I wondered if Ellis noticed and figured
that he probably did. He didn't miss anything.

'Very well,' he said, still curt. 'We'll be back. With a warrant.
So you might want to call your lawyer now. Have a good day, Ms
Medina.'

TWENTY-FIVE

heard the outside door click shut behind Detectives Ellis and Castillo and leaned against the inside door as if I needed it to hold me up, fighting panic. Ellis *knew*. Somehow he knew I had the icon because someone had either phoned in an anonymous tip or an informant he worked with had told him. However he'd managed to find out, he didn't have enough information to get a judge to agree to sign a search warrant and that bought me some time – though probably not much.

I climbed the stairs again, and when I reached the foyer, I stared at my key-keeper. I owned two keys to the studio – mine and a guest key. But there was one more person who had a copy of that key because I'd never bothered to change the lock when I took over the lease of the studio. Someone I hadn't thought about until just now.

Max.

He was home when I rang the bell. He took one look at my face and said, 'I think you'd better come inside.'

'What's going on?' he asked as he led me into his living room. 'Sit. You look awful, Sophie. Can I get you a glass of water? A brandy?'

I sat on the sofa, and he sat next to me. 'Nothing, thanks.'

'You'd better talk to me, darlin'. Tell me what this is all about.'

'Someone hit me over the head last night in the alley as I was walking over to my studio. A friend took me to the ER. I've got a concussion, but I'm OK.' A bald-faced lie because I was anything but OK. Especially because of what I was about to ask him.

Max looked me over as if I'd suddenly become something delicate and fragile that he was afraid might break. 'My God. This city isn't safe *anywhere* anymore. Thank God the guy didn't have a weapon. Even kids in elementary school carry guns now. Children. It's insanity. We need to get motion sensor lights in the alley – I should have done it as soon as the crime rate started going up after the pandemic. I'll call the company we used for the gallery and get

someone over here.' He paused to take a breath from his rant about
DC crime. 'What is it? There's something else.'

'Do you have your key to the studio?'

He looked taken aback, and I knew it was not what he was
expecting me to say. 'Did you lose yours when he knocked you
out? Of course I have it. It's with the other keys on the key rack in
the pantry.'

'Could I borrow it?'

He came back a moment later and, from the stricken look on his
face, I knew he'd figured it out. 'It's not there,' he said in a hoarse
voice. 'But you knew that already.'

'I did. You know who took it, don't you?'

After a long moment, he said, 'It could only have been Gil.'

'That's what I thought.'

He left the room again and returned with the brandy bottle and
two glasses. 'I think we might need this to get through what you're
going to tell me. At least I know *I* need a drink.'

He sat down and poured two hefty shots, handing one to me.
'Go ahead. Tell me everything.'

I told him plenty – especially about my tripod being the murder
weapon and about Ellis questioning me – but I didn't tell him
everything. I didn't say a word about Danny, who I now knew was
innocent of the murder of Robbie Blake. Though I did tell him that
I knew the icon had been stolen, where it had come from and that
Robbie had known full well that it was plundered art. Surprisingly,
Max didn't ask how I knew. So I went on, my heart heavy with
sadness and dread and the realization of what I'd figured out and
what I still had to ask him.

'Gil knew about the icon, and he knew Robbie trafficked in stolen
art.' I swallowed hard and my voice cracked. 'Did you know, too,
Max?'

He knocked back his brandy and helped himself to another. 'When
you came by the other day, we'd been arguing.'

'I heard you.'

'I thought you did.'

'I didn't hear what you were saying.'

'A few days ago, I found . . . some items in our warehouse that
were under a tarp. I knew we hadn't ordered them. I knew they
weren't ours. So I confronted Gil.'

'They were stolen?'

He nodded.

'*Gil* was Robbie's dealer?'

'I have no idea – since I didn't know about Robbie, it never occurred to me to ask. He just said he'd move everything out, store it somewhere else. I asked him how long this had been going on and he said, "A while." I still don't know any of the details. For a day or two, I kept thinking I didn't *want* to know. My God, the business. Our reputation. What he's done could destroy everything we've built.'

'Because it's *illegal*.'

'I know. Believe me, I *know*.'

'He took the key so he could put the icon he took from the kiot in Robbie's house in my studio,' I said. 'I found it last night after I got home from the ER.'

Max turned pale and said as if he couldn't believe it, 'Gil hit you with enough force to give you a concussion.'

'Yes. Apparently, I nearly caught him as he was leaving the studio. He came up behind me in the dark – I never saw who it was. A friend took me to the GW Emergency Room and then spent last night making sure I was OK after the doctor said I could go home.'

He shook his head, still stunned. And now angry. 'You're going to press charges? Because that's assault. Along with breaking and entering.'

'I need to prove it was him first. And there's more.'

He closed his eyes as if he wanted to shut out this whole nightmare story that now involved him as well. 'Go on.'

'Just before I came over here, Detective Ellis and another detective showed up at my door. Gil must have phoned in an anonymous tip about the icon, but Ellis didn't have a search warrant, so I didn't let them in. I haven't got much time, Max.'

'What do you want to do?' His voice was grim.

'Make a couple of phone calls. You make one and I'll make one.'

Max called Gil and asked him to stop by, telling him they needed to finish the conversation they'd been having the other day. He thought it best to do it at his apartment where they'd have some privacy, rather than in the gallery.

Gil bought it.

I heard their voices when he got there forty-five minutes later and then Gil saying something about needing a glass of water to take some medication. I was waiting in the pantry when he slipped into the kitchen and opened the door to put my studio key back on the key rack.

'Hello, Gil,' I said. 'I'll take that.'

'What . . . are you doing here?'

Max had followed him into the kitchen. 'I think you'd better explain what *you're* doing here.'

The stunned look on Gil's face disappeared, replaced by anger. 'You *asked* me to come over. What is this? An ambush? What do you two think you're doing?'

'You took this key so you could put the icon you stole from Robbie's house in my studio last night,' I said. 'To make it look even more like I was guilty of killing him. Because after all, as we both know, my tripod was the murder weapon. You used it when you hit Robbie over the head.'

Gil's eyes flickered from me to Max. 'You two are crazy. You're both out of your minds. I've got nothing to say to either of you.'

'How long have you been supplying Robbie with stolen art, Gil? How long has this been going on? How long have you been running your side business through our gallery?' Max asked, his voice tight with fury. 'This is going to destroy us. Not just you. *Both of us.*'

'You can't prove anything,' he said to Max in a snide tone. 'Nor you, Sophie. You're just throwing darts and hoping something you say hits a target. I'm leaving.' He turned to go.

He meant it. He was going to walk out of here right now. We had nothing. He'd said nothing.

'Before you go,' I said. 'You got Olivia involved, too. Her career will be over once this is out.'

He stopped and turned around to face us again. '*Leave her out of this.* She doesn't know anything.'

'I think she knows plenty,' I said. 'I know for a fact she knew exactly what was going on, that you were selling Robbie stolen art – or at least some of the stolen art he owned. Olivia and Robbie were close; they were lovers. Of course, she knew.'

I didn't know with absolute certainty whether Olivia knew anything, but he didn't need to know that.

'They weren't *that* close,' he said, and it sounded like a sneer. 'You're mistaken. She told me some things . . . things no one else knows.'

The motives for most crimes people commit boil down to a

handful of reasons: greed, anger, revenge, ideology . . . and lust or jealousy.

The day after Robbie was murdered when Max and Gil came by the studio, Gil said he'd learned about Robbie's death the following day when Max called him. But the other day when they'd been drinking on Max's deck, he said he'd already stopped by Olivia's apartment because he'd known Robbie was dead. One of those statements was a lie because both couldn't be true. The puzzle pieces came together and now I knew why Gil killed Robbie: jealousy.

'You're in love with her,' I said. 'Did you think if you killed Robbie that Olivia would turn to you?'

'Shut up.'

'Is *that* why you did it? Because of Olivia? You didn't have to kill him, for God's sake,' Max said.

At first, I thought Gil wasn't going to answer. But I'd goaded him by bringing up Olivia and Max had backed me up. Gil's eyes flashed with anger.

'He treated her like dirt, used her when he needed her. She didn't deserve it. All the other women he'd sleep with, he'd throw them in her face, humiliating her. When I confronted him about it, he just laughed at me, told me he could do whatever he wanted, and she'd forgive anything. He was making a fool of her . . . I couldn't stand it.'

'She's planning his funeral. She's executrix of his estate. He trusted her,' I said. 'He trusted her with everything.'

'He still screwed other women. Olivia was like, I don't know . . . his accountant, his bookkeeper. *That's* how he thought of her.'

'So you were defending Olivia when you went to see Robbie that day,' Max said, in a soothing voice. Calming him down. Trying to get him to talk. Because so far he still hadn't actually admitted anything.

'Of course I was. Who else was going to do it? Certainly not *you.*' He stabbed his finger angrily at Max's chest. 'You were only too happy to have Robbie as a friend, with his incredible wealth and connections and philanthropic do-gooding – you didn't care what he did to her, so you turned a blind eye. I *didn't.*'

'Did Robbie know you loved Olivia?' I needed to steer him away from his combustible remarks about Max before the tension between them erupted into something more.

'He guessed. He laughed at me. Told me she was out of my

league.' Gil's voice brimmed over with bitterness at having been mocked. Scorned.

'So you lost your temper? That's when you hit him?' *Go slow. Be gentle. Just get him to admit it.* I gave him an encouraging nod, as if I understood him.

'*It was an accident.* He provoked me; he did it deliberately.'

'Why did you take the icon?' Max's voice was tight, clipped. He was probably still simmering over Gil's dig about his relationship with Robbie.

'He was going to sell it. He said the stories about it having some kind of mystical power creeped him out. I told him it was too risky to move it – it was too hot. I said if he wanted to get rid of it, he should sell it back to me, but he told me he already had a buyer who was coming over and was going to pay him twice what he paid me.'

Neither Max nor I had seen the bulge under his jacket where the gun was. He pulled it out. 'I'm getting out of town, out of the country. I'm leaving today. And you two have become loose ends.'

He raised his arm and aimed the gun at Max. 'Sorry, partner. I wasn't expecting to have to do this.'

Two quick shots. I think I screamed. Then Gil doubled over, slumping to the ground, as Joe Ellis kicked the gun out of his hand, and suddenly the kitchen was filled with DC police officers holding shields and dressed as if they were ready for a riot.

'You shot me,' Gil screamed. 'You shot me. I'm bleeding, goddammit. Do something.'

'Shut up,' Ellis said, growling at him. 'I nicked you in the arm before you could pull the trigger. You'll live, buddy. Don't worry. You'll still be able to stand trial for murder.' To two of the officers who were crowding around us, he said, 'Call EMS and get him out of here.'

'If you'd shown up even a few seconds later,' I said to Ellis, my heart still racing, 'you'd be calling EMS for Max and me.'

'Don't worry. We wouldn't have let anything happen to you. I told you that.'

'Can I take my wire off now?' I asked. 'I assume you got everything – his confession?'

Ellis nodded.

'Now what happens?' Max said.

'Now we have Robson Blake's killer in custody, so I imagine

there'll be a press conference later today when the chief announces it, probably along with the mayor,' he said. 'It'll be a big deal. And thank you.'

'I'm glad you believed me when I called you and told you about the icon being in my studio,' I said.

'Someone from the FBI Art Fraud Squad will take possession of it,' he said. 'Probably later today. In the meantime, one of my people will babysit it until that happens.'

'I presume it will be returned to the church in Kyiv?'

'The State Department will handle that,' he said. 'But, yes, I'm sure it will go back where it belongs.'

'What about . . .?' Max paused and swallowed painfully. 'The rest of the stolen art? My partner was running a side business I knew nothing about until this past weekend, when I discovered some items in the warehouse that belongs to my gallery that I knew weren't ours.'

Ellis gave him a skeptical look like, *Buddy, it's the story of my life: everybody says they had no idea what was going on right under their nose and that they're innocent.* 'You're not charged with anything at this time, Mr Katzer, but your warehouse is now a crime scene and will be off limits until we can investigate everything that's in there.'

'How long will that be?'

'As long as it takes.'

Max pressed his lips together and nodded, looking distraught and angry and fearful, and I knew he was contemplating the damage Gil had done to his reputation and his business, and wondering whether it might ever be repaired. And whether he'd face any collateral charges.

'It's going to be OK.' I slid my arm around his waist.

'No, it's not,' he said. 'Once word gets out that Robbie owned an icon he knew was stolen – especially the circumstances surrounding that particular icon and the fact there's blood on his hands – all hell is going to break loose at every museum and cultural institution that has a plaque next to a work of art that says "donated by" or "on loan from the collection of" and his name. With all the stories and scandals in the mainstream news about stolen art being repatriated and returned to its rightful owners – after decades, even centuries – this is going to set off a tsunami that will rock the art world for a long time. Every curator will be scrambling to verify the provenance of what he gave or loaned them.'

Ellis looked at both of us. 'Do either of you know anything about other items Robson Blake owned that were also stolen?'

Max shook his head and I said, 'Nothing specific, except the icon.'

He zeroed in on me. 'Do you know something else, Ms Medina, that you should be sharing with me? Maybe *general* details about stolen items in Mr Blake's collection, since you say you don't know anything specific?'

I thought of Danny and Enrique Navarro. There was still no reason to bring Danny into this and I wasn't about to tell him about Navarro who, number one, I still didn't trust, and number two, *would* bring up Danny.

'The answer to your question,' I said in a firm *this-is-all-I-know* voice, 'is no.'

TWENTY-SIX

He showed up the same way he'd arrived the first time. Broke into my studio and waited until I walked in the day after the press conference announcing that Robbie Blake's murderer was in custody.

'Well, hello, Houdini.' I let the irritation and anger seep into my voice 'We have to stop meeting like this.'

He held out his arms like a supplicant. 'I'm sorry, Sophie. I really am.'

'It's a little late for "sorry," Danny. Where the hell have you been?'

'I left town for a few days,' he said. 'There was no way I was going to contact you – it was too dangerous. I know how it must have looked.'

'Do you really? It *looked* like you might have been guilty of murder, that's how it looked to *me*. To Detective Ellis, on the other hand, it *looked* like *I* was guilty of murder. My tripod was the murder weapon, and from his misbegotten but understandable point of view, he thought I knew way too much about the missing icon, including the fact that I knew it was stolen. Last but not least, Gil Tessier, who *did* kill Robbie, broke into this studio – though, unlike you, he used a key – and left the icon upstairs in the bedroom: another nail in the coffin to pin the murder on me. Ellis found out, of course. Almost immediately. So guess what he thought *then*?' I was still standing in the doorway, so furious with him I was practically shaking.

He closed his eyes. 'I didn't know it was that bad. I don't know what I can say or do to make it up to you.'

'I was *that close* to getting arrested as an accessory to murder if Ellis learned about you and connected the two of us.' I held up my thumb and forefinger so there was no daylight between them. 'Or worse.'

'Which is why I took off,' he said. 'Because I was there that day.'

'What?'

'I was at Blake's home. After I left you that night, we got wind that he was planning to sell the icon, and already had a buyer lined up. If it vanished again, who knew when we'd find it? So we moved up the timeline. It was too risky to get word to you.'

I walked into the room and headed straight for the kitchen and the bottle of Scotch. There was still about half left after his last visit.

'What did you do?' I found two glasses, got ice for my glass and took the same seat as the other night. I poured our drinks and handed him a Scotch, neat.

'Thank you.' He raised his glass. 'We got lucky – in a way. There was a dry-cleaning truck in the neighborhood. I took a guess the driver would make a stop at Blake's house.'

'You took Robbie's dry-cleaning and delivered it yourself? That's it? That was your plan?'

'We kind of made it up as we went along. I told the guy I was Mr Blake's new assistant when he was a couple doors down from the house and said I'd save him a stop, so he gave it to me. I tipped him really well.'

'And you walked into Robbie's house with his dry-cleaning, just like that?'

'The driver had left his jacket with the company logo on it and a cap on a hook in his truck. One of my guys, uh, borrowed them for a while when the driver was making another delivery. Returned them later after I was done with them.'

'Danny.' I shook my head. '*Jesus*. Then what?'

'The front door to Blake's house was unlocked. I walked right in.'

'Just like I did,' I said. 'What happened next?'

'We'd already hacked into his security system and discovered his cameras were off. When I found him – in the library, like you said – he was dead, and the icon was gone. So I took off.'

'Perhaps he really did have a female visitor he didn't want recorded earlier that afternoon so he turned the cameras off early.'

He swallowed some Scotch. 'My guess is he didn't want whoever was buying the icon to be seen on camera.'

'So Gil's visit wasn't recorded, either,' I said.

'No.'

'What happens now?' I asked.

'I need to lie low for a while after all this,' he said. 'I'm leaving. Again.'

'Enrique Navarro met up with me. He knew about Robbie dealing in stolen art. He found out when he saw a painting Robbie owned that he knew had been stolen from a Spanish museum. He did more research on other items Robbie owned; they were friends, and apparently, Robbie showed off a lot of his new acquisitions to Navarro. He discovered even more items that were stolen. He told me he wanted to hook up with you and share information,' I said.

Danny shook his head. 'The FBI and Interpol will be going over Robbie's entire collection with a magnifying glass. Their investigation will blow anything Navarro has out of the water. What he knows won't matter anymore.'

'Maybe that will be the end of him contacting me to get to you. Though I suspect he'll be devastated. He thought he had an Ortega y Gasset-winning scoop. He was counting on it.'

'It's a cold, cruel world sometimes.'

'Isn't it just.' I set my glass down. 'So this is goodbye? Au revoir – until we meet again? Adios – go with God? Goodbye – have a nice life? Which is it, Danny?'

'Right now, it's goodbye for a while.'

'I won't hear from you, will I?'

'I'll be in touch if I can.'

'Sure.' Which meant I'd hear from him every once in a blue moon. Maybe. And maybe then we could finally talk about Antonio, and he could tell me all the things I never knew about my father – *our* father. At least, we could start talking about that.

'I've got a friend who is going to be dropping by my apartment soon. He's passing through on his way to London. I should go.'

'Which is my cue to take off.' He got up and came over to me, pulling me up and kissing me on the forehead. 'Goodbye, Sophie.'

'Goodbye, Danny.'

He slipped out the door as he'd done last time, closing it with a sharp click.

And then he was gone, and I was alone.

The fallout from Robbie Blake's murder and the discovery that he had been dealing in plundered and looted art rocked the art world, just as Max predicted. Grace, who was writing the story for the *Trib*, told me the Senate Foreign Relations Committee had decided to hold hearings on the impact of stolen art on US foreign policy as a national security issue – specifically the sale of looted art and antiquities to fund war efforts such as the Russian invasion of Ukraine or to provide cash for international terrorist organizations. Ben, she said, was working flat out to prepare for the hearings which the chairman wanted to take place as soon as possible.

'Ben says the chairman wants to – and I quote – strike while the iron's hot and there's so much prurient interest in the Blake murder,' she said. 'Plus, Robbie Blake's affair with Olivia Sage and how she destroyed her professional reputation by establishing false provenance for some of the stolen art he bought and owned. So they're expecting massive public interest and press coverage for these hearings, or at least hoping for it. Everyone loves a scandal.'

Jack had filled us both in on the devastating fallout for Olivia. Losing her tenured position and being fired by the university were the least of it. She was also facing multiple counts of forging documents to falsify ownership of stolen art and antiquities as well as possession of stolen and plundered art, both of which would probably mean she'd serve time in jail. When we asked if he'd seen her, he said yes, a bit tersely, and left it at that. If he'd heard her confession, I suspected what she'd told him was an exception to the rule that most sins were boring.

I shared more information with Grace about what I'd learned about Robbie's dealings in plundered art, plus I told her about my searches with ArtRevive, which had come back confirming the two icons pictured in Olivia's books on Byzantine art were, in fact, stolen. But for some reason, I clammed up and didn't say a word about Danny. I did introduce her to Valerie Zhou at the International Consortium of Investigative Journalists, who I knew would also keep mum about Danny – and about Enrique Navarro. But Grace knew there was something else I wasn't telling her – she always knew. For once, she didn't push me to talk about it and I was grateful.

After the news broke about Gil Tessier's arrest, I drove out to Mayfield and spent a night with Harry and my mother, mostly talking about the murder and how I'd nearly ended up as a suspect. Not one word about my last visit or Antonio's letters, which I knew would be one of those unresolved issues that would simmer below the surface of my complicated relationship with my mother. If we were careful and never made an accidental slip that brought up the subject, we could avoid another disastrous blowup. It wasn't a solution, but it was the way things were between us: a lot of landmines that we were constantly vigilant to step around or, occasionally, step over. For my part, I didn't talk about meeting Danny, especially not about my half-brother's current occupation as an international art thief. My mother wasn't the only one to keep family secrets.

The night Perry spent with me before he left for London was nothing like the white-hot night we'd spent in bed the last time he was here. Landon had left a piece of paper on Nick's bedside table where he'd scribbled notes about my condition every time he woke me up, and I'd forgotten it was there. Perry found it, of course. And had a few questions.

'We were fully dressed. I had a *concussion*. My head hurt like hell. He's a doctor and he did me a favor waking me up every hour all night so I didn't have to stay in the hospital.'

'You slept with him?'

'I slept *next to him*. It's not the same thing. You may have found his notes, but he found your condoms in the bathroom. Which came up indirectly as a subject of conversation over breakfast. So, you're even. Sort of.'

'Oh.'

The next morning, he kissed me goodbye as his cab pulled up in front of the house and I tasted resignation in his kiss.

'Perry—'

'Don't say it,' he said. 'I'm not pushing you, but you know what I want. We don't have to go over this again. And I don't want to say goodbye after an argument. I'd better go before I blow it.'

I kissed him back. 'Thank you.'

'Think about it, Medina,' he said before his cab drove off.

The day of the soccer camp was about as perfect a spring day in Washington as you could ask for. Landon, who had come by the apartment a few days earlier to bring Harriet over and help her get acclimated, came with me. This time, he watched on the sidelines as I took photos of the players from Real Madrid and DC United working with the kids, whose faces lit up with such pure joy that it was probably one of the most memorable and heartwarming events I've ever photographed. A large crowd had gathered on the Mall to watch and cheer the kids on, and when it was over and autographs had been signed and uniforms and balls and cleats had been handed out to each of the participants, Finn Hathaway came over to me and said, 'Well? Now aren't you glad you said yes?'

'I am,' I said. 'It was fantastic. Thank you for asking me.'

'No one knew you were Antonio Medina's daughter,' he said. 'Just like I promised.'

When I got home, I downloaded my pictures with Harriet curled up in a tiny ball and purring contentedly on my lap. Finn hadn't been quite right. I zoomed in on one of the photos of the crowd. I had seen him, but I hadn't been sure if I was right or not.

He hadn't been able to stay away, either. Someone did know I was Antonio's daughter.

Danny.

Acknowledgments

I owe thanks to many people who helped me with my research for this book; as usual, if it's wrong, it's on me, and if it's right, they said it. They are: Hossein Amirsadeghi; April Arnold, Deepwood Veterinary Clinic; Reverend Doctor Peter Barlow; Andy Braddel, Vice President & Managing Director of Global Media Services, Associated Press; Cathy Brannon; Julio Cortez, Pulitzer Prize-winning photographer & Chief Photographer, Associated Press; Rosemarie Forsythe; Fr Donald Heet, OSFS; Maximillian Katzer, Senior Director, Commercial Property Management at Denver International Airport (who also loaned me his name); André de Nesnera; Peter de Nesnera; Crystal Nosal, Media Relations, Metropolitan Washington Airports Authority; Rebekah Oakes, Historian, U.S. Patent and Trademark Office; MPO Jim Smith, Fairfax County Police Department; and David Swinson. Since this is a work of fiction, I did take some liberties with a few facts to make them fit the story I wanted to write, so, again, blame me if it's wrong.

As usual, huge thanks to Donna Andrews, John Gilstrap, Alan Orloff and Art Taylor, my critique group buddies for the last thirteen years, affectionately known as the Rumpus Writers, for their constructive comments and help with early drafts of this book.

Many of the instances of stolen or plundered art that I wrote about were taken from news accounts of incidents that really happened as I was working on the manuscript for *Dodge and Burn* – which gives you an idea of just how common art plunder, looting and theft have become. Without exception, all the articles cited below – if you want to know more about the *real* story – appeared in print in 2022 and 2023.

The relationship between Olivia Sage and Robson Blake was loosely based on a fascinating three-part series in *The Denver Post* published December 1, 2022, and written by journalist Sam Tabachnik: 'Unmasking "The Scholar": The Colorado woman who helped a global art smuggling operation flourish for decades: An investigation into how Emma C. Bunker helped Douglas Latchford sell stolen Cambodian antiquities.' A mysterious man in a white lab coat accompanied by Russian soldiers *did* appear in the Ukrainian city of Melitopol at the Museum of Local History and, using tweezers, extracted the most valuable items of Scythian gold in the museum's collection. For more information on this bizarre heist, please read: 'As Russians Steal Ukraine's Art, They Attack Its Identity, Too' by Jeffrey Gettleman and Oleksandra Mykolyshyn in the January 14, 2023 edition of *The New York Times*. The Iranian sculpture hacked out of an ancient rock relief that Rex Morgenthau mentioned to Sophie and Vince Kirby was described in an article on April 3, 2023 on the artnews.com website: 'Agents Seized an Ancient Iranian Carving at a London Airport. Before Being Repatriated, It Will Go on View at the British Museum.' The story about art stolen from a church in Cuenca that Enrique Navarro describes to Sophie was loosely based on several articles, including 'With a Stolen Fragment Restored, This Stunning Seventeenth-century Tapestry Is Made Whole' by Nora McGreevy, published on March 22, 2022 in *Smithsonian Magazine*, and 'Final piece of seventeenth-century tapestry stolen forty-two years ago found by Spanish police' by Sam Jones, in a February 21, 2022 article in *The Guardian*. The story about a painting believed to have been destroyed during World War I that appeared in a photo taken in actress and singer Madonna's London home for a 2015 issue of *Paris Match* and was subsequently spotted by an art expert from Amiens, France, was written about extensively. 'Madge Mystery: Painting spotted on Madonna's wall is lost masterpiece that vanished in WWI, say French experts – and they want it back' by Jon Rogers appeared in the January 18, 2023 issue of *The Sun* and 'A French City Appeals to Madonna for Clues About a Long-Lost Painting' written by Jenny Gross, appeared in the January 18, 2023 issue of *The New York Times*. It's also true, as Darius Zahiri points out to Sophie, that on occasion thieves have no idea whether what they've stolen is the real thing or a fake or forgery – including Scythian gold that was stolen from Ukraine. For more information on that stranger-than-fiction story, please read 'Police in Spain Seized Greco-Scythian Artifacts That Were Allegedly Stolen From Ukraine – But Experts Doubt Their Authenticity' by Adam Schrader in the October 25, 2023 online issue of Artnet News. If, in fact, the eleven pieces of gold jewelry turn out to be real, the estimated value is over sixty-three million dollars. Finally, the extraordinary story of the top-secret mission to smuggle fragile icons out of Ukraine by train and bring them to the Louvre appeared on the artnet.com website on June 15, 2023 in an article by Jo Lawson-Tancred entitled 'The Louvre Has Displayed Sacred Treasures Rescued From Ukraine as Part of Its Partnership With Local Museums.'

The account of the eviction of the largest homeless camp in Washington, DC, was described in detail in *The Washington Post* in Marisa J. Lang's June 27, 2023 article: 'D.C. cleared scores of homeless from McPherson Square. Then kept evicting them.' Fr Jack O'Hara's talk with Sophie explaining that listening to confession is nothing like she imagines because "sins are really boring" was stolen from a talk given by Fr. Joe Newman, Provincial of the Toledo-Detroit Province, Oblates of St. Francis de Sales. I owe huge thanks to AP Pulitzer Prizing winning chief photographer Julio Cortez for telling me that a photojournalist often takes pictures of people on the best days of their lives or the worst ones, a line I knew Sophie had to say. Julio also provided a poignant first-hand account of coaching soccer to a group of migrant and homeless kids that I borrowed from heavily. Finally, to learn more about the valuable and important work of the International Consortium of Investigative Journalists visit their website at www.icij.org

At Severn House, I owe thanks to my wonderful editor Rachel Slatter for, well, everything: deft, thoughtful editing, the right advice and guidance always delivered gently, and a lovely, sly sense of humor. Also huge thanks to Tina Pietron, Assistant Editor, and Martin Brown, Senior Brand Manager, who never ceases to amaze me with how skillfully he looks after so many authors but always makes me feel as if he has all the time in the world for me. And thanks to Piers Tilbury, Head of Design, for yet another gorgeous cover. None of this would be possible without Dominick Abel, my agent for nineteen wonderful years – thanks and love.

A full heart and so much love to my husband, André de Nesnera, for more than words can say and for always, always believing in me.